CORRUPTION IN OUR MIDST

CORRUPTION IN OUR MIDST

AN ADAM DARBY THRILLER

KENDALL CARLTON

Dedicated to my wonderful wife, Susan.

This book would not have been possible

without her love, support, and encouragement.

CONTENTS

CORRUPTION IN OUR MIDST

CHAPTER ONE
NORTHERN MONTANA WILDERNESS

His eyes fluttered open and then closed. He was lying in the weeds and rocks near a small gurgling creek. His head was pounding and even though it hurt to open his eyes, he forced them open, a little. The sun was low in the western sky and filtered through the dense woods dappling the ground surrounding him with long shadows. The only sounds he heard were the chattering of some birds and the babbling of the nearby creek. He lay still for a while and took an inventory of his body. Everything moved as it should, but his whole body hurt. Slowly he sat up and looked around. He looked at his feet and one foot was in the cold water of the creek and a sharp rock was pressed into his buttocks. He rolled over and gently stood up from all fours. There was an old, smooth tree trunk that had been lying near the creek for years. He shuffled over to the tree trunk and sat down. His brain was foggy, and he couldn't remember anything since... at least a day ago, and he had no idea where he was. Leaning forward with his head in his hands, he tried to remember. There was something there, just out of reach, but it was escaping him.

He stood on shaky legs and slowly walked around the area to get his bearings. The air was cool and damp on his skin, but that didn't help him determine where he was. He checked his pockets, and they were all empty. No wallet, keys, phone - nothing. As he was walking around, he found an old trail that followed the creek. A quick inspection showed plenty of deer and elk tracks but no human footprints. His mind was racing, trying to understand where he was and how he got there.

His mind began to clear a little and his predicament began to take the priority in his thoughts. He knew, if he was going to survive, he needed to find his way to civilization, but first he needed to find some shelter.

The woods were dense with lots of deadfall. He gathered some branches and built a rickety lean-to. He stepped back and looked at the lean-to and thought, *It'll work. Hopefully, it won't rain.*

He tried to get a fire started the old-fashioned way but wasn't successful. It was dark and cold, and he didn't sleep much. He tossed and turned on the hard ground and shivered throughout the night.

As the sun was rising in the east, the forest sounds came to life. He stood and stretched his achy joints. His headache was still there but wasn't pounding anymore, just a dull ache. The nearby trail headed northwest or southeast. He stood on the trail and looked in both directions. He didn't know where he was but decided to go southeast.

He had been hiking all day and was extremely tired. He didn't know the time, but the sun was getting low in the west. *I need to find shelter again,* he was thinking as he crested a small hill.

The view was spectacular. In the distance, he noticed a silvery plume of smoke. *It must be a cabin or camp,* he thought with great anticipation. A short while later, he found a faint trail leading toward the source of the smoke. As he got closer, he decided that he needed to use extreme caution—walking quietly trying not to make a sound. Moving slowly, he ascended a small rise, stopped, and lay down just below the crest. Carefully, he looked over the crest of the rise and saw a cabin with warm light shining from the windows and smoke curling out of the fireplace.

The cabin was made of logs with old chinking to keep the cold out and a stone fireplace. The cabin was quite old. The front porch was clean with two rocking chairs. *Caution is my friend*, so he stepped off the trail and found a place to sit and watch for a while. There was movement inside what looked like a kitchen area. No movement was noticed outside the cabin. There was an old 4x4 vehicle that he could only see part of behind the cabin. It was probably red when it was new but had lightened from the sun to a pale pink color. After what felt like an hour, he decided to approach the cabin and knock on the door. Slowly he walked toward the front door of the cabin keeping a wary eye out for a big ferocious dog, but there wasn't one. The first step on the front porch squeaked and he stopped. His heart was racing. He reminded himself that he was not in danger yet...

He knocked on the cabin door and it was answered by a dog barking. Not the big ferocious bark that he was expecting but the high-pitched bark of a small lap dog, perhaps a poodle. The door opened and he was greeted by an old woman. She had a round welcoming face and shoulder-length gray hair. She was a little overweight, and she looked like the grandmother every child dreamed of. Adam expected her to be holding a plate of cookies for just such an occasion. Instead, she held a small white dog with white curly hair and a pink bow on her head. A wonderful aroma enveloped him as the door opened. The woman was visibly taken aback by his appearance and concerned for his well-being.

"Are you okay?" she asked.

"Good evening, ma'am. My name is Adam Darby. I don't know where I am or how I got here. It appears I was beaten and dumped in the woods, but I don't remember anything for the last couple of days," Adam said.

"Come in, please," she said as she motioned Adam to a large soft, leather chair by the fireplace and rushed to the kitchen. The fire was warm on his tired, aching body. She brought a glass of water and a sandwich on a small plate and set them on the table next to him. "Please eat and drink. You look like it has been days since you have eaten. How long have you been lost?" she asked with concern in her voice. "By the way, my name is Mary. Mary Parke."

"Hi, Mary. Thank you so much for helping me. Where am I?" Adam asked.

"My cabin is near the town of Yaak, Montana."

"What day is it? I don't remember anything since September eighth."

"Well Adam, today is September tenth. You don't remember anything since September eighth?"

"I woke up in the woods by a creek yesterday afternoon. I spent the night in the woods and found you today. Did you say we are in Montana?"

"Yes, Northern Montana, not far from the Canadian border."

Adam's head was pounding, and he began to feel dizzy. "Montana?" Adam asked with a look of disbelief. "The last place that I remember being in was Ottawa, Ontario. I work for the CIA and was working surveillance. I can't say too much for security concerns, but my work is of national importance to the United States," Adam said as he took a bite of the ham and cheese sandwich. "Boy, this is the best ham and cheese sandwich that I have ever had."

"Thank you," she said. "You have no idea what happened to you in Ottawa and how you ended up in the Kootenai National Forest? Let me check that wound on your head. I used to be a nurse before I met my husband, and I retired to come live here." She took a damp rag and gently cleaned the wound on Adam's head. "It looks like you took a nasty blow on your head."

"Where is your husband?" Adam asked, wondering if he would be home and what he would say about him being here.

"Paul passed away a little over a year ago, God rest his soul. He was such a kind and generous man. He retired from the NSA and would have loved to talk shop with you," Mary said as she contin-ued to dress his wounds.

She is making sure that I don't have a weapon.

"I think that you should stay the night here. Tomorrow I can take you to town," Mary said.

"Thank you so much for your hospitality. Why do you trust me and believe the crazy story that I told?" Adam asked, wondering why she didn't shoot first and ask questions later.

"When Paul was working for the NSA, there were many things that he could not tell me. There were times that he was deep undercover, and I wouldn't see him for weeks or even months. One time he was gone over a year. I had to learn who to trust and, more importantly, who not to trust. There was and still is a pos-sibility that one of the enemies he investigated could be trying to find him," she looked around the room deep in memories. "Paul taught me how to take care of myself," she said with a faraway look in her eyes.

"I need to talk to the office. Do you have a telephone?" Adam asked.

"No, not here. One of the reasons Paul and I moved to this remote area was for protection and isolation. His work always presented danger to him and me, so it was safer for us to be here. Sometimes I get lonely out here now that Paul is gone, but I know that he wanted me to stay here, so I talk to him and enjoy the quiet life he provided me. I go into town once a week to stock up on supplies. I was planning on going tomorrow so we can go together."

"I am a little concerned to be seen since I was dumped here. Maybe they are still looking for me. I don't have any money or identification. I will need a secure place to make some phone calls," Adam said.

Mary walked back to the kitchen deep in thought and returned with a steaming cup of hot chocolate with frothy whipped cream about to cascade from the sides of the cup. "Here, drink this. It will help you sleep. I know a safe place to take you. His name is Johnny and lives near town. He is someone that Paul always trusted, and he has a telephone. We will stop there tomorrow morning on the way to town," she said. "Now, finish your hot chocolate. I still have Paul's clothes. I will find something clean for you to change into."

Mary left the room and returned a few minutes later. "I put the clothes in the bathroom over there. Go get cleaned up and I will make up the couch for you."

Adam stiffly stood up from his chair by the fireplace, thanked Mary for everything, and went into the bathroom. It was small, but comfortable. To Adam's surprise, there was a new toothbrush and a razor waiting for him. The shower was hot and steamy on his tender skin but felt oh so good. After the shower, Adam shaved and ran his fingers through his hair. As he looked in the mirror, he saw a man that had been betrayed, but his light brown wavy hair and green eyes were still the same. He was exhausted and there were dark circles under his eyes. He put his hand under the cold water and took a drink. He dressed in Paul's clothes that Mary put out for him. They fit fine but were a little short. When Adam returned to the living room the couch was covered with a patchwork quilt made with high quality fabric and by loving hands. "Mary, did you make this quilt?" Adam asked.

"Yes, it is one of the things I do that brings me great satisfaction. I usually make a few a year to raise money for the local church I attend," Mary said.

"It looks very comfortable. I'm sure I will sleep well. Thank you again for all you have done for me," Adam told her gratefully. His head was starting to feel light as his body was trying to fall asleep before he even sat down.

Mary walked toward her room and turned off the light. "Goodnight," she said.

"Goodnight," Adam said as he instantly fell asleep.

Adam awoke to the morning light and the smell of bacon and coffee in the kitchen. He got up and padded to the bathroom. When he came out, Mary said, "It looks like you slept well. How are you feeling?"

Adam smiled. "Much better. It smells wonderful in here. I'm famished."

"Come sit at the table and have some breakfast," Mary said.

Adam sat down at an old wooden table with comfortable chairs. The smell of eggs and bacon excited his senses, and his brain began to fire on all cylinders at the bubbling sound of the percolator and aroma of brewing coffee. Adam started to remember something about the night of the attack, but as soon as it was beginning to clearly show itself, it disappeared. "Are you alright?" Mary asked.

"Yes. I thought I started to remember something, but it wasn't clear," Adam said with confusion expressed on his face.

"I could see that you were deep in thought about something and there was confusion in your eyes," Mary expressed in a motherly way and placed a huge plate of bacon, eggs, and fried potatoes in front of him. "How do you like your coffee?" Mary asked.

"Black please," Adam said.

"Eat up. It is good to see a man eat a hearty breakfast," Mary said as she laughed.

Adam chuckled and said that this was the best breakfast a man could ask for. When he could eat no more, he tried to help with the cleanup, but she told him in no uncertain terms to sit down and she would take care of it. When she finished, she took him to the closet by the front door and found one of Paul's old barn jackets and gave it to him. She grabbed her purse from the hook by the front door. "Let's go."

They went outside and she locked the door and, to his surprise, slid a hidden panel back and exposed a high-tech security system. She set it and closed the nearly invisible hidden panel.

"That panel is so well hidden. If I had not seen it with my own eyes, I would not have believed it," Adam said.

"Paul designed and built the security system for our protection. I knew when you were watching the cabin before you came to the door. Or the dog barked," she said with a grin.

"Why did you trust me?" Adam asked.

"I have a feeling about you, and you remind me of my late-husband Paul. I also contacted a friend to run a background check on you to make sure you were who you said you were." She took me around to the back of the cabin and we got into an old, faded Ford Bronco. "Buckle up," she said as she started the Bronco. It started with a quick, deep-throaty exhaust note. Adam could tell it wasn't an average old, worn-out vehicle as it appeared from the outside. They took off with a jolt and were bouncing down the road toward town. The road was narrow, but relatively smooth. They crossed a small creek. *Is this the creek that I woke up next to a couple of days ago?*

About ten miles down the road Mary slowed and made a left turn on a smaller road that consisted of two single tracks for the tires. After a half mile or so, they came upon a gate. The gate was rustic but well maintained. Adam started to get out to open the gate and Mary said, "Stay inside."

She rolled her window down and stared up at a nearby tree knowing that there was a camouflaged speaker and microphone concealed there. "Hi JJ. It's Mary. I have a guy with me that needs our help."

A voice replied in a static staccato asking, "Do you trust him?"

"Yes, JJ."

"Okay, I'll open the gate," the voice said. The gate silently opened, and they drove through.

"I thought his name was Johnny," Adam asked.

"It is, but we have a security system of words to indicate

danger. If I would have said 'Yes, Johnny,' he would have known that I did not trust you." Mary said.

"Paul sure did everything to keep you safe," Adam said.

"He sure did. Here we are," Mary said as they arrived at the cabin and got out. The cabin was not all that different from Mary's but older looking. As they approached the front door, it was opened by an older man with a thick gray mane of hair, plaid shirt, blue jeans, and cowboy boots—exactly, what Adam would expect. The man held out his hand and said in a deep resonant voice, "Hi, I'm Johnny Fox."

Johnny extended his hand to Adam, and they shook hands with a strong, firm grip. "I'm Adam Darby. It's a pleasure to meet you."

"Please come in," Johnny said as he motioned them inside.

The cabin was warm and comfortable. A crackling fire was in the fireplace. Outside the windows there was a grove of aspen trees glowing a golden yellow in the crisp fall air. He led them across the room to a door that looked like it could be a closet and opened it. There were stairs going down to a basement. He turned on the light and descended the stairs. The walls were unfinished concrete. By one wall was a stack of random lumber that they were walking toward. Johnny pulled and turned one piece of wood and to Adam's surprise the stack of lumber was a door leading to a secret room. A light turned on automatically as they entered the room, and the door closed behind them with a solid thump. There were four comfortable leather armchairs in the room. Along one wall were several computer monitors and other high-tech electronic equipment. The walls were finished with dark wood. One wall had a door leading somewhere.

"Have a seat and tell us your story and what you need help with," Johnny said.

Adam relayed the events of the last few days as he remembered them. As he was telling the story of what happened, something foggy in his brain was trying to tell him something. Adam paused and closed his eyes and tried to focus on that distant feeling. He could not put his finger on it, but he did remember feeling a prick in the back of his neck.

"That's it!" Adam said as he felt the back of his neck.

"What is?" Mary asked.

"I remember feeling a prick in the back of my neck. Mary, can you look to see if you see an injection point from a hypodermic needle?" Adam asked.

Mary looked where Adam was pointing. She used a magnifying glass to inspect his neck. "It looks like there is a faint spot resembling a mark from an injection needle."

Johnny went over to look. "I think you're right Mary. That does look like an injection mark a few days old. It seems clear that whoever did this to you sedated you and dropped you in the woods. Since it has been less than forty-eight hours since you woke up, we should be able to determine what they used to knock you out. Do you mind if I take a small blood sample?" Johnny asked.

"No, go ahead," Adam replied.

"When I was with the NSA, I worked in forensics and electronic surveillance. I have all the necessary equipment to test that here. I have found that there are certain chemical makeups of sedation drugs favored by different groups worldwide. We may be able to determine who did this based on this chemical makeup, but it must be done quickly, because it dilutes in the human body very quickly," Johnny said.

"I think that is a great idea. Please, go ahead." Adam put out his left arm as Johnny quickly stepped across the room to a cabinet and pulled out a black Pelican plastic case. Johnny put the case on the table in front of Adam and opened it. Inside there was the expected blood-drawing equipment in addition to several bottles. Johnny handed gloves to Mary. "Can you draw the blood sample?"

Mary put on the gloves and cleaned a spot near his elbow on the inside of his arm. She tied a rubber tourniquet around his upper arm to plump up the veins. She injected a syringe into his vein and drew a small amount of blood into a vial. She removed the syringe, placed a bandage over the injection site, and handed the vial to Johnny.

Then he put a drop of blood on each slide and mixed each drop with a drop of a different chemical. He took the slide over to a microscope in the corner of the room. Next to the microscope was a color chart. He turned on a computer monitor, accessed a program, and then focused the image of the blood drops. As he checked each one it came up negative. The last one showed a positive match.

"Hmmm... That is interesting," he mused and looked up from his microscope and turned to the others.

"This match is the last one that I thought it would be. It is a very rarely used sedative and is only manufactured in Islamabad, Pakistan by a company called Laila Pharmaceuticals. This company is led by a suspected terrorist backer named Muhammed Suleiman. Very little is known about this person. He leads a hidden life. The only time that this drug has been found in a victim was following the hijacking and subsequent crash of Air France flight 3496 in Morocco. The pilots' bodies were recovered immediately from the crash site and this same test was completed. The results of your test and the tests from the pilots are an exact match. Unfortunately, they died prior to waking up from this sedative. Does this help trying to determine who did this to you?"

"It might. I was investigating a group of Chinese nationals that have suspected ties to an organization named Chinese Peoples State or 'CPS.' This organization's goal is to make China the only world superpower. They have a particular hatred of the United States and Europe. They have many of the same enemies as radical Muslim terrorist organizations," Adam said.

CHAPTER TWO

OTTAWA, ONTARIO, CANADA

Two days earlier, operative Chang Huang from the Chinese Peoples State (CPS) was driving a black Mercedes S-Class luxury sedan through Ottawa. Chang Huang looked like a well-dressed wealthy businessman from China. His dark suit was expensive and fit perfectly in every way. The dark color contrasted nicely with his salt-and-pepper hair. His cell phone rang as he was driving to a non-descript suburban house on the northeast side of Ottawa. He answered the call. "Yes?"

The caller did not identify himself, but Chang knew his boss's voice. "You have been compromised. My source in the CIA revealed that an agent has been tracking you and is currently surveilling the safe house."

"Understood. We will eliminate the threat," Chang said as he ended the call.

Chang called his partner, Pak Huo, and instructed him to find and eliminate the CIA agent. Pak Huo was a thin wiry man with short black hair and black eyes. He had a menacing look but didn't look physically dangerous. Nothing could have been further from the truth. Huo and Chang had worked together for many years and knew each other better than most married couples. Chang knew about the surveillance but ignored it knowing that Huo would take care of it.

The sun had just set, and it was getting dark. The air was still warm but was cooling down. The streetlights were just coming on as Chang parked his rental car in the driveway of the safe house. He was wearing an expensive suit but hidden in his pocket was a compact 9mm Heckler and Koch handgun. As he exited the car, another car pulled up from the opposite direction, pulled into the driveway of a house down the street and parked in the garage, then closed the door.

As Chang walked to the front door, Huo went inside a house down the street. Leaving all the lights off, he went upstairs and looked out the window at the street. He identified the surveillance car and saw the agent watching the safe house. He went downstairs and slipped out the back door. Huo walked down the alley and then around to the street in front of the house.

Adam was sitting in a dark blue Chevrolet Malibu sedan several houses down from the Chinese safe house that Chang entered. From the moment that Chang arrived, Adam was photographing and listening to Chang. He did not notice Huo park in the garage down the street. Had he noticed the driver, he would have recognized him. In the back of Adam's mind, he was thinking, *Where is Huo? They are always near each other. After Chang enters the house, I'll look for him.*

The day had been hot, so Adam had the driver's-side window down for a bit of ventilation. Huo silently approached Adam's car from behind making sure that he was not visible in any of the mirrors. Adam was so intent on the photography that he did not notice Huo approaching from behind.

Huo slipped up to the side of the car and jabbed an epi pen filled with a sedative that he acquired in Pakistan from Laila Pharmaceuticals. The sedative delivery was fast, and the reaction was even faster. Within two seconds, Adam was slumped over the steering wheel. Huo pulled him from the driver's seat and stuffed him into the back seat. He did not bother to tie him up since he knew the sedative would keep him out for at least twenty-four hours. He slipped into the driver's seat and drove Adam's car toward Pendleton Airport on the east side of Ottawa.

On the way to the airport, Huo pulled into a deserted park with many trees. He wound through the park and stopped in a secluded place and dragged Adam from the back seat and heaved him into the trunk. He removed all identification and weapons from Adam's body. Huo double checked to make sure that all weapons were found and removed. Once satisfied, he put everything into a duffel bag, gently closed the trunk and continued to the airport.

Huo arrived at the executive terminal showed his credentials to the guard and was waved through without so much as a glance in the back seat of the vehicle. He drove to the hangar that housed the Learjet 75. The pilots were waiting with the door open and flight plan ready. Adam was loaded into the aircraft and Huo took his seat. A moment later, dressed in black tactical gear and carrying two large bags, Joachim Smith arrived and settled in across from Huo.

"*You are five minutes late!*" Huo fumed. The door was closed, and the jet engines began to spin as the startup procedure began.

The business jet was registered to a straw corporation called STS Enterprises. Huo's false identity was recorded as the CEO of

STS Enterprises. The flight plan was to fly directly to Vancouver, British Columbia, then continue to Shanghai, China. The passenger list only listed Huo and the pilots. The other two would not be on board when the jet landed in Vancouver.

The jet reached its cruising altitude of fifty thousand feet with a flight time of just over three and a half hours. Joachim Smith finished his drink and unbuckled his seat belt. Joachim Smith was not his real name—a mercenary for hire with an extensive resume of special operations work. His specialty is black ops and deep penetration via sky diving from very high altitudes. Joachim laid his equipment out and began to set everything in place. The air at fifty thousand feet was very cold, so he wrestled an insulated suit and harness on Adam's inert body. He then donned his insulated suit and harness.

"Ten minutes to drop point," the pilot said over the intercom.

Joachim turned on the oxygen bottle and tested the flow for both him and Adam. Satisfied that all was well, he dragged Adam to the door. The plane slowed and the pilot said, "five minutes to drop." The plane slowed and dropped altitude until it was near stall speed. Joachim hooked his harness to Adam and held him by the door.

"Thirty seconds to drop. Open the door," the intercom squawked.

Huo opened the door. The blast of icy wind took his breath away. Joachim pulled his goggles over his eyes and put Adam's over his eyes.

"Drop in five, four, three..."

Joachim started his tracking system on his wrist.

"One. Go, go, go!" Joachim pushed Adam out the door and fell with him.

The air rushed by, and Joachim could faintly hear the jet speeding away as it picked up speed. The sound of the wind was deafening, and the dark seemed endless. There were pinpricks of light down below. Joachim looked at his altimeter: thirty thousand feet. He still had twenty-five thousand feet to go before deploying the parachute. The wind was calm, and he was on course for his destination. At fifteen thousand feet, Joachim began to make out more detail of the ground below. At ten thousand feet, he made some adjustments to his trajectory, then pulled the cord to deploy the parachute at exactly five thousand feet. The chute deployed with a jerk. Joachim pulled down his night vision goggles that were connected to his tracking device. His landing zone was visible and clear.

The landing was going to be one of the most difficult of Joachim's sky diving career since Adam was unconscious. He came in as slowly as possible and landed without too much difficulty. Near the landing zone was a Jeep Wrangler hidden in the brush. It was painted flat black, had large tires, and was difficult to see in the dark. Joachim unhooked his harness from Adam and took off the insulated suit. Once the equipment was packed away, Joachim loaded Adam into the passenger seat of the jeep. One last look around with a flashlight to make sure there wasn't any evidence of his being there. They were good to go.

Joachim started the Jeep and drove back to the dirt road he came in on. He then drove for another ten miles and took a small side road. After a mile or so, he stopped. He threw Adam over his shoulder and hiked out into the woods for a mile or so and stopped by a creek in some dense woods. He looked around and was satisfied that the body wouldn't be found easily. He dumped Adam's body on the ground by the creek.

The sunrise was only an hour away and Joachim headed back to the Jeep. Before driving away, Joachim unlocked his cell phone and checked his numbered account and found that his fee had already been received. He smiled as he set his phone on the seat next to him, started the Jeep, and began his long drive home.

CHAPTER THREE

WASHINGTON, DC

Sitting at his large desk in his well-worn, leather chair, CIA Deputy Director Dirk Stevens had just finished a long meeting with the Senate Intelligence Committee answering their never-ending questions, some of which were beyond their comprehension. With a deep sigh, he ran his hand across his balding head and rubbed his eyes. He was getting too old for the never-ending meeting schedule. *It will end soon,* he thought. *Retirement to the Caribbean will be a welcome relief to the rat race.*

His belly rubbed against his desk drawer as he slid his mouse across his desk, activating the screen on his computer. After the fingerprint scan and extensive login procedure, he began reading his email. At that moment his personal cell phone began buzzing on the desk. The screen showed an unknown number from Montana. He almost didn't answer the call, suspecting that it was probably a scam call.

He answered the call, just to see who it was and to avoid reading any more email on Friday afternoon. "Hello," he said.

"Deputy Director Stevens, this is Adam Darcy," Adam said.

"Adam, where are you? Your cover was blown, and you disappeared. We thought you were kidnapped and murdered."

"I'm okay and am in Montana. This isn't a secure line, so I will explain later. Right now, I need money, identification, weapons, and transportation back to Washington. I was compromised. I tried to contact my parents to let them know that I was okay, but both of their phones went straight to voicemail. I need to know if my parents are okay," Adam said.

"We suspected that you were compromised. I had your parents moved to a safe house and they are being protected. What is the closest city to you?"

"Spokane is about three hours away."

"I will send an agent and car from the field office in Spokane."

"I will meet them in four hours at Yaak River General Store. Make sure that they are using counter surveillance. I need to remain dark."

"I will have a company jet ready in Spokane. See you soon. Call me when you arrive, and we will debrief then."

"Thanks. See you soon," Adam said as he ended the call.

CIA Deputy Director Stevens leaned back in his chair and sighed. He leaned forward and opened the bottom drawer of his desk, lifted the false bottom, and removed another cell phone. That one was a burner phone intended for one time communication. It was to be destroyed and disposed of after one call so it couldn't be tracked.

He pocketed the burner phone, logged out of his computer, and left his office. He locked the door behind him. As he passed his administrative assistant, Janet, he said, "See you Monday, Janet. Have a great weekend!"

He took the elevator down to the third level of the parking garage and found his black BMW 530i M-Spec. He always smiled when he saw his car. As a matter of habit, he walked around the car, looking for anything that might indicate that it had been tampered with. Seeing nothing, he unlocked the car and slid into the driver's seat. The car started with a ferocious growl and settled into a smooth, deep rumbling idle. The grin appeared on his face again.

Exiting the parking garage, Stevens drove through Foggy Bottom toward the Potomac River, crossed into Virginia on Highway 66, passed Arlington National Cemetery, and headed south to his home in Alexandria. He opened his garage door and pulled in.

Stevens had divorced from his wife many years before and lived alone. He didn't have any children. His home was in a quiet neighborhood with stately homes and large lawns. He worked most of the time, so he didn't have more than a passing knowledge of his neighbors.

Once inside his home, he stopped at the buffet and poured himself three fingers of Kentucky Bourbon from his home stock. He took the glass to his office, sat down, and removed the burner phone from his pocket, dialing a number from memory to make the call.

The call was answered on the second ring. "Wentworth?"

"I warned the Chinese that our agent was putting the pieces together about their part of our plan. They abducted him and left him for dead in a wilderness. Somehow, he managed to survive, and he just contacted me. I have sent an asset to eliminate him," Stevens said.

"He is proving more difficult than we thought. Make sure that he is eliminated," Wentworth said as he ended the call.

Stevens removed the SIM card and battery from the phone and broke it in half. He sighed again and swallowed the rest of the bourbon in one tip of the glass. Pocketing the used burner, he headed back to the garage and sat in his car. He backed out of the garage and headed out to dinner. As he crossed the Potomac, he rolled the window down, glanced in his mirrors, and tossed the burner over the railing. He kept the broken SIM card and disposed of it in a trash can at a gas station when he filled up the BMW with premium fuel.

CHAPTER FOUR

NORTHERN MONTANA

Adam watched as a black Chevy Tahoe with dark windows slowly drove through Yaak, Montana, then turned around and pulled up to the general store and parked. The driver waited in the Tahoe for a few minutes, then exited the vehicle and went in the store. Adam could tell that the man didn't belong there and assumed that he was his contact. Adam waited for the man to come out of the store.

A few minutes later, the man exited the store with a bag of snacks and a soft drink. He slowly walked toward his own vehicle while observing his surroundings. Adam could tell he was a professional and decided to approach him. He was still nervous and had a feeling that something was off. He continued watching from his concealed location. Adam started walking toward the store from across the street. The man saw Adam and paused, stared at him, and waved him over.

As Adam was crossing the street, the man partially concealed behind the Tahoe, smoothly reached behind his back and removed his Sig Sauer P320 and screwed on the silencer. Suddenly, he leveled the handgun, its bullets chambered in a .45 ACP caliber cartridge, and fired over the hood of the Tahoe. The gun spat in a "pfft," and Adam disappeared.

Adam detected the tell-tale sign of movement in the man's extra-large shoulders and dove into the ditch on the side of the road just as the .45 caliber bullet radiated heat onto Adam's face as it narrowly missed his head. He lay in the ditch a moment, his heart racing and breathing like he just ran up a mountain. Adam removed the Smith & Wesson M&P Shield—that Johnny loaned him—from his waistband and peeked over the edge of the ditch. From ground level, he saw the man's feet under the Tahoe. From a prone position, he aimed and fired two shots. The first shot hit the man in the ankle under the Tahoe. The man fell and Adam fired a third shot into the man's forehead, killing him instantly.

Adam ran to the Tahoe, grabbed the man's wallet and gun, jumped in the Tahoe and took off with rocks and dirt flying everywhere. Adam knew that the county sheriff would have been called and there was a description of the Tahoe from the store cashier. Ten miles down the road, Adam began to watch for a dirt side road. He saw one on the left and slammed on the brakes. He hit the dirt in a slide and controlled the Tahoe enough to straighten it out and barely kept it on the road. He flew down the road a mile and then slowed to allow the dust to settle. It was almost dark, and he needed to find a hiding spot. He saw a stand of trees with an overgrown two-track road heading toward them that hadn't been used in a long time. It looked rough and muddy, so he shifted into four-wheel drive and slowly crawled over the rough surface. Once behind the trees, he found a spot to abandon the Tahoe.

An inventory of the Tahoe revealed that there was only half a bottle of water and a bag with a backup Sig Sauer P320 and two hundred rounds of ammunition. The wallet had a credit card and two hundred dollars in cash. He took the cash and gun and left the rest in the Tahoe. The credit card could be tracked. Nothing else would help. He wiped down all the surfaces, left the keys in the ignition, and started hiking.

When he approached the highway, he concealed himself behind some bushes and used his burner phone to call Johnny. He answered on the first ring. Adam explained what happened and that the only person who knew where he was, other than Johnny and Mary, was CIA Deputy Director Stevens, who sent him on the mission to Ottawa.

He asked for a ride and gave Johnny his location.

Johnny appeared about thirty minutes later in a 1956 Chevrolet Pickup. Johnny waited a few minutes knowing Adam was waiting elsewhere and being vigilant.

Adam was concealed behind some brush and spent a few moments making sure that Johnny wasn't followed. When he was comfortable that they weren't being observed, he ran to the truck. Johnny had the window down and yelled, "Get in!" Johnny put the truck in gear and drove away. The dim headlights barely lit the road.

Adam breathed a sigh of relief as they drove and got farther from where he ditched the Tahoe. He turned to Johnny. "Thank you for helping me again."

"No problem," Johnny said as he took them on a long journey through the mountain backroads. After a time of silence, Johnny said, "So, clearly, you're being setup and are now a target. Do you have anyone who you can trust?"

"I thought that I could trust Stevens, but now, I don't know who to trust," Adam said, then paused in thought. "I asked Stevens if my parents were safe, and he assured me that they were in a safe house being protected. I thought that was good, but now,

I think that they are being held against their will and will be used as leverage to get to me."

Johnny focused on the road and after a few moments said, "If you want, I can help you. I am retired and off grid. I don't care about the politicians and the corruption in DC. In fact, I would relish being able to take them down. Would you like my help?"

"I would. You and Mary helped me when I suddenly showed up on your doorstep. I think that I can trust you," Adam said.

"Okay, what do you know so far?" Johnny asked.

Adam was quiet thinking for a moment trying to decide what he could say. His mission was top secret, and he couldn't discuss it. He also knew that he had been betrayed by Deputy Director Stevens. "I'm not sure how much I can say about my mission. It was top secret and I reported directly to the deputy director."

"Even though I am officially retired from the NSA, I still maintain my top-secret clearance and consult for all the alphabet organizations."

Realizing that he didn't have much choice and Johnny technically had the clearance to discuss the details with, Adam decided to take the risk and reveal his mission to Johnny. "My mission was to track Chang Huang and Pak Hou from the Chinese Peoples State. They are suspected of working to smuggle a biological weapon and releasing it in North America. We think that the Chinese are planning an attack in the United States and Canada to release a virus into the atmosphere that will sicken and kill untold numbers. The COVID-19 virus was a test to see how the US and the world would respond to such an incident. We also suspect that the Chinese Spy Balloon incident was a test of a possible distribution system. Now, I suspect that there is corruption within the US government. Stevens must be involved, and I'll bet that there are others as well. Why didn't the military shoot down the spy balloon when it was first found? There are a lot of questions that we don't know the answers to yet. We need to figure this out. But first, where are my parents?" Adam asked as they were pulling up to Johnny's cabin.

Johnny and Adam got out of the truck and walked to the front door of the cabin. Johnny pressed a knot in the log near the door and with a faint audible click, a small, concealed door opened to reveal a fingerprint reader. He placed one of his fingers on the reader and the red light turned green. He gently closed the concealed door and unlocked the front door with a key. "The key looks old school but has a biometric reader that the lock must authenticate before the bolt will retract with the key mechanism."

They stepped into the cabin and the lights turned on automatically. Johnny turned to Adam and said, "I have some contacts that I can check with. I should be able to find where your parents are being held. Give me all the information that you know, and I will go to work on that. In the meantime, you need to get some rest. The guest room is yours. There are extra clothes in the closet and toiletries in the bathroom. We will have an initial plan in the morning to discuss."

Johnny showed Adam to the guest room. "Thank you so much for your help, Johnny. I don't know how I can repay you for your generosity."

"You're welcome. It's what we do. Get some rest," Johnny said as he closed the door.

Adam lay on the bed and was asleep instantly.

CHAPTER FIVE

NORTHERN MONTANA

Adam awoke and sat on the edge of the bed. He rubbed his eyes and could smell the aroma of freshly brewed coffee. He went to the bathroom and took a steaming hot shower, shaved, and brushed his teeth. He picked some clothes and dressed. When he emerged from the room, Johnny was already hard at work typing furiously at his workstation. He turned when he heard Adam and offered him a cup of hot coffee with a frothy topping of whipped cream.

After the first sip of hot coffee, Adam exclaimed that was probably the best coffee that he had ever tasted. Johnny grinned and kept working for a few minutes and then turned his chair toward Adam.

"I have something on your parents. I checked the last location of your parents' phones, and they were at their home the last time that they pinged the cell towers. I then took that time and checked any other cell phones that pinged from that location close to that time. I tracked those phones to a house in Spencer, West Virginia. I have some friends in Virginia that we can have surveil the house to get eyes on the situation. They are en route to Spencer as we speak."

Adam's priority was to secure his parents. "I need to get to West Virginia as soon as possible. Do you have any suggestions?"

"I do. My younger brother, Ian, is a retired Air Force pilot and was basically born with wings. He has several airplanes. He made a lot of money after he retired from the Air Force flying covert missions for the alphabet organizations. He lives an hour from here and has his own runway on his ranch. I knew that you would need to get to West Virginia quickly, so I called him, and he is fueling up the Learjet now. If you are ready, we can go there now," Johnny said.

"That sounds great. Why are you helping me like this?" Adam asked.

"You will find out more when we reach Ian's ranch. I can tell you this: we have a group of retired guys that are looking for ways to get back in the game and help the people of the United States. We are all patriots and have a broad range of experience," Johnny said.

Johnny and Adam headed out the door and got in Johnny's pickup. As they were driving, Johnny explained that his brother Ian had assembled a team of trustworthy retired special ops assets that would assist Adam in securing his family. Ian would also be able to kit the mission from his extensive armory. The drive flew by as Johnny and Adam discussed the mission and how to accomplish their goal of securing Adam's parents, rooting out the corruption, and protecting the United States.

Johnny pulled up to the large entry edifice of Ian's ranch. The multi-thousand-acre ranch was fenced with a secure gate. There was a keypad for entry, but it was really a biometric scanner. Johnny opened the window and looked at the keypad with a flashing red light. In a moment, the light turned green, and the gate opened to allow entry. The road was paved and winding through open meadows and rolling hills. No buildings were visible from the gate. Adam looked around and only spotted one camera but knew that there were probably more. About a mile down the drive as they crested a small rise, the house came into view. It was a beautiful large log home with an imposing stone fireplace that sat on the edge of a valley. A large hangar and barn were also visible in the distance. They parked in front of the large garage attached to the main house.

As they were exiting the vehicle, Ian opened one of the four garage doors and walked out. Ian looked nothing like his brother Johnny; he was fit, clean shaven, and had salt-and-pepper hair. He was dressed in designer jeans and a crisp button-down shirt with Ray Ban Aviators sticking out of his pocket. The brothers greeted with a rough hug and back slapping. Ian turned to Adam and put his hand out and introduced himself.

"Johnny called me and told me your story," Ian said. "Please come in. We'll discuss the plan before wheels up."

CHAPTER SIX

NORTHERN MONTANA

Adam followed Ian and Johnny to the house and entered through the garage door. They made their way to the great room and Ian motioned for them to take a seat in front of the fireplace. The room was warm with a roaring fire in the fireplace and the leather couches wrapped Adam in comfort. He looked around and thought that it was the kind of room that he could spend the day reading and relaxing in without a care in the world. *Not today.* Ian came back in with three men following him. Ian introduced the men: David Stone, Tuck Landry, and Beck Michaels.

David was a retired Marine Force Recon commander. He was muscular with broad shoulders; his hair was black with hints of silver cut in a military style. His expertise was reconnaissance and piloting aircraft.

Tuck was a retired Navy Seal. He was wearing black tactical clothing and wore a full beard. His hair was brown, not yet show-ing any signs of gray. Although he wasn't a large man, he exuded a strength that would frighten most men. The scar on the left side of his face, from a knife fight in Iraq, made him look even more menacing. His expertise was infiltration, especially in the Middle East and his knowledge of the Arabic language. He was also an expert diver, sniper, knife fighting, and all things firearms.

Beck was a retired CIA agent. His hair was mostly gray. He was dressed in chinos, a button-down shirt, and a sport coat. He came from a wealthy business and political family and had many contacts in Washington, DC. He was an expert tactical planner and had extensive resources.

Ian then introduced himself. He was a retired Air Force Fighter Pilot who graduated from the United States Air Force Academy. He was an expert pilot and could pilot anything that flies. He had extensive experience flying covert missions.

Adam was impressed with all the men and was honored to have them helping him. Many would say the men were the best of the best and they fiercely loved their country.

After the introductions, Ian continued to say that each of the men in the room had seen the corruption in governments and the hatred of freedom in many of the world's communist and theocratic countries. They had been discussing ways to "get back in the game" as a private organization. Although each man was wealthy due to their special skills and the covert work that they had completed around the world before retirement, they needed and found a benefactor to fund their expensive missions.

"Since Johnny called last night, we have been setting everything up for this to be our first mission. We would like you to be on the team as lead on this rescue mission. If it goes well and the team unanimously agrees, you can join the team. We will need you to sign an NDA before we continue," Ian explained to Adam.

Adam said, "This is a lot to take in, but I like the sound of it. I will sign the NDA and we can get down to business."

Ian presented the NDA to Adam. It was simple and straight forward. The organization didn't have an official name and their identities or missions couldn't be revealed.

"Okay, now that the legal business is out of the way you need to know that we will not take on a mission unless we unanimously agree that it is a worthy cause. We have all talked before this meeting and have agreed to help you with this mission. We believe your story and have other data to indicate that there is likely corruption at the highest levels in the United States. This must be stopped before it's too late. Adam, please tell us your story and then we will discuss the plan," said Ian.

Adam told the story to the team. Even though he didn't know any of the team members until that day, he knew that they were trustworthy and that he wanted to be part of the team. The CIA probably processed his employment as missing-in-action or deceased, and he would need a new job anyway after it was all over.

They discussed the plan. Ian would fly the team to West Virginia International Field in Charleston, West Virginia. Two SUVs would be waiting in a hangar at the airport for them. Adam, Beck, and Ian would be in one SUV and David and Tuck would be in the second one. They would be outfitted before boarding the Learjet. Johnny would support them from Montana.

The next stop was the extensive armory located in the hangar that housed the Learjet 60. Each man picked his weapons, body armor, and comms. Outfitted with top shelf Heckler and Koch handguns and rifles all chambered in 5.56 mm, KaBar knives, flash bang and smoke grenades, along with silencers and a sniper rifle, completed the kit. Ian also chose to include a surveillance drone for overwatch.

They boarded the plane and Ian completed the pre-flight checklist. They stowed their gear and buckled in. Ian taxied to the end of the runway and took off. After they reached their cruising altitude of forty thousand feet and leveled off, they discussed the details of the mission. Adam made sure that each member of the team knew the details about his parents. His father, Ken, was eighty years old and healthy; his mother, Susie, was seventy-nine and was diagnosed with Parkinson's disease fifteen years before. His father cared for her, but the stress of being detained was probably difficult for her. Hopefully, she had her medications. If not, they would need to get her stabilized as soon as possible. They decided that they should bring a wheelchair in the SUV, blankets, and sedatives.

They arrived at West Virginia International Airport at midnight. They loaded the SUVs with their kits and supplies. There was fresh coffee in the hangar when they arrived, so they all loaded up with large to-go cups. They had a one-hour drive to reach Spencer, West Virginia.

During the drive, Adam called Johnny to get the latest update from his people surveilling the location. Johnny was sitting at his workstation in Montana when his encrypted cell phone rang. The screen showed that Adam was calling. He swiped his finger across the screen and waited a moment for the encryption to synchronize on both phones.

"Hi Adam, I have you on the way to Spencer," Johnny said.

"Hey Johnny. What is the latest from the team in Spencer?" Adam asked.

"They currently have eyes on the house. It has been quiet with little activity. They have identified two agents that regularly patrol the outside. Their thermal imaging shows one agent inside and two other individuals that are assumed to be your parents. They are moving about, so it doesn't look like they are being held against their will," Johnny said.

"Firepower, cameras, security system?" Adam asked.

"There may be rifles inside, and I would assume that there are. The agents that have been observed outside are sure to have concealed weapons. There are doorbell cameras in front and back. I will take control of the cameras and security system just before entry. I am monitoring those systems now. No additional counter surveillance has been found," Johnny said.

"Any other information?" Adam asked.

"That's all for now. There is a school nearby that was permanently closed a couple of years ago. The parking area is not easily visible from the road. Use that as your staging area. Ian can provide real time overwatch from there. When you activate your comms, I will be providing information from here," Johnny said.

"Sounds good, talk to you soon," Adam said.

"Copy that," Johnny said as he ended the call.

Adam turned to Ian and said, "Ian, what are your thoughts?"

"Sounds straight forward," Ian said.

As the two vehicles pulled into Spencer at 1:45 a.m., there was not a vehicle in sight. They pulled into the parking lot at the vacant school and parked close to the building out of sight.

The men exited the vehicles and kitted up for the night raid. Ian set up the drone and completed his pre-flight check. Adam gathered everyone to give last-minute instructions.

"Is everyone ready?" Adam asked and received affirmative replies. "Okay, the house is two blocks away. Does everyone have the location pinned on your wrist-mounted GPS?" Adam asked and again received affirmative replies. "Okay, as we discussed on the flight, Beck and David, leave your vehicle a block from the house and approach the back from the alley. Tuck and I will approach from the front. Ian will have our vehicle here and provide overwatch from the drone imaging. The surveillance team will monitor for any counter surveillance. They will be on comms. We will wait for the outside patrols to emerge and then take them down.

"Only use the force necessary to subdue them. Injections of Propofol will keep them sleeping while we escape. Once they are down, we will enter the house. Johnny will have taken control of the security and cameras and will be on comms. Priority is to secure the house by neutralizing the inside guard and securing my parents. They may be surprised and think that we are the enemy, so be careful.

"My Dad's name is Ken and my mom is Susie. She has Parkinson's Disease and is very sensitive to stress and will likely be very anxious. I will reveal myself to her as soon as possible to relieve her concerns. Once they are secured, Ian will pick us up out front. Beck and David, make your way back to your vehicle and head back to the airport. Everyone clear? Any questions?" Adam received affirmative replies. "Ian, send up the drone. Let's head out," Adam said.

CHAPTER SEVEN

SPENCER, WEST VIRGINIA

The street was dark and quiet. A few porch lights lit the front yards of random houses. The houses were modest one-story homes made of brick construction. The neighborhood was well-kept but was showing its age. Large trees shaded the road and yards of the homes. Dressed in black, they were fully kitted for the rescue. They looked more like soldiers on a battlefield instead of sneaking through the small-town neighborhood. Adam and Tuck made themselves known to the surveillance team and continued in the shadows on the cool night. They took up positions out of sight at the corner of the front yard of the target house. "Team one in place," Adam spoke quietly into the throat microphone of his communications device.

David and Beck made their way to the back of the target house. They were behind the fence out of sight. "Team two in place," David said.

"Overwatch in place," Ian said, pausing a moment as he double checked the drone's imaging. "Thermal imaging shows all guards inside - standby. Guard one is moving toward the front door and guard two is moving toward the back door. Visual confirmation, guards one and two exiting the house."

"I have eyes on guard one," Adam said. "Guard one walking around the east side of the house," Adam, in point position, moved silently with Tuck watching behind them. Adam moved within two meters of the guard and sprang at the back of the guard. He wrapped his right arm around the guard's neck from behind. The guard was struggling, and Adam continued to pull tighter into the sleeper hold. Tuck grabbed him and injected the full syringe into his left arm. The guard began to weaken and was asleep in seconds. The entire struggle only lasted fifteen seconds, but it felt like fifteen minutes. Adam's heart was pounding as he gently lowered the guard to the ground and said, "Guard one down." Tuck used flexicuffs to bind the guard and pulled him into the bushes so he wouldn't be seen from the street.

David and Beck jumped the fence and David landed on the second guard and brought him down. Beck was ready and injected him. He was out in ten seconds.

Beck flex-cuffed the guard and hid him behind a backyard shed. "Guard two is down," David said. David and Beck moved to the back door and had their backs to the wall on either side of the door. "Team two at back door, ready to enter," David said.

"Moving to your six," Tuck said as he and Adam moved in behind them. They decided to enter through the back door since the front door was more exposed. The back door had a patio cover, and they were more concealed from any unwanted sightings from a neighbor with insomnia.

Adam placed his hand on Beck's back and Tuck moved in behind David. David took the lead and carefully checked the doorknob to see if the door was locked. It was and Adam asked, "Ian, where is the guard inside?"

"Everyone inside is in two of the bedrooms," Ian said. "It looks like the last inside guard is sleeping while the other two keep watch."

David nodded to Beck, and he removed his lock picking tools. "Johnny, is the security system disarmed?" Adam asked.

"Yes, you are good to go," Johnny said.

Beck picked the lock and had the door open in twenty seconds. David grabbed the doorknob and slowly turned the knob and quietly opened the door. Beck and Adam held their rifles at the ready and Tuck was keeping an eye behind them. The door opened quietly and all four entered the house in formation.

"I have your thermal signatures just entering the house. There are two thermal signatures in the first room on the left. The other thermal signature is on the right at the end of the hallway," Ian said.

Adam and Tuck moved silently and cleared the kitchen and living room. Adam said, "Living room and kitchen clear." They moved to the first door on the left after clearing the kitchen and living room and waited.

David and Beck moved to the last bedroom also on the left and entered to clear the room. "Bedroom three, clear," David said. David and Beck moved to the bedroom on the right and nodded to Adam and Tuck. Adam held up three fingers and counted down. When he closed his fist, the teams moved into each room simultaneously.

David and Beck entered bedroom two with their rifles leading the way. They were quiet, but the guard awakened. Beck jumped onto the guard and pinned her to the bed. David was about to inject the guard, but she said, "If you are helping the Darbys, I have information for you. Please take me with you and I will share what I know. What is happening here is wrong, but I have not been able to get them away."

"Beck, cuff and gag her and we will check with the rest of the team. Guard three secured and will be coming with us. She says she has information for us. If it is not good, we will dump her," David said.

Adam and Tuck entered bedroom one and both of Adam's parents were sleeping in the bed. When Adam saw his parents sleeping peacefully, his eyes were near tears, with the knowledge that they were safe. Adam went to his mother and Tuck went to Adam's father. They gently awakened them.

"Adam, what are you doing here? We thought you were dead!" Susie exclaimed with a start and a trembling voice. She was shaking, not only with the emotional surprise of finding out that her son was alive, but the stress of the last few days had taken a toll on her.

"I'll explain later, but for now keep quiet, get up, and get dressed quickly. Get your medications and Dad, get your hearing aids and glasses. We need to leave in one minute." Into his comms, Adam said, "My parents are secure. Ian, we need pick up in one minute."

Ken and Susie quickly got dressed and grabbed what they needed. All seven people headed to the front door and lined up. Adam took the lead with Ken and Susie behind; Tuck had the prisoner held in front of him. David and Beck waited. Adam said to David and Beck, "See you soon," not wanting to give the prisoner any information about their destination.

Opening the front door just a crack, Adam watched for Ian. In a few moments, Ian pulled up to the front of the house. Ian said, "Front clear." Adam exited the front door and looked both ways then motioned for his parents and Tuck bringing the prisoner to follow him.

They rushed to the SUV and piled in. Ken climbed into the third seat and Adam put his mom into the front passenger seat. Adam climbed in the back door and slid all the way across, and Tuck pushed the prisoner in while Adam had his gun trained on her. Tuck jumped in and slammed the door.

At that moment, while Adam was holding his gun on the female agent, their eyes met and were locked together. A spark in Adam's brain caused him to blink rapidly a few times. He continued to stare at the woman and his brain and emotions were pulling at each other. He was attracted to her but shouldn't be since she was holding his parents hostage. He shook his head and turned to look at his mother in the front seat. His mind was racing, and his heart was still pounding.

"*Go, go, go!*" Tuck yelled.

The drone was still idling high above the house. Ian pressed a pre-programmed button on the tablet attached to the dash to send the drone to a preset location just outside of town in a roadside pullout. Ian drove out of town, pulled into the pullout and skidded to a stop. He jumped out, grabbed the drone, put it in the cargo area of the Tahoe, and jumped back into the driver's seat. He threw the Tahoe into drive and pulled back onto the road with dirt and rocks flying from the rear wheels. The big SUV was back up to the speed limit in a few seconds.

Once the teams were on their way back to the airport, the surveillance teams that Johnny had watching the safehouse prepared to leave. They stayed for forty-five minutes to warn the teams if there was any law enforcement activity. It was clear after forty-five minutes, so they left. Johnny also monitored for any law enforcement activity on the police scanner. Nothing.

On the drive to the airport, Adam removed the gag from the prisoner and asked, "What is your name and who do you work for?"

The woman had beautiful full lips and a great figure. Her dark brown hair was messy and her face free of makeup. Her dark brown eyes kept pulling Adam into them as he watched her. It was like there was a lightning storm in his head and his heart was thundering.

"My name is Ally, and I work for the CIA. Are you Adam Darby? I was told that you had been killed and that we were to protect your parents from the assassins that killed you. I knew something was wrong when Deputy Director Stevens told us that this mission was off the books. He told us that we needed to grab your parents in the middle of the night without letting them know. It was to be a kidnapping 'for their protection.' This isn't the way that we do things."

"Anyway, while we have been holding them at the safe house in Spencer, I have been doing some investigating into Deputy Director Stevens. From what I found he may have some connections to the Chinese Peoples State. I had a friend do some deep digging and we found that this corruption goes much higher than Stevens. We still need to do more investigation, but this needs to be exposed. I want to help you expose this corruption and bring them down. Stevens is a prick! He told me that if I performed this mission well, then I could become his 'assistant' and we could work 'closely together.' He said all of this while undressing me with his eyes. What a jackass!"

Adam's dad, Ken, spoke up from the back seat. "Adam, I believe her. She was very good to us and made sure that we were well taken care of. The other two treated us like prisoners. When the others were outside, she told us that we were going to escape as soon as we could get away from them. She also was very kind and helped your mom with keeping her medications on schedule."

Adam's mom, Susie, turned toward the back of the SUV and said, "Adam, your dad's right. I would have been in a bad way without her help."

"Okay, we will take you with us, but we will have to keep you restrained until we verify your story. Is that okay with you? If not, we will sedate you and leave you in the woods," Adam said.

"I understand," Ally said.

Adam pulled his cell phone from his pocket and called Johnny. "Johnny, I need you to do a thorough background check on Ally, umm. Ally, what is your last name?" Adam said as he looked at Ally.

Ally replied, "Grace. Allison Cherie Grace."

Adam continued with Johnny. "Her full name is Allison Cherie Grace. Please check her out. She maintains that she works for the CIA and found some dirt on Stevens and connections to the Chinese. We will keep her restrained until we return and get your report."

"Got it. I will have the information in a couple of hours," Johnny said.

"Thanks Johnny. We'll speak again soon," Adam said has he ended the call.

Ian pulled up to the gates of the private aviation area of the West Virginia International Airport. Ian entered the gate code and they slowly drove to their hangar. When they arrived, the hangar door was already open and Ian pulled in. David and Beck were already there.

Ian opened the back of the Tahoe and placed the drone back into its Pelican case and moved it to the Learjet. He then poured a large cup of coffee from the machine in the hangar. Beck started the pot when they arrived, so it was hot and fresh. Because it was 4:00 a.m., they had been up all night, and he had to fly three hours, he needed the caffeine boost. With the large coffee cup in hand, he began the preflight checklist. As he walked around the plane, the team loaded the gear into the luggage compartment of the Learjet. Adam escorted his parents and Ally into the aircraft and got them seated. The rest of the team boarded the plane and took their seats.

Ian completed his preflight check and David used the tug to move the plane from the hangar to the apron on the tarmac. David moved the tug back into the hangar and closed the door. He boarded the plane and made sure that all seatbelts were buckled. David took his seat in the cockpit with Ian, and they began the startup procedure. The jet engines slowly spun up to speed with a high-pitched whine. When the engines were at operating temperature, Ian pushed the throttles forward and contacted air traffic control for takeoff clearance.

CHAPTER EIGHT

SKIES OVER UNITED STATES

As the flight to Ian's ranch in Montana reached its cruising altitude of forty thousand feet, Adam moved to a seat across from his parents. They were holding hands and his mother looked very anxious. Softly, Adam told the story of how he was abducted in Ottawa and his journey to civilization. He told them of his chance encounter with Mary and how she introduced him to Johnny. The details of the attempt on his life and the corruption uncovered were left vague. They were relieved to know that Adam was alive and well. Tears and hugs were shared, and a feeling of love and peace surrounded them.

Ally was still restrained and watched as Adam spoke to his parents. They were several seats away and speaking softly, so she could not hear what they were saying. It was clear to her that their family bond was strong and their love for one another was deep. The emotional connection that she witnessed caused unexpected feelings to bubble up inside her. She turned her head to look out the window at the dark sky and a tear rolled down her cheek as she thought of her parents and their tragic deaths.

During Adam's conversation with his parents, he noticed that Ally was watching him. He tried to ignore her and focus on his parents. While he mostly succeeded, his mind kept drifting toward her. After he finished his discussion with his parents, they asked for pillows and blankets. He gave them what they needed, and they drifted off in airplane-sleep mode: not too deep, but light sleep came as they came down from the adrenaline rush of the rescue and finding out that Adam was still alive. They continued to hold hands and Susie's head was resting on Ken's shoulder.

Ally continued to stare out the window and saw that the sky was beginning to lighten a little behind them. She wondered where they were going but, even with the unknown circumstances, she knew that she had done the right thing. She would likely be fired from the CIA, but she couldn't be a part of the corruption that she had witnessed. She thought about how she would explain what she found and what she suspected was happening. She was still looking out the window when she sensed someone. Adam sat in the seat next to her. A lightning bolt of energy exploded within her. She turned toward Adam and he smiled at her. The smile was bright and his eyes a penetrating green. She thought that she could get lost staring into those eyes. *Stop it,* she said to herself.

Adam spoke softly to Ally and asked her why she so easily surrendered to them and gave them information. She told him that since she was a little girl, she wanted to be a spy. She loved spy movies and pretended to be a spy, saving people from "bad guys." She always believed that the United States was the "good guys" and that everyone in law enforcement and intelligence was a good guy. She talked about going to Georgetown and studying for dual degrees in political science and computer science. She was recruited as a junior to work at the CIA as an intern. That led to a permanent position as a special agent after graduating. The training program at The Farm was intense, but she was top of her class. She was trained to evade interrogation techniques and mislead the enemy if she were captured. After the incident with Deputy Director Stevens, she was disenchanted and felt betrayed by her own people.

Adam listened to Ally and watched her for any signs of deception. It was hard to stay focused; his attention was pulled to her long dark hair, brown eyes, and beautiful lips. As they talked, Adam could not find any tells that would indicate that she was deceiving him, unless she was extremely good at lying. Adam remained cautious and thought about all the information that she told him. He had the same training she received at The Farm a year earlier. He too was top of his class and knew what it took to accomplish that feat. Adam thanked her for her honesty and sharing her story. He moved back to his seat and continued to think about her as he began to doze off.

Adam woke with a start when the wheels touched down at the ranch in Montana. He rubbed his eyes and looked around the cabin. Everyone was waking up and getting ready to deplane.

Ian taxied the Learjet to the tarmac in front of the hangar and shut down the engines. Once the shutdown was complete, he stood, exited the cockpit, and stretched. He was tired but felt more alive than he had in a long time. He opened the door and stairs and motioned to everyone that they could deplane. Each person exited the aircraft, with Ken and Adam helping Susie to negotiate the stairs. A wheelchair was brought out for Susie, and she sat down gratefully.

Ian addressed Ken and Susie. "This is my ranch. I called ahead and had one of my guest cabins prepared for you. It is close to the main house and there is easy access between them. You are my guests, and it is my honor to host you for as long as needed. This is a safe place that is completely off grid. Please let me or any of my staff know if you need anything and we will take care of it."

Ken and Susie thanked Ian as one of his staff led them to an awaiting ATV to take them to their cabin.

Ian turned to the rest of the team and said, "The rest of us have some business to discuss before we hit the rack. Please join me in the hangar conference room." The conference room was decorated in the lodge style of the main house. The large table that could seat twelve was constructed of a huge, live-edge slab of black walnut. There were plush leather chairs surrounding the table and a bank of TV screens on one wall. Ian sat down and thumbed a remote turning on the wall of TV screens while the rest of the team and Ally found their seats.

An image of Johnny at his workstation appeared in the center screen. Johnny said, "Great to see you all. The first thing that we need to discuss is Ally. Ally, thank you for joining us and offering to help us with this mission. I did a thorough background check and additional vetting through my contacts. You were born in Miami, Florida and graduated from South Miami High School with top honors. Your father was a lawyer who graduated from Miami University originally from Connecticut and your mother was of Cuban descent and was a homemaker. After high school, you went to Georgetown and completed bachelor of science degrees in political science and computer science. You were recruited by the CIA in your junior year with an internship. You graduated top of your class from CIA training at The Farm. Your career was on the fast track. I spoke with some of my old contacts, and they all spoke very highly of you. I found out that you were on a special mission at the request of Deputy Director Stevens. Does that sound correct?"

Ally confirmed the information.

"Adam relayed the information that you provided him on the flight. Will you please give us a detailed briefing for the rest of the team?" Johnny said.

Ally took thirty minutes presenting her initial findings to the team and the motivation for her providing this information to the team. Adam then suggested that they remove the restraints from Ally and accept her onto the team for the assignment. He was hopeful that there would be more missions that they could work on together.

The team voted unanimously to accept Ally on the condition that she sign the NDA that Adam signed earlier. She agreed and the restraints were removed. She rubbed her wrists, grateful to be released and told the team that she understood and appreciated their cautiousness.

Ian then welcomed Ally to the team and his ranch. "Adam and Ally, we have accommodations prepared for you in the bunk house that you'll share with the rest of the team. You'll each have your own guest suite. I had my staff go to town and get some clothes for each of you. Please make yourselves at home here. We'll reconvene for a mission planning meeting at 5:00 p.m. Breakfast is waiting for us in the main house."

The team all stood and headed to the main house in side-by-side ATVs and joined Adam's parents for breakfast. After breakfast they all adjourned to their rooms for some much-needed rest.

CHAPTER NINE

WASHINGTON, DC

Deputy Director Stevens was sitting at his desk preparing for his next meeting with the Congressional Intelligence Oversight Committee. It was the part of the job he loathed, working with the politicians. The meeting would be the next day and would last the better part of the day. His secretary, Janet, knocked on his door and Stevens looked up, saw her through the door window, and motioned her in. She brought in a tray with lunch for Stevens. She placed the tray with a sandwich, chips, and diet soda on his desk and left his office closing the door behind her.

He was reviewing his presentation when his cell phone rang. He looked at the phone lying screen up on his desk and saw the caller identification and frowned. He swiped the answer bar on the screen and said brusquely. "Stevens." The caller was one of the agents that was guarding Adam Darby's parents. He reported that Ken and Susie Darby were gone, and Agent Grace was also missing and assumed kidnapped by the intruders. Also, nothing was recorded on any of their cameras, and their laptops were the only items missing. Stevens fumed and slammed his fist on his desk.

"How hard is it to watch a couple of senior citizens?" he yelled as he hung up the phone. He immediately grabbed a burner phone

from his desk and shut down his computer. He stormed out of his office without eating the lunch that Janet had just delivered. He didn't say a word to her as he headed to the elevator.

In the parking garage, he pressed the "unlock" button on his key fob and climbed into his car, forgetting to check for anything out of place before opening the door. He left the parking garage with tires squealing and headed for Virginia.

Once out of the DC metro area and into the endless sea of brake lights, the heated anger began to subside. The farther he drove, the calmer he became. The view of the Potomac alongside George Washington Memorial Parkway was stunning and produced a feeling of calm as the powerful BMW ate the miles. He pulled into the trailhead parking lot at the Mount Vernon Trail Potomac Overlook and got out of the car. He walked along the trail and found a bench looking over the mighty river. He plopped down on the bench and let out a sigh and thought, *this is getting out of hand. First, Adam Darby was not lost in the woods and then was not killed when I sent an assassin after him. Now Adam's parents—who were the backup plan to blackmail Adam—are gone. The rescue of his parents must have been Adam Darby. But how did he have the resources to pull off such a brazen rescue attempt so quickly? When I spoke with Adam, he was deep in northern Montana without any money, credit cards, or identification. Who did Adam know who could pull this together?*

The more he thought about it, the more he couldn't wrap his mind around what happened. He pulled out the burner phone to call Wentworth. It was a difficult call to make. He had to report another setback. Not a major one but one that needed to be reported nonetheless. He took a deep breath and pressed speed dial number "one."

The call connected and was answered. "What is it now, Stevens? I didn't expect another call from you so soon." Stevens replied and told Wentworth what he knew.

"You need to find and neutralize Darby. It must be your top priority!" Wentworth said in his deep sonorous voice.

Stevens said, "I'm working on it and will get my best people to find him, but I need to be careful and not pull too many company assets into our plan. I will use anonymous contractors for the hit. The more people working on any aspect of our plan, the more risk that someone may start putting the pieces together. Granted, we have many pieces to sort through, but we need to minimize the risk."

"Just get it done, Stevens. We have a lot riding on this," Wentworth yelled as he immediately ended the call.

Stevens looked at the phone and put it back in his pocket and watched a man, rowing a scull, glide through the water heading upstream. Once they passed and no one was on the trail to his left or right, he removed the burner phone from his pocket and took out the SIM card. He broke the phone and threw it as far as he could into the Potomac. He broke the SIM in two and dropped it in a trash can at the parking lot where he left his car. He walked around his BMW and—finding nothing out of place—unlocked the door and started the massive engine.

He pulled out of the parking lot and headed to Route 1 and slammed the accelerator to the floor. The engine snarled and accelerated up the on-ramp, hitting one hundred miles per hour before he merged into the traffic. He smiled as he quickly changed lanes to the left-most lane. After a couple of miles at one hundred twenty miles per hour, he slowed to a more orderly pace and kept up with traffic. The speed and power of his car represented the power that he craved. He would gain this power and wealth once the plan with Wentworth was complete.

CHAPTER TEN

GENEVA, SWITZERLAND

Liam Wentworth, the CEO of DanZe Pharmaceuticals, called a meeting of his advisors in his headquarters building in Geneva, Switzerland. DanZe Pharmaceuticals was a research and development pharmaceutical company that was on the edge of a breakthrough for the treatment of communicable diseases. Their process would allow a near-real-time implementation of a drug that could be used to treat viruses. Their testing of the drug with the COVID-19 pandemic proved that it would work. Even though the virus could have been stopped with their product, it wasn't time to release it. The fast tracking of the COVID-19 vaccines was a trial run to get approval without the years waiting. It was going to make DanZe Pharmaceuticals the most valuable corporation on the planet and the most powerful.

The meeting included a secure video call with Qi Limpon, the head of the Chinese Peoples State, his head of security, Tomas Finn, and his second in command, Alex Giovanni.

Liam Wentworth was already a very rich man, but money wasn't all he craved. He was a man of power, and that power gave him the satisfaction that he was the best and no one could or would beat him. He was a risk taker and was willing to kill as many people as it took to become the most powerful man in the world. He always dressed in the highest quality suits, custom made by the best tailor in Switzerland. His dark hair would have been graying, but he made sure that it was colored and styled perfectly. His dark eyes squinted as he focused on the task at hand during the upcoming meeting.

The meeting was to take place in the private conference room connected to Wentworth's office. The office was located on the top floor of the DanZe building and overlooked Lake Geneva. The view was spectacular. Tomas Finn was the first to arrive, followed closely by Alex Giovanni. The three took their seats at the conference room table and Wentworth pressed a button on the remote. A screen lowered from the ceiling and the image of Qi Limpon was displayed.

Wentworth said, "Welcome to the meeting, Qi. We have a few items to discuss. First, I would like to get a report from you about the distribution of the virus and the security of the distribution plan. The assets that I have in place in the United States military and CIA were successful in letting the balloon drift across the United States and destroying the proof-of-concept distribution system. Qi, did the data collection and distribution system work as we planned?"

"Thank you for the warm greeting, Liam. Yes, the distribution system worked flawlessly. The data link to the balloon also worked as planned. My team has thoroughly analyzed every aspect of the data. The distribution was projected to directly reach thirty percent of the United States population with the six balloons we are planning on releasing within twenty four hours. The prevailing winds and person-to-person infection rates are projected to reach eighty percent of the population within one week. On the next topic of operational security, there was a CIA agent that was surveilling our primary ground agents in Canada. Thanks to Liam's assets in the CIA, we knew he was there. We captured and drugged him. He was released within a remote region of the northwestern United States. The drug should have made him forget anything during his detainment. Unfortunately, he found his way out of the wilderness, even though he should have died of exposure. This shouldn't be a problem. We don't think that he knew anything about the operation, just monitoring a known CPS asset," Limpon said.

"Thank you, Qi. I know that you are confident that he didn't know anything, but to be on the safe side, we need to neutralize him. I have already asked my highly placed asset in the CIA to get this completed as soon as possible. His first attempt was unsuccessful and his backup plan of using the agent's parents for blackmail has also failed with their rescue. Although, we don't have proof that this agent rescued his parents, it is the most logical conclusion.

"Qi, please prepare a plan to have someone from your team find this agent and take him out. He is a loose end that we need to tie off."

"What is the status of the new virus? Will it be ready for the planned distribution date?" Wentworth asked.

"Yes, the production is on track to be completed by the end of the week. I visited our lab in Wuhan yesterday and the scientists have been successful delivering the virus to monkeys and stopping the spread using your product. There was a twenty percent death rate without treatment as we planned," Qi said.

"Thank you, Qi. That is good news. Everything is going according to plan. Tomas, any concerns on security here or with our distribution system?" Wentworth asked.

"No concerns with security, here, in China, or at the FDA. Our asset there is putting everything in place to fast track through the approval process," Tomas Finn said.

"Alex, please give us an update on the vaccine production," Wentworth asked.

"The production plan is ready," Alex Giovanni said.

Wentworth looked at each one of the men and said with a smile, "Good work gentlemen. This will make us very, very rich! Thank you for your updates."

Wentworth ended the meeting, returned to his desk, and turned his chair and stared out of the floor-to-ceiling windows watching the boats come and go on the smooth, dark blue water of Lake Geneva. He savored the thought of the plan coming together. He turned back to his desk and called his secretary and asked her to request a meeting with United States President Grange.

CHAPTER ELEVEN

NORTHERN MONTANA

At 5:00 p.m., Adam and team had all gathered in the hangar conference room. Ian, seated at the head of the table, picked up the remote control and powered on the screens. Johnny was again in the center screen.

Ian welcomed everyone to the meeting. "Hi everyone. I hope you all were able to rest some after the long night. Hello Johnny, thanks for joining us. Let's get started. Johnny, since you have been working on this all day, please give us an update."

"I spoke with Ally after our meeting to get more details on her investigation. Based on this information, I can confirm that Deputy Director Stevens appears to be compromised. The trick will be to determine who he is working with. I was able to get his personal cell phone number and have been tracking it. It is encrypted, so we can't tell who he is talking to or what is being said, but we can triangulate the location of the phone and log incoming or outgoing calls. I am sure that he is not using his personal cell phone for communication with his conspirators, so the calls themselves are probably not important to our mission. My guess is that he is using one time use burner phones. Those are nearly impossible to track since they are only online when they are powered on and in use. By constantly monitoring his personal cell phone's location and comparing that to other phones in the same location, we can grab the burner calls," Johnny said as he looked around the room to make sure everyone was following. They all gave nods of understanding.

"Today, Stevens received a call on his personal cell phone at 12:23 this afternoon while he was in the office. The call was short. Immediately afterward, he left the office. I tracked his cell phone and he stopped at the Mount Vernon Trail Potomac Overlook in Virginia. He was stopped for thirty minutes. During that time, I logged a call from the same location from a burner phone. It came online just before the call and went offline just after the call which lasted five minutes. I was able to trace the call being received by a cell phone in Geneva, Switzerland. I checked the location of the receiving phone, and it was located within the DanZe Pharmaceuticals building. I am now tracking that phone as well. This phone is registered to DanZe Pharmaceuticals. We will need to hack into the DanZe system to determine who the phone is assigned to. I have a hacker friend of mine working on that."

"Thank you, Johnny, that is good work and very helpful. Okay, it sounds like we need to develop a plan," Ian said as he looked around the room for acknowledgement from the team.

Adam spoke up. "I think that we need to have a two-pronged approach. One, let's follow Stevens and see if we can get a bug in his car and house. I'm doubtful that he will speak in those locations, but it might prove useful. A tracker on his car would also be useful. Two, we should send a team to Geneva to run a surveillance operation on the receiver of these calls."

"That sounds like the start of a good plan, Adam," Ian said. "Other comments?"

"Stevens knows both Adam and me, so we should go to Geneva. Tuck and Beck can go to DC to watch Stevens," Ally said.

Tuck and Beck both nodded in agreement.

Adam looked at Ally and thought a moment, agreed, and asked, "What resources do we have for surveillance?"

Ian pulled the keyboard on the table closer to him and said, "We have a large armory here at the ranch that includes electronics and imaging capabilities. We have commercial products and some in-house designed state-of-the-art devices." Ian quickly typed a few commands and a list of items appeared on the screen. "These are the items that we have immediately available in the armory. The bugs and tracking devices have new proprietary technology that makes them extremely difficult to detect. These are fully vetted prototype devices that will eventually be offered to the alphabet agencies in the US, but for now we are the only ones with access to them." Ian grinned as he looked at the stunned faces in the room. "Johnny was instrumental in the design of these devices and is fully up to speed on their operation. He will be on site in two hours to train you in their operation."

"I will be co-pilot for Ian on the flights. I have my pilot certification for the Learjet and will back up either team," David said.

"Thanks, David. There will be a lot of flying and I'll appreciate the company. One more item that we need to discuss. Since Adam and Ally will be traveling to Geneva, they will need new identities. Johnny has already created these and will bring them with him." Ian stood up, turned around, and touched a hidden release button on the wall behind him. A secret compartment opened revealing a safe. Ian put his palm on the palm reader and a green light flashed on the display. He then put his eye on the eyepiece and a retinal scanner scanned his unique retinal pattern. The second green light flashed and the safe automatically opened slowly. Ian reached in, pulled out a stack of US dollars, Euros, and credit cards. He riffled through the safe for a moment and found some Swiss Fracs. He gave them to Adam and Ally to split between them, then he closed the safe and the hidden compartment door. "Next, we will go to the hangar and visit the armory. Each of you will stock up on the items that you will need. I will file a flight plan for a departure at 7:00 tomorrow morning. Johnny, thanks for joining. We'll see you in a couple of hours," Ian said.

The meeting adjourned, and as they exited the hangar conference room, they saw that the house staff prepared a barbecue meal and set up tables in the hangar. They were all famished since they slept through lunch and immediately plated their meals at the buffet. There were smoked pork ribs, pulled pork, and beef brisket. The smell was amazing and there was not much talk while they were eating. After the meal, the excitement of seeing the technology was palpable. They all stood, and Ian led them to the armory. The door was concealed so well that they couldn't tell there was a door there. Ian pressed the hidden switch and the concealed door opened with a whoosh revealing a large safe like door that had the same palm and retinal scans required for entry. Ian opened the door to the armory and stood to the side allowing the team to enter. They each picked their desired sidearms, body armor, and ammunition. Then they chose optics and listening devices.

They all turned as Johnny walked in with a huge smile on his face. Adam introduced Johnny to Ally since it was the first time meeting her in person. Johnny handed passports and cover story packs to Adam and Ally and said, "Review these and memorize all the details. Let's get to the bugs first." Johnny opened a drawer and removed a small Pelican box and moved to the table and opened it. Inside the box was a smartphone and twelve small black disc shaped devices and twelve similar-looking devices with a clear dot in the center. Johnny removed the cell phone and showed the team.

"This is a custom cell phone that will connect anywhere in the world. It uses cellular and wireless networks and if not available connects via satellite if there is a clear view of the sky. There is no known way to trace these devices. There is a pre-installed app that automatically connects to the audio and video bugs in the case. The transmissions are very difficult to detect and are completely encrypted, visible only to these specific devices. That means that each device can see and hear any bug that has been placed. If you notice, there are six stickers in the lid of the box. These are tracking devices and can easily be concealed on a vehicle, clothing, computer, or anything that you stick it to. The trackers also connect to the smartphone and utilize the same app. I can see and hear all devices at my workstation. You will each have comms and I will stay in communication with each of you during your missions."

"These are like nothing I have ever seen in the CIA," Adam exclaimed.

Ian handed out duffle bags to each of the team members. They loaded up and exited the armory. After Ian closed and secured the armory, they all loaded their gear bags into the Learjet's cargo area and headed to the main house in their side-by-side ATVs.

They gathered in the main living room around the massive fireplace. Ian offered everyone a drink. They kicked back, enjoying their drinks and lively discussion. After a couple of hours, yawns were starting and Ian said, "I would like to thank each of you for your expertise and enthusiasm. It is truly a pleasure to work with each of you. Please stay as long as you like. I am headed to bed; I have a long flight tomorrow." He smiled and waved as he exited the living room heading down the hallway to his suite. The rest of the team said their goodnights and headed to their rooms.

Adam took a long shower. He was mentally prepared for the trip and decided to stop at his parents' cabin first thing in the morning and say goodbye to them. Seconds after his head hit the pillow, Adam went to sleep.

CHAPTER TWELVE

NORTHERN MONTANA

Adam awoke at 5:00 a.m. feeling well rested. He got up and decided to go for a quick run to get the day started. He looked in the closet and found that there was a pair of running shoes in his size and he found some exercise clothes in the dresser. He quickly dressed and laced up his shoes. He stepped outside into the cool brisk air and shivered slightly in the morning's pre-light dawn. After a few quick stretches, he took off and ran at a leisurely pace down to the hangar and then ran the length of the runway and back for a three-mile run. Satisfied that he was fully awake and ready for the day, he jogged to his parents' cabin and told them the plan and would see them later. He then went back to his room, showered, and dressed for the day.

At 6:45 a.m., Adam and the team gathered at the hangar, grabbed large coffees in to-go cups, and boarded the Learjet. Their flight plan had them landing at the Manassas Regional Airport to drop off Tuck and Beck. They would then fuel up for the long transatlantic flight to Bern, Switzerland. The airports were chosen to throw off any tracking, as unlikely as it may be.

Ian completed his pre-flight checklist with David, and they boarded the Learjet. The ground crew pushed the Learjet out of the hangar. Ian and David checked that everything was working properly and that the area was clear around the aircraft. They started the engines and allowed them to reach operating temperature. Moments later, the jet leapt from the ground and was ascending to their cruising altitude.

Ian landed at the Manassas Regional Airport, taxied to the private terminal, and parked the Learjet in the assigned spot then shut down the jet engines. Once the shutdown was complete, he called for the rental car and the fuel truck. The driver left the rental car near the door of the Learjet and quickly departed. Tuck and Beck waited for the driver to leave and opened the door of the aircraft. They opened the cargo area and grabbed their duffels and put them in the trunk of the car.

The car was a silver Toyota Camry four-door sedan that was one of the most common cars on the road. They would be nearly invisible. They put their gear in the trunk and headed out of the airport.

The fuel truck arrived as they were driving away. Ian met the fuel truck, and they began fueling the Learjet. The rest of the team stayed on board. The flight would take around eight hours. It took thirty minutes to finish fueling the Learjet and another fifteen minutes to clear for departure.

Ian taxied to the end of the runway, looked over at David, and said, "Do you want to take her up?"

David smiled and said, "I thought you'd never ask."

Air traffic control gave them permission to takeoff and David pushed the throttles to the max and they were airborne in less than half a mile. They continued to climb reaching their cruising altitude of forty-five thousand feet. David engaged the autopilot and looked over at Ian and said, "That was fun!"

In the cabin of the aircraft, Adam and Ally sat facing each other. Adam said, "Tell me your cover story." He smiled at her, feeling the excitement of the upcoming mission and something else. "We have a long flight and should be knowledgeable about our partner's history."

"My name is Sierra Johnson, thirty-five years old, born in Davenport, Iowa. I attended Iowa State University and graduated with a degree in Mass Communications. I am an only child. My father passed away in 2012 and my mother is in a nursing home. I work as a freelance journalist and publish exposé news articles in various publications. I have been married to Andrew Johnson for eight years and live in Atlanta, Georgia."

"Great, my name is Andrew Johnson. You must be my wife!" Adam laughed.

They both laughed and Adam got up and said, "Would you like something to drink and a snack?"

Ally requested a Diet Coke and cookies. Adam went to the galley and brought back the soft drinks and a bag of cookies. He placed them on the table between them. They each took a sip and grabbed a cookie.

"Okay, husband, tell me your story," she said with a grin.

"My name is Andrew Johnson, and I was born in Phoenix, Arizona. I am 36 years old and attended Iowa State. I graduated with a degree in business and went on to get an MBA. I work as a junior executive at Peachfield Pharmaceuticals. I work with the logistics team. We live in Atlanta in a suburb called Riverdale. I work remotely most of the time and only spend a few weeks in the office each year. We mix work and vacation in our many travels."

"Where did we get married?" Adam asked.

"We had a destination wedding in Estes Park, Colorado. We got married in an outdoor chapel overlooking the Rocky Mountain National Park. It was in September, so the Aspen trees were displaying their magnificent golden autumn leaves. Our honeymoon was there and in Grand Lake, Colorado. We stayed in a lake house for a week," Ally said.

"Good, it sounds like our cover stories match. Hopefully, we will only use them to pass through customs. Now, what are we doing in Geneva? Since we are landing in Bern, we will need to get to Geneva for the mission. We have two options. One, we rent a car and drive, or two, we rent a boat and sail across the lake. The car will be faster, but the boat will provide an additional layer of security for us and our gear. What do you think, Ally?" Adam asked.

"I agree with your assessment. I have a little experience sailing. How about you, Adam?"

"I do as well. I got my sailing certification a couple of years ago in the Caribbean. It would be good to get some more sailing practice. Let's do the sail. Should be easy, since it is not on the open sea. Let's call Johnny and get him to make the arrangements."

Adam picked up the built-in phone and dialed Johnny. The satellite phone built into the plane was encrypted and took a minute to create a secure connection. Johnny answered, "Hi Adam and Ally. Or should I say, 'Mr. and Mrs. Johnson?'"

"Hi Johnny!" they laughed.

"Trying to get used to being married to a drop-dead gorgeous woman," Adam said as he smiled. He noticed that Ally blushed a little at the comment.

"Before we get to why you called, I just received some news regarding the owner of the phone in Geneva. It is assigned to the CEO of DanZe Pharmaceuticals, Liam Wentworth. His schedule shows him traveling and returning to Geneva next week, so you have a few days to get in place before he arrives," Johnny said.

"Great news, and that fits perfectly with our plan and the reason that we called. We will be landing in Bern and need to travel to Geneva. We thought about driving and getting a place to stay, but then came up with the idea that we charter a sailing yacht. That would give us a secure place to stay and more anonymity. Can you help find a charter boat?" Adam asked.

"That is a good idea. Can either of you sail?" Johnny asked.

"Yes, I got a captain's certification for monohull sailboats a couple of years ago. Ally has some experience and will make a great first mate," Adam said.

"Perfect. I will set that up and send you the details. I agree with your security assessment of that method. I will also make arrangements for a car to be at the marina in Geneva. You will have the option of leaving the boat there and driving back to Bern as soon as you get the information that you need. Does that work for you two?"

"Yes, that will work," Ally said.

"Great, I will get on it. Have a safe flight, bye," Johnny said as he ended the call.

Adam hung up the phone and said, "Okay, I think that we are all set. We should make a list of necessities that we will need on the sail and pick it up before arriving at the boat. Then let's get some rest before we land."

CHAPTER THIRTEEN

WASHINGTON, DC

Tuck and Beck were driving to Washington, DC and discussing their plan to track CIA Deputy Director Stevens. Tuck was driving and Beck said, "We should get an update from Johnny to see where Stevens is now."

"Sounds good. Give him a call," Tuck said.

Beck dialed Johnny's number on his encrypted phone and when the call was connected, Johnny answered almost immediately. "Hi Beck and Tuck."

"Do you have an update on Stevens' location?" Beck asked.

"I do. He is at the office. Surveillance of CIA headquarters is not advised. I would suggest that you wait for movement at least three miles away from the building. I have been monitoring his movements over the last couple of days and he usually goes to his home when he leaves the office, if not he usually goes somewhere in the same direction. There is a shopping mall on the way and that would be a good place to wait. I will call you when he is moving and let you know when and what direction to go. We will keep you far enough back so that you are not spotted. It is okay to lose sight of him, since I will be following the cell phone pings, but it would be best if you can keep eyes on him if he powers down his phone for some reason. He hasn't done that, so I don't expect him to, but it's better to be safe. I just sent you directions to the shopping mall. You might want to pick up something to eat on the way. He usually leaves the office around 5:00 p.m.," Johnny said.

"Perfect, thanks for the help, Johnny," Beck said as he hung up the phone and turned to Tuck. "Sounds like a day of waiting."

Beck received the location of the shopping mall and entered it into the GPS unit in the car while Tuck drove in that direction. They stopped at a coffee shop on the way to get much-needed caffeine. When they got to the shopping mall, they found a nearby pizza restaurant and ordered an extra-large, three-meat pizza and sodas to go. They parked in a shaded parking spot at the mall with easy access to the exit and the nearby freeway. They enjoyed their pizza and soda.

The day was sunny and warm, but not too hot, which was nice. They sat in the car with the windows open and chatted about life and occasional ideas for tracking Stevens. Late afternoon, Johnny called, and Beck answered. "Hi Johnny."

"Okay, guys. Stevens is moving. He is heading in your direction. With the traffic, it will take him twenty-five minutes to reach you. Go ahead and put your comms in and we will connect through those. Check in when you are connected," Johnny said.

"Beck here."

"Tuck here."

"Johnny here." Johnny disconnected the call and continued communicating through their secure comms. Twenty minutes later, Johnny said, "Okay, head out to Route 1 and wait for my word to enter the highway. He drives a Black BMW 530i M-Spec with Virginia plates."

Tuck drove to a convenience store next the highway entrance, pulled in, and parked near the exit. "In place near the highway entrance," Tuck said so that Johnny would know that they were in place and ready.

A couple of minutes later Johnny said, "Go, and navigate to the middle lane. He drives fast. I expect him to be in the left lane and pass you, then you can follow him."

"Got him in the mirror. He is going past now. Visually verified that it is Stevens," Tuck said as he kept driving. A few cars passed him. He merged into the left lane and followed four cars back. "He is changing lanes. Looks like he is going to exit. Beck, watch him carefully, there is a lot of traffic."

"He is exiting and turning right," Beck said.

Tuck exited and turned right. Stevens drove for about a mile down the road and pulled into a bar.

"He pulled into what looks like a bar on the right. Drive past and park when you can," Beck said. Beck pulled out the tracking devices and activated the first and second tracker. A block past the bar, Tuck pulled into a shopping center with a large grocery store. "Wait here, I will be back in fifteen minutes or less."

Beck jumped out of the car and walked down the street toward the bar's parking lot. The large BMW was sitting in the parking lot. Beck walked past the bar and looked for anything amiss. A minute later, he untied one shoe and began to walk back through the parking lot and pretended to notice his shoe untied, then bent down to tie his shoe behind the BMW. As he tied his shoe, he placed the tracker under the rear bumper. He then went into the bar, he stopped just inside the door and let his eyes adjust to the darkness. He saw Stevens sitting at the bar and an empty stool next to him. Beck strolled over, took a seat next to Stevens, and ordered a beer.

"Nice day, today," Beck said to Stevens while facing the mirror behind the bar.

Stevens glanced over and said, "Sure is."

"I'm on vacation with the family and needed a quick break. Do you live around here?" Beck asked.

"Not too far from here," Stevens said cordially.

"I'm taking the family out to dinner tonight; do you have any suggestions for a nice restaurant?" Beck asked.

"Go down to the waterfront. There is a seafood restaurant there called "Rey's." It is fantastic. Look for the hammerhead shark on the sign," Stevens said.

"Thanks, that sounds like the place to go. I appreciate the recommendation."

Just then, Beck pulled his phone out of his pocket as if it just rang and was on vibrate. He looked at the screen at an angle so that Stevens could not see it. He looked at Stevens and said, "I have to take this."

Stevens shrugged and Beck acted like he answered the phone.

"Hi Babe. Yeah, I will be back in a few minutes. I was just talking to a guy. Heading that way now. How does seafood sound for dinner? Love you." Beck turned back to Stevens and finished his beer. "I gotta go. Can't keep the wife waiting, you know." Beck stood up and patted Stevens on the back and thanked him again, slipping the tracker under the collar of his coat as he left the bar.

Once outside he walked back to the car where Tuck was waiting. He got in the car and Tuck pulled out and drove away.

"Nice job," Tuck said.

They drove to a chain hotel nearby and parked. They disconnected from the comms and went inside and got two adjoining rooms.

Once in the rooms, they pulled out their laptops and connected to the internet through a secure satellite communication protocol that Johnny set up and then they connected to Johnny. Johnny appeared in the corner of the screen. He provided them with two auxiliary screens, and they displayed the location of Stevens's car on a map and the other had the audio of the bug on Stevens's coat.

"Good work Beck. I have audio and tracking on the car. I will monitor and let you know the next steps. Get some rest. You may need it," Johnny said.

"Thanks, Johnny," they said at the same time.

CHAPTER FOURTEEN

GENEVA, SWITZERLAND

Liam Wentworth was sitting at his desk on the top floor of the DanZe tower. He was deep in thought about his plan and the results from the meeting that he had that morning. He looked up when he heard a knock on his office door.

"Come in," he said.

His secretary opened the door quietly and looked in and said, "The president of the United States is on line one."

"Thank you," Wentworth said while waiting for her to close the door. He picked up the phone on his desk and answered. "This is Liam Wentworth."

"Thank you for answering Mr. Wentworth. Please hold a moment for the president," the voice said. Wentworth knew the protocol and held for a few moments waiting for the president to come on the line.

There was a series of clicks and the president said, "Liam, so good to hear from you! I only have a few minutes before my next briefing."

Liam wouldn't need long. "Hello, Mr. President. I have finalized the plans."

"I understand. I will be on location this weekend. See you then," the president said and then ended the call.

It was precisely the conversation that Liam expected. He called his secretary into his office. She knocked on the door and was invited in. Liam said to her, "I need to fly to San Antonio, Texas immediately. Please have the jet prepared for departure in two hours."

"Yes, sir," she said as she quickly exited the office.

Wentworth picked up his jacket and briefcase and left his office, glancing at his secretary on the way to the elevator. "Your driver is pulling up out front now," she said. Wentworth nodded without saying anything to her as he pressed the "down" button for the elevator.

At the front door, the driver was holding open the door of the black Mercedes limousine. He stepped inside and sat on the plush leather seat. He instructed the driver to take him to his house. He sat back and closed his eyes as the driver pulled into traffic.

The driver parked the limousine in the front, circular driveway of Wentworth's house and opened the rear door for him. He stepped out of the limousine and entered his house. It wouldn't take long to gather his things for the short trip to the United States. He quickly packed a small bag and grabbed a couple of burner phones.

Back in the limousine, he instructed the driver to take him to the hangar that housed his Gulfstream G800. The driver pulled up to the hangar. The huge door opened slowly; he drove inside and parked next to the sleek jet.

Wentworth loved his jet. He loved the luxury, speed, and power that it exuded. It was one of the most expensive private business class jets in the world and fit his needs perfectly. He walked around the beautiful aircraft and marveled at the clean lines and sleek look. He chatted with the pilots and maintenance crew, then boarded the aircraft and sat in his favorite plush leather armchair. He raised the footrest and leaned back beginning to relax for the first time all day.

The pilots boarded the jet a few minutes later along with the flight attendant. The captain said, "We will push back in just a few minutes."

After the plane was airborne, the flight attendant, who was also Wentworth's mistress served him dinner of filet mignon, asparagus, and baby potatoes. Coupled with a nice red wine, they enjoyed dinner together before retiring to the small bedroom in the back of the aircraft.

The flight arrived in San Antonio fourteen hours later and pulled into a private hangar. When Wentworth deplaned from the Gulfstream, there was a new black Chevrolet Suburban waiting next to the jet. The driver opened the door, and he sat in the back seat. The driver got in and said that it would take two hours to reach the president's ranch.

Two hours later, the driver turned off the highway onto a driveway entering the president's ranch. There was an arched entry edifice with the name "Rockin G" at the top. The Rockin G ranch was in the hill country of central Texas and consisted of one thousand acres of rolling hills. The driveway wound into the ranch for a mile or so before rounding a corner revealing the large ranch house with a wide wrap-a-round porch. The driver parked the Suburban in front of the house and opened the rear door for Liam.

President Grange was standing on the porch waiting for the Suburban to park. He was dressed in jeans and a checkered shirt. His perfectly groomed gray hair and blue eyes were welcoming. It was easy to see why he was so popular with the voters. He exuded confidence and looked trustworthy. His lust for power and wealth were well hidden from his public persona.

Wentworth stepped out onto the gravel drive and was greeted by President Grange. "Hi Liam, welcome to my ranch. I hope you enjoy your stay here. I know that it will be productive. You've had a long flight. Please follow me and I will take you to your accommodations."

"It is nice to see you Mr. President," Wentworth said as they started walking toward the house side by side.

"Let's dispense with the formalities. Please, call me Joe," the president said as they walked toward the guest suite. "Here are your accommodations," the president said as he opened the door and motioned for Wentworth to enter. The bedroom was large with a king-size bed and sitting area. The floor-to-ceiling windows revealed a view for miles with nothing visible except for game and brush. The attached bathroom was large and relaxing with spa amenities. "Please freshen up and get some rest. Let's talk more over dinner. Please meet me in the dining room at 5:00 p.m." The president left Wentworth in the guest suite.

At 5:00 p.m., Wentworth was rested and ready for the discussion that would finalize his plans to become the wealthiest and most powerful man in the world. He left the guest suite and made his way to the dining room and was seated at the table. The president entered a few moments later and sat across the table from him.

"Thank you for joining me at my ranch. I hope you have enjoyed the guest suite."

"I have. Thank you for your hospitality."

"Ah, here is our dinner," Grange said and motioned to the servers to begin.

The servers brought in reverse seared smoked tomahawk rib-eye steaks, with smoked sweet potatoes and a large chef's salad. Chilled wine was sitting in an ice bucket and ready to be served. Grange poured the wine, and they began to eat with some small talk.

After dinner, Grange said, "Let's move into the den and get down to business." They moved to the den and sat in large leather chairs facing each other with a roaring fire in the fireplace.

Wentworth began. "I met with my team and the Chinese. The distribution system is in place and has been tested. The virus and distribution system are ready. The vaccine has been tested extensively on animal and human trials. It has a ninety percent efficacy. Here is a copy of the report from my team." He handed the packet to the president as he said, "Needless to say, this report needs to be destroyed once you have read it. We must keep this project secure for it to work as expected."

"This looks good, Liam. What are the details of the plan?"

"First, the Chinese Peoples State assets have loaded the virus, distribution system, and the balloons on ships that are in route to be in position off the west coast of the United States and Canada ready to launch the balloons once given the go ahead. The distribution systems on the balloons will be charged on the ship and the balloons will be launched. The balloons have all the telemetry needed for the Chinese to know their exact location. The release of the virus is managed by a complex algorithm. There will be six balloons released that will traverse the country, releasing the virus over populated areas. We expect the virus to be propagated to eighty percent of the people in the United States within one week. The virus will be severe and make people very sick, but only a few will die. You will drive the pharmaceutical companies to fast track a vaccine. We will come to the table approximately three months after the release with a vaccine that will stop the virus. Your team will need to distribute the vaccine to the American people. DanZe will offer the vaccine at a reduced rate to the United States and the world. Even at the reduced rate we will receive over one-hundred-billion dollars in revenue. You will receive an additional ten million into your numbered offshore account. It will take approximately six more months to get the vaccine distributed and the virus under control. That will take us to the end of your second term as president. You will leave office with the legacy of stopping the pandemic."

"I have a question; it won't be hard to figure out that the Chinese balloons are the source of the virus. There will be calls to go to war with China," Grange said.

"You are correct. As a distraction, we have Islamic terrorists in place in ten cities across the United States to set a series of synchronized bombings. They won't do much damage and have minimal casualties but will be a distraction from the balloons. You are already fighting terrorism; this will cause you to put together a task force to track them down and eliminate them. You won't find many, but enough to make you look like the hero. There will be trace elements of the virus in the explosive residue that will point to the virus being distributed by the Islamic terrorists," Wentworth said.

"I don't like knowing that some Americans will be killed in the operation." Grange paused then he grinned and said, "Twenty million dollars sure helps to assuage the guilt."

Wentworth smiled, knowing that he had the president with his lust for power and wealth.

CHAPTER FIFTEEN

BERN, SWITZERLAND

The Learjet touched down in Bern, Switzerland on a cool, clear night and taxied to the private hangar that was already prepared for them. As Ian and David shut down the jet engines outside the hangar, the ground crew quickly began preparations for refueling and moving the plane inside the hangar. A blue Skoda Octavia was waiting at the hangar for Adam and Ally.

They exited the aircraft as the crew were getting ready to move the jet into the hangar, grabbed their luggage, and loaded it into the waiting car. There was very little traffic that late at night. They exited the airport and headed toward one of the airport hotels. Johnny had booked two adjacent rooms at the hotel, and they checked in for the rest of the night.

Adam awoke with the sun shining through the break in the curtain. He opened his eyes and sat on the edge of the bed. With a stretch and a scratch, he stood and walked to the window and pulled the curtain back. It was a beautiful sunny day in Switzerland. He gazed at the aquamarine water in the Aare River and the green fields and trees for a few moments, allowing his mind to focus on the beauty of his surroundings. The blue sky was dotted with small, puffy white clouds. The landscape was peaceful and serene. *No wonder the Swiss were always a neutral and peaceful country,* Adam thought. He padded to the bathroom, took a hot shower, and dressed for the day.

Adam walked to Ally's room and knocked on the door. A moment later the peephole darkened as Ally checked to see who was there, and seeing only Adam, she opened the door with a smile. She was dressed for the day and her bags were ready to go. "Come in," she said as she motioned to him. She turned toward her laptop on the desk and said, "I have been up working for a while. I ordered our supplies. They will be ready to pick up as soon as we arrive at the marina. I have also plotted our course across Lake Geneva."

"You have been busy," Adam said with a grin. "We can call Johnny for last minute details from the car. Are you ready to leave?"

"I spoke with Johnny this morning and have all the information about the yacht rental and the details on Liam Wentworth's location. He flew to the United States and is currently at President Grange's ranch in Texas," Ally said.

"President Grange," Adam said with disbelief. "Is he our missing piece to the high-level corruption of this plot?"

"It looks like it. Hopefully, we will find more details once we surveil Wentworth."

"This conspiracy is getting huge."

"It is. Let's get moving so that we can get setup in Geneva and find out what this conspiracy is all about."

"It looks like it will be about an hour drive to get to the marina. We should be able to shove off in about two hours," Adam replied.

"Let's go," Ally said as she slipped her laptop into her backpack. They headed out the door and stopped at Adam's room as he grabbed his bags.

The drive from Bern to Lake Geneva was stunning. The small farming communities and villages were idyllic. During the drive, their conversation was of the mission and discussing the plan. Adam kept glancing at Ally as they drove. There was an excitement in him that he wasn't sure about.

They picked up their supplies and completed the rental agreement for the yacht with the understanding that they would be leaving the yacht in Geneva. They strolled down the dock to the slip where the yacht was moored and loaded their supplies. The lake was calm with a slight breeze. Adam and Ally stowed their supplies and checked that the vessel was ready to sail. Adam fired up the diesel engine and, while it was warming up, he and Ally prepared to sail. Ally cast off the lines and Adam piloted the boat out of the marina. Once on the lake, they shut off the engine, hoisted the sails, and adjusted the trim.

Once the boat's sails were trimmed, the quiet gliding of the boat across the lake was refreshing. The air was cool, and jackets were required. As they sailed toward Geneva, they discussed the plan some more. It would take two days of sailing to reach Geneva and they planned to spend the night in a marina in Saint-Prex.

In Saint-Prex, they docked the sailboat in the assigned slip and went ashore to enjoy a nice dinner while watching the sunset over the lake. Back in the yacht, they decided to check in with Johnny. Adam pulled his cell phone out of his pocket, called Johnny and put it on speaker.

After the third ring, Johnny answered. "Hi Adam, I see you are in Saint-Prex. I hope you are enjoying the sail and brief break from the mission."

Adam laughed. "Hi Johnny, Ally is here with me, and I have you on speaker. We are in the yacht, so we can speak freely. What have you got for us?"

"Let's get right to it. Liam Wentworth's pilot has filed a flight plan returning to Geneva leaving today. I assume Wentworth has left the president's ranch and is heading back to San Antonio and will board his jet and fly directly back to Geneva. I estimate his arrival back to Geneva tomorrow afternoon," Johnny said.

"Ally told me he was with the president this morning. Why was he visiting the president of the United States at his Texas ranch? Could the conspiracy go all the way to the president?" Adam said.

"It could be, but we don't know the agenda for their meeting. It does sound suspicious, especially since the meeting was held at his ranch and not at the White House," Johnny said.

"Let's hope that our surveillance of Wentworth will reveal the reason for the call with Stevens and President Grange," Ally said.

Adam appeared deep in thought and said, "I think that we need to leave Saint-Prex tonight to arrive in Geneva in the morning so that we can place some bugs in his office. Tomorrow is Sunday, so that should be a good time to enter his office to place the bugs. Johnny, please send us what you can find on the building and security. Also, can you locate his car and send us his home address? We will see what we can place before he arrives. If there is anything that you can do to delay his arrival, it would be helpful."

"Okay, I will get to work on that. Have a safe sail tonight and I will talk to you in the morning," Johnny said and ended the call.

Adam turned to Ally. "Are you okay with a night sail?"

She smiled back at him, his heart thumped in his chest, and he swallowed hard.

Ally looked at Adam slyly and said, "Sure. We can take four-hour shifts to get a little rest." She turned and headed to the bow to begin removing the dock lines.

Adam was stunned and stared at her as she moved, admiring her exquisite beauty. He shook his head and started the diesel engine and began entering the coordinates into the chart plotter. Once Ally had cast off the lines, he increased the throttle just above idle and began slowly moving out of the marina. There was just enough breeze to sail, so he shut down the engine and asked Ally to help him raise the sails. As Adam was trimming the sails for the best speed, Ally went below deck and brewed a pot of coffee.

While the coffee was brewing, Ally put on a heavier sweater and jacket, then poured the coffee into two large spill-proof insulated mugs. She climbed up to the cockpit and handed Adam a mug, which he accepted gratefully. She then sat next to Adam at the helm. They were quiet and enjoyed the sound of the boat gliding through the water and the multitude of stars above them on the clear night.

Adam was more enamored with Ally than the beauty of the night sail. He was looking at her as she stared up at the stars and he put his arm around her as she snuggled into his shoulder. Adam's heart began to beat wildly, and he felt totally content with her by his side.

"I have never seen the stars so beautiful before," she said.

Adam smiled and said as he stared at her, "They are more beautiful with you here."

Ally turned toward Adam, smiled and said, "That is the most romantic thing that has ever been said to me. It makes me feel special."

"You are very beautiful and very special. I know that we have only known each other a few days, but I feel a connection with you that I haven't felt before. It scares me a bit, because of the business that we are in, but it also energizes me knowing that we are in this together," Adam said.

"I feel the same way," Ally said as she gazed into Adam's eyes. "Let's enjoy this night sail and not think about work until we arrive in Geneva."

After a quiet pause, Adam said in a gentle voice, "I know you are an only child, tell me about your parents."

Ally's face suddenly fell, and she looked down with her eyes and stared at her feet. Quietly she said, "My parents are both gone. They passed away when I was in college. A drunk driver crossed the center line one night and killed them instantly."

Adam's eyes were wide and held a look of concern. He wrapped his arm around her and said in a comforting voice, "I'm so sorry, Ally. That must be hard."

"It is and I will always miss them," she said.

Adam squinted his eyes and tilted his head. Ally straightened up and looked at Adam questioningly. Adam held his finger to his lips and strained to listen. He whispered to Ally, "Please get the binoculars. I think I hear a motor approaching."

Ally opened a hatch and handed the binoculars to Adam, and he scanned the horizon a couple of times. Then he saw it. A faint outline of a speed boat heading directly toward them. He handed the binoculars to Ally and pointed in the direction to look. It took a moment, and she saw it too. "What do you think?" she asked.

"I think it is too late for a speed boat to be running fast and it is unlikely they are heading for us randomly. Take the helm. I'll get the weapons ready."

Ally took the helm and kept them on course while Adam went below deck. Although it was a surveillance mission, they brought plenty of firepower. Adam grabbed their handguns and screwed on the silencers. He also assembled a sniper rifle with motion stabilization and silencer. It was a custom-made sniper rifle with built-in precision optics and electronically controlled gyro stabilization so that they could shoot accurately from the moving boat. He came back on deck and handed Ally her handgun.

"I can take the sniper rifle. I did CIA sniper training and scored at the top of my class," Ally said.

"That sounds good to me. I'm sure you are a better shot than I am. I was just average in my training. Do you think the coach roof would be a good place?"

"Yes, I do. Please grab a cushion for me to rest the rifle on," Ally said as she climbed up on the coach roof. Adam handed her the cushion and she settled in and aimed in the direction of the speed boat quickly approaching. She was peering through the image-enhanced optics and said to Adam, "You were right. I can see two armed men on board."

"Keep them in your sights. If there is a threat, take them out."

"Okay, keep us on a steady course," Ally said has she watched. The boat was getting within range of the weapons the men were carrying and she saw them chambering their rifles and raising them to their shoulders.

Ally had a bead on the driver of the boat and held her breath as a shot from the approaching boat rang out. The bullet pinged and whistled as it ricocheted off the side of the aluminum mast above her. She focused her mind and slowly let out a breath and gently squeezed the trigger. Her aim was dead on, the windscreen of the speedboat shattered, and the driver flew to the back of the boat in a cloud of red mist. The speedboat began a slow turn before the other man was able to get it back under control. Ally had already anticipated that the man would grab the wheel, so she kept her aim on the wheel. As soon as the man stepped to the wheel, she fired again. Like the first man, he also disappeared in a red cloud. The speedboat was still going at full throttle headed toward them. She fired several rounds into the engine area before they heard the engine cough and sputter then it was quiet. The speed boat slowed to a stop.

Adam heaved to and dropped the sails. He started the diesel engine and motored toward the speedboat. They lashed the boats together and boarded the speedboat. Adam searched the men. No identification was found, but they did take their cell phones. Adam found some rope and tied the men to the boat while Ally found the sea cocks and loosened them. Adam unleashed the boat and Ally removed the seacocks to flood the speed boat. It was rapidly filling with water as she jumped aboard the sailboat. Adam motored a short distance away and stopped.

Their adrenaline was maxed out and they sat holding each other as they watched the speedboat get lower in the water. When it disappeared beneath the inky black water, Adam looked at Ally. "Nice shooting." After a moment, he said, "I wonder how they found us? We need to call Johnny in the morning and let him know."

They sat in silence until their heart rates slowed. Ally turned to Adam. "I'm not going to be able to sleep after that attack. That was the first time I had to kill another human. I know they were trying to kill us, and I didn't hesitate to take them out, but I still need to process my feelings."

Adam took a moment to look directly into her eyes and softly said, "I experienced similar feelings when I first had to kill an enemy. It is never easy, but necessary in our line of work. I watched you focus on the task and analyze the actions of the assassins that were trying to kill us, and you didn't hesitate. You took the shots after they fired the first round at us. Your rock-solid performance under that pressure shows your professionalism and extraordinary strength of character. You saved our lives. I am not sure that I could have hit two for two like you did."

Ally leaned into Adam's shoulder, and they embraced for a long time. She sobbed into his shirt. She didn't move until the tears stopped and her composure began to return. She pulled back from Adam enough to look him in the eyes. "I'd do it all over again for you." Her eyes misted over again, and Adam gently kissed her on the forehead. Without opening her eyes, she coyly said, "Is that all I'm going to get?"

Slowly, Adam leaned toward Ally and gently kissed her on the lips. Slow at first, but the sparks that they had been feeling began to ignite in a passion that cemented their feelings for each other. After several minutes, they pulled back and stared into each other's eyes and smiled.

"We better get going if we are going to make it to Geneva by morning," Adam said. He stood and helped up Ally. Together they raised the sails and set their heading for Geneva.

CHAPTER SIXTEEN

GENEVA, SWITZERLAND

The sun had risen an hour earlier as the sailboat approached the marina in Geneva. Adam and Ally reefed the sails. Adam started the engines and Ally put out the fenders. They radioed the marina and were directed to the slip they had reserved. Adam gently piloted the yacht into the slip and Ally expertly tied them off. Adam shut down the engine and looked around.

Adam opened the compartment at the helm station and pulled out the binoculars. "Johnny's email showed us that the tall building there is the DanZe Pharmaceuticals headquarters. Based on the floor plans he provided the top corner office facing us is Wentworth's office. I think that it is time to take a walk," Adam said.

Ally went below and changed her clothes and packed their supplies in a backpack that would not look out of place for a tourist. She handed them up to Adam and they locked up the cabin and stepped onto the dock.

They stopped at the Marina office and checked in and got a cup of the complimentary coffee. They left the office holding hands.

They walked down the street toward the DanZe tower and found a coffee shop across the street. They stopped in and sat at a table that had a view of the building and ordered breakfast. They observed that there were two security guards inside the front door at the reception desk. Since it was Sunday, no foot traffic entered or exited the building. The guards also stayed seated watching their computer monitors.

"We should call Johnny after breakfast to see if he can get us into the building. If he can briefly turn off the security system on the emergency exit doors, we can quickly slip in and go up the stairs. We also need to know if there are cameras in the building," Adam said.

"My guess is that they have cameras on the entrances and on the labs but probably not in the office areas. Hopefully, Johnny can access them and put them in a loop," Ally replied.

As they finished their breakfast, they walked down to the street to a lakeside park and found a bench facing the lake that was secluded. Adam fished his phone out of his pocket while Ally accessed the data files that Johnny sent. Adam called Johnny and put it on speaker so that they both could hear but kept the volume low so that it wouldn't be easily overheard.

"Hi Adam and Ally," Johnny answered. "How was your sail?"

"We were attacked by two men in a speedboat early last night. Ally took them out with the sniper rifle. She also stopped the boat with some well-placed shots into the engine. We boarded the boat and searched the men and the boat. They didn't have any identification on them, but we photographed them and took their phones. They are currently at the bottom of the lake with the speedboat. The rest of the night sail was uneventful," Adam said and smiled as Ally winked at him. "What can you tell us about the security of the DanZe tower?" Adam asked.

"There are cameras on the entrances and the labs where confidential work happens. I can loop those. Your best bet for entrance is through an emergency exit at the fire escape on the back of the building. I will momentarily release the electronic lock and spoof the sensor so that the guards don't know the door opened. That will get you in. Looping the cameras is proving to be difficult, but I almost have it working. I should be ready in an hour. I sent the layout of the building to your phones. What I don't know is what Wentworth's office security is like. It is likely just a standard lock that you can pick. Hopefully it is not a biometric reader or pass-code lock. When you get there let me know if there is anything that I can do to help gain entrance."

"That sounds good. We will study the layout and text when we are ready to enter." Adam waited for Johnny to acknowledge and ended the call.

Ally looked at Adam. "After we study the plans," she said, "we should walk around the waterfront before making our way back towards the building. If there are any surveillance measures, that should help to reduce any sightings of us in the area. I have stud-ied the maps of the area and have chosen a route to approach the building from the back."

"That makes sense. Show me the floor plan of the building," Adam said as Ally leaned close to Adam and showed him her phone screen. She spoke quietly, making it look like they were looking at photos of their honeymoon in Switzerland. Once they finished, Adam said, "Looks pretty straight forward, let's go for our walk now."

After their walk around the lakefront, they approached the building from the back and stopped in a secluded spot in an alley that contained a couple of trash dumpsters. Adam pulled out his phone and looked at Ally and said, "Is your phone on silent? Comms ready?"

She nodded to confirm. Adam checked his phone and texted Johnny letting him know that they were ready and could be at the door in thirty seconds and that their comms were ready."

Johnny spoke a moment later through the comms. "Go."

Adam and Ally quickly approached the door with their heads on a swivel. Not noting anyone watching, Adam tried the door and it opened. They slipped inside, closed the door quietly, and looked around. They quickly made their way to the stairwell, stepped inside, and carefully climbed the stairs heading for the top floor. They stopped at the last door and waited a few seconds to catch their breath after the long climb. Adam subvocalized into his throat mic that they were ready to enter the top floor. "It is clear from what I can see," Johnny said.

Adam held up three fingers and looked intently into Ally's eyes. He slowly dropped each finger and then slowly opened the door and peeked through. Nothing. He opened it more and still not seeing anyone, he stepped through the door and entered Wentworth's reception area. Ally kept watch while Adam checked the office door. It was locked, but it was a simple door lock. Adam pulled his lock pick kit from his front pocket and had the door open in twenty seconds.

Adam and Ally entered the office and Ally kept watch at the door. Adam removed listening devices and placed them on the phone, desk, and various places around the room and in the conference room that was attached. Once they were all activated, Johnny said in their comms, "I have signals from each of the bugs." No response was required.

Adam checked the desk, careful not to disturb anything. Not seeing anything that could help him, he rose to leave. Johnny said,

"Can you place a data sniffer anywhere on the network cabling on his computer?"

Adam looked around. "There is a docking station."

"Perfect. Stick one to the bottom near the network cables," Johnny said.

Adam carefully lifted the docking station and placed the data sniffer. He carefully returned it to the exact location it was previously and said, "Done." Johnny acknowledged that it was working.

Adam turned to Ally and gestured that it was time to go. They locked the office door and headed back the way they came. At the ground floor Adam said to Johnny, "We are ready to exit."

"The door will unlock in ten seconds," Johnny said.

Adam and Ally peeked out the door and rushed to the exit door. It opened and they moved quickly to the dumpsters. "Johnny, is everything okay?" Ally said.

"I'm looking now. Everything is back in place and no movement from the guards. It looks like the infiltration was successful. You better get moving," Johnny said.

Adam and Ally removed their comms and turned and walked away in a different direction from where they arrived. They walked along the waterfront area stopping in shops and getting a drink. When they were sure that they were not followed, they headed back to the marina.

Adam and Ally boarded the sailboat and made some sand-wiches. When Ally served the sandwiches, Adam pulled out his phone and called Johnny.

"Hi Adam," Johnny answered.

"Hi Johnny. We are back on the boat. Do you have signals from the bugs?" Adam asked.

"Yes, the signals from the bugs are strong. Also, the sniffer on the docking station is on and waiting for data. Good work. Now the next target. I have a possible location of Wentworth's car. He is driven in a limousine that is stored in a garage at his home. The chauffeur lives in an apartment above the garage, so that will make this infiltration more difficult. His home is well secured. The perimeter of the house is fenced with cameras and motion sensors. There is a single guard at the gate, and it looks like one guard who patrols the property. These two guards swap locations every two hours."

"Okay, this will take some planning. For the car tracker, we could easily intercept it at a traffic stop and place a tracker. To place bugs inside the house will be more difficult. What can you do to disable the security system, Johnny?" Ally said.

"His security system is advanced, but I can hack it. It will take a couple of hours to be ready," Johnny said.

"What time is Wentworth due back?" Adam asked.

"His flight is due to arrive in Geneva at 4:00 p.m. local time," Johnny said.

"That is only four hours from now. We may be able to place a tracker on the car as it drives to the airport to pick him up. How about we intercept the car a couple of blocks from the house. I can distract the driver while Adam places a tracker on the back of the car. Then we can enter the house and place bugs inside," Ally said.

"It's a good plan. The timing will be tight. Johnny, is there anyone in the house other than the guards?" Adam asked.

"Yes, his wife is there. She doesn't secure her online presence, so I reviewed the latest social media posts and found out that she attends tennis lessons this afternoon at 3:00 p.m. She should be leaving around 2:30 p.m."

"The difficulty will be entering the property without being seen in broad daylight. Have you reviewed the satellite images around the property?" Adam asked.

"Yes, I have. The house is in an area with other large estates, so that helps. There is a wooded open space behind the property. I would recommend entering from that side. You can park in a lot near the open space trailhead. There are security cameras there, so make sure that your faces are not visible to the cameras."

"Ally is pulling up the images now. I like the plan. We will need to move fast to coordinate each step. Thank you, Johnny. We will put comms in just before the operation begins," Adam said.

"I will have eyes on the estate and will disable the security system just before entry. Stay safe out there," Johnny said as he ended the call.

CHAPTER SEVENTEEN

GENEVA, SWITZERLAND

Ally reviewed the location on the map and satellite images. She picked a likely intersection to distract the limousine driver so that Adam could place the tracker on the car. She then went into her berth and changed clothes. She was wearing a short skirt and a low-cut, tight blouse. She did her hair and makeup. She also packed a dark sweater and yoga pants in a small bag. After a last-minute check in the mirror, she emerged from her berth. Adam was sitting on the settee in the main cabin. He looked up as he heard the door open. His eyes opened wide, and a flush of red formed in his cheeks. With his mouth slightly agape, he muttered slowly, "Wow! You look amazing!"

Ally smiled and did a slow pirouette while enjoying the attention that Adam displayed. She said coyly while batting her eyes, "Do you like what you see?"

Adam stood and said, "I do." He leaned in and pulled her close for a long hug. Then he held her at arm's length and said, "If you don't get the drivers attention, I don't know what will!"

Ally beamed and said, "We better get going so we aren't late. The car should be waiting in the marina parking lot, and we can pick up the keys from the marina store."

Adam gestured for her to head up the companion way and he followed locking the cabin. They stepped off the boat and made their way to the marina store carrying their backpacks containing their supplies.

Once again, the car that Johnny reserved was a nondescript car. This time the car was a white Citroen C4. It would not stand out in traffic. Adam drove and Ally used the GPS on her phone to direct Adam to the intersection where they would distract the limousine driver and place the tracker. Adam found a parking space at a local market a block from the intersection. As they parked Adam called Johnny to let him know that they were on comms and getting into position. Adam left the car first to get into location and a minute later, Ally got out of the car.

Ally stood next to the car and smoothed out her skirt and made sure her blouse enhanced her curves. She checked her hair in the reflection on the door glass. She locked the car and walked to the bus stop at the intersection. "I am approaching the bus stop. Where is the limo, Johnny?"

"He is pulling out of the estate now. Adam are you ready with the tracker? You should have a visual in three minutes," Johnny said.

Adam acknowledged that he was ready, and the tracker was activated.

"Thirty seconds," Johnny said.

Ally stood and picked up the shopping bag that she brought with her. She glanced up and saw the driver in position. She turned to walk away and spilled the bag containing fruit that rolled into the street in front of the limousine. The limousine slammed on his brakes and put his flashers on. She looked at the driver and smiled bending over in front of the car to pick up the fruit, making sure that the driver had the best view of her back side.

As Ally was distracting the driver, Adam stepped off the curb and knelt behind the limousine and quickly placed the tracker under the edge of the rear bumper. He stood up palming an orange and walked toward Ally and handed it to her. He continued walking down the sidewalk.

Ally looked again at the driver and leaned forward toward him, smiled, and mouthed, "Merci." She turned back to the sidewalk and continued walking away from the limousine in the opposite direction from their car.

Adam reached the car and pulled out of the parking lot. He picked up Ally a block down the road. She got in the passenger seat and smiled at Adam.

"How'd I do?" she asked.

Adam was still awed over her looks and smiled. His grin said it all. She smiled as she said, "Don't look. I need to take this skirt off and change to pants."

Adam tried to keep his eyes on the road and get to their destination without looking. He did steal a glance and saw her toned legs but looked back at the road quickly.

"All done. We are almost to the trailhead," Ally said.

Johnny was still listening on the communication devices. "Alright you two. Let's focus on the next step in the mission. The tracking device is working properly, and the limousine is nearing the private terminal at the airport. You will need to move quickly."

Adam pulled into the trailhead parking lot and parked the car. "Johnny, we are in the parking lot at the trailhead."

They exited the car. Adam and Ally grabbed their backpacks from the trunk of the car. They were wearing wide brimmed hiking hats to obscure their faces from the security cameras and began their hike. "Johnny, we're on the trail now. Do you have our locations?"

"Yes, I am following you. I have live satellite images monitoring the estate. In fifty meters, step off the trail and head north for two hundred meters through the trees. It looks dense from above. Stop when you see the back of the estate but keep concealed so we can time your approach," Johnny said.

"I don't see anyone on the trail," said Ally. "We are stepping off and heading north through the trees."

After a few minutes they found a concealed location near the rear of Wentworth's estate. "We are in position and can view the estate," Adam said.

Johnny replied, "Okay, I have your location. The guard is moving around the front of the house. He will pass through the backyard in a minute. He will continue around the house and then relieve the guard at the gate. That guard will then enter the front of the house. That will be our best entry time. Ally, I want you to stay in position and monitor the perimeter in case Adam needs backup or a distraction. Adam you will have fifteen minutes before the guards start another patrol. I will disarm and loop the camera in thirty seconds. Be ready to move in one minute."

Adam and Ally both acknowledged that they were ready.

Adam pulled his backpack straps tight and waited for Johnny's signal to proceed.

"Go, go, go!" Johnny said.

Adam sprinted to the back wall of the estate and quickly scaled the wall. "Clear," Adam said as he peeked over the wall. He scaled the wall and landed quietly on the other side. He sprinted to the back door. "Are we clear inside, Johnny?"

"Yes, both guards are out front. No thermal signatures inside. Once inside take the first right to get to the office."

Adam acknowledged and opened the back door. He moved silently to the office and slipped inside. He placed several bugs in concealed locations and then placed a data sniffer on the laptop docking station. "Johnny, are the bugs and sniffer activated?"

"Yes, all working as expected. Find the master bedroom and place a bug there also. It should be upstairs at the end of the hallway."

Adam carefully exited the office and slipped up the stairs moving quickly to the master bedroom and placed several more bugs. "Done and heading out now."

"You have thirty seconds for the guard to clear the backyard," Johnny said.

Adam paused at the back door, being sure to keep himself concealed from sight.

"Clear," Johnny said.

Adam opened the door a crack and verified that the guard was out of sight. It was clear, so he closed the door softly and sprinted across the yard and scaled the wall. He had just landed on the other side when Johnny said urgently, "Adam, the guard turned around. Get down!"

Adam fell to the ground and lay still in the tall grass. Ally saw what was happening and she slipped out of the bushes and began to call, "Heidi! Where are you?" The guard asked her what she was doing. She replied in French, that her little dog, Heidi, escaped while they were hiking on the trail. She asked if he saw her and continued to call for the dog. The guard said he didn't see the dog and she continued to look for the dog and disappeared back into the trees.

The guard admired Ally's figure and watched her until she disappeared in the trees. He shook his head and smiled and then continued his patrol after reporting to his colleague what happened. As soon as he disappeared around the corner of the house, Johnny reported, "Adam, you are clear now. The security system is back on and cameras online."

Adam and Ally met in the trees and had a quick hug. "Good improvising, Ally. That distraction kept me from being observed. By the way, that guard was ogling you when you walked away." Adam smiled as he told her. She shrugged her shoulders and grabbed his hand as they walked away.

"The bugs are active and ready. We should get some good information from them. I have a satellite in place and am watching the trail. Two people with a dog are approaching, so stay back and stay still."

They dropped and lay still on the ground behind some trees and waited until they passed. They waited another couple of minutes so that the dog wouldn't hear them exit the woods. As they approached the parking area, they pulled their hats down tight and kept their heads down. They approached the car, threw their packs in the trunk, drove away, and turned off their communication devices.

"Would you like to stop somewhere for dinner on our way back to the boat?" Adam asked.

"I'd love to. I would like to change first. Let's head back to the boat and change, then go out for a nice dinner," Ally answered.

CHAPTER EIGHTEEN

GENEVA, SWITZERLAND

Wentworth's jet touched down in Geneva just as the sun was setting and rolled to a stop in front of his hangar. The pilots shut down the jet engines and the ground crew attached the tug to move the jet into the hangar. The jet was in the hangar in a matter of minutes. The pilots exited the cockpit and greeted Wentworth as they moved to unlatch and open the door. Once the door was opened, they gestured for Wentworth to exit the aircraft.

Wentworth unlatched his seatbelt, grabbed his briefcase, and exited the aircraft. His driver, who was waiting by the limo, opened the back door.

"Where to?" the driver asked.

"Take me to the office. I have a few things to take care of there. You can wait for me; I won't be long."

"Yes sir," the driver said.

The car pulled out of the hangar and the driver exited the private aviation area. It took thirty minutes to navigate the traffic and pull up to the front of the DanZe building. The driver double-parked and opened the door for Wentworth to exit the car. "I will be parked in the garage. Call me when you are ready to be picked up," the driver said as Wentworth was walking away.

Wentworth just waved his hand behind him at the driver, dismissing him.

Wentworth entered his office and, since it was after 5:00 p.m., his secretary was off for the day. *Just as well*, he thought. *I don't need any distractions.* He unlocked his office door and sat at his large desk and turned his chair to take in the evening view. *It's been a long day,* he thought as he took a moment to focus on the task ahead. He turned his chair around and placed his briefcase on the desk. He removed his laptop and docked it to the docking station. While he was waiting for it to boot up, he went to the minibar in the middle of his extensive floor-to-ceiling bookshelf and picked up a Glencairn-cut crystal whiskey glass and poured three fingers of Macallan Thirty Year Double Cask Scotch. He returned to his desk. *It was time.*

He took a drink and entered his password to log in to the DanZe network. Little did he know that every keystroke and data transfer from his computer was being monitored and saved. Wentworth navigated the internet to an email server that provided free email addresses. He entered the login information and turned off any history tracking for the website. He thought he was being secure, and normally it would have been sufficient, but with the data sniffer that Adam placed earlier, everything was about to become known.

The email address was shared with his contact from an Islamic terrorist organization based in Yemen. He did not know the name of the organization or who he was connecting with, and he didn't care. It was the least secure portion of his planning and why he only allowed himself to be the contact. The only others who knew about the terrorist attack distractions were President Grange and

Deputy Director Stevens. They didn't know anything other than they were coming.

Wentworth clicked the new email screen and entered a message to his contact. The message was asking for confirmation of their readiness for the attacks and that the finalized bombing date would be coming within the week—the locations having been already established across the United States. There was no destination email address entered and the draft was saved. The contact would check the email account daily and would read and delete the draft and respond likewise. It was the most secure way to communicate since no data was sent over the internet.

Wentworth logged out of the email account and verified that there was no history of the session saved on his computer, he closed his laptop and took a deep breath. He turned his chair and stood near the window and stared out over Lake Geneva and the marina below.

It will be nice to retire and spend the rest of my life sailing from one exotic location to another. I might even bring my wife.

He chuckled at his inside joke. He decided to call his wife and let her know he was on his way home, although he knew she didn't care. Maybe she would be amiable to his advances that night.

He sent a text to the driver and packed his laptop into his briefcase, locked his office, and headed to the elevator.

The next morning, Wentworth returned to the office and logged into his computer. He decided to check the email account and found an acknowledgement from his contact. He had no way of knowing that he was communicating with Johnny.

CHAPTER NINETEEN

GENEVA, SWITZERLAND

Johnny was communicating with the terrorist contact acting as Wentworth and communicating with Wentworth acting as the terrorist contact. Johnny was controlling both sides of the communication and would be able to stop the pending attack.

Johnny was collecting so much information from Wentworth's office and home that he asked his friend Mary to come over and help him organize it. She was all too happy to help.

Johnny sent a text message to Adam and Ally to call when they returned to the sailboat. Adam called Johnny.

"Hi Adam and Ally. I have Mary here; she is helping me organize all the information that we are receiving from Wentworth's data sniffer and bugs. There is a lot coming in, but I can give you a brief rundown of what we know so far.

"Wentworth created an email draft to a contact in Yemen asking for verification of their readiness for the upcoming attacks in the United States. He is communicating securely by creating a draft and not sending it. The recipient will log in to the same email account, read the draft, delete it, and create a new draft as a reply. A virtual dead drop if you will. I was able to clone the email account and now I am controlling both sides of the conversation.

We should be able to stop the terrorist attacks before they happen now. I will keep working on this and get the right entities involved to apprehend the terror cells that are in place. That is the biggest news so far. We also found out that Wentworth's marriage is a sham and only for looks. She wants his money and status; he wants her as arm candy. No surprise there either. As we learn more, we will let you know."

"So does this mean that Stevens is colluding with Wentworth to have terrorists attack his own country?" Ally asked.

"I'm not sure yet. I am tracking Stevens as well and nothing out of the ordinary has been found yet. I would guess that there are multiple things going on here. Stay in Geneva and keep an eye on the DanZe building and who comes and goes. I suggest that you place a camera somewhere where we can get images of the people coming and going into the building. I will run facial recognition on them to see if we have others involved," Johnny said.

Adam replied, "We will place a couple of cameras tonight."

"Good, that will help. Get some rest, you had a long day. We are going to keep working on the analysis of the data that we are getting. Goodbye," Johnny said as he ended the call.

Adam looked at Ally and said, "Get some sleep. We will go out at 2:30 a.m. to place the cameras. Do you have some ideas on where to place them?"

"While we were talking, I pulled up the pictures that we took this morning on our stroll. There are a couple of large planters with trees flanking either side of the front door. We can pretend that we are drunk and stumble up to them and place the cameras and then stumble off without alerting the guards inside," Ally said.

"That is a great plan. You get some sleep first; I will keep watch and wake you at 2:15 a.m. I will sleep afterward while you keep watch."

"Okay." Ally yawned. "That sounds good to me. I'll be out before my head hits the pillow."

Ally was breathing deeply as Adam approached her, although she had been moaning and twitching as she slept. Adam looked at her and knew at that moment she was the one. In the short time that he had known her, he felt a deep connection with her and sensed that she felt the same way. He gently shook her shoulder and said quietly in a husky voice, "Wake up, sleepyhead."

Ally blinked her eyes several times and saw Adam looking down at her. Her heart skipped a beat, and she wanted to pull him down to her, but it wasn't the time for that. *I have only known him for a few days,* she thought. *What am I thinking?* She shook her head and sat up. Adam handed her a steaming mug of coffee and she took it gratefully. "Here are some clothes for tonight's mission," Adam said as he handed her the pile of clothes that he had prepared for her to wear that smelled atrociously.

"Where did you get these? They stink," Ally said while pinching her nose.

"They were in the hanging locker, and I found some old liquor and beer bottles on the dock that I poured on them. We need to look and smell the part." Adam smiled and said, "Your hair looks the part already." Ally smacked him in the shoulder.

"Give me a minute to get dressed. I will meet you topside. You look awful, also." Ally said laughing. "This is the worst part of this job..." she muttered as she closed the door to her berth.

At 2:30 a.m., they were quietly walking down the dock toward the street. When they got close enough to see the front of the DanZe building they collapsed onto a bench. Adam pulled a couple of beer bottles out of his pockets and handed one to Ally and whispered, "I cleaned them and put sparkling water in them so we can drink them and spill some as we stumble around."

"Thanks," Ally took a sip and leaned into Adam. It was partially an act, but not all of it. "What do you see?"

"The guards are at the desk watching the monitors and looking at their phones."

"Okay, then drag me on, Mr. Drunk guy."

Adam shakily stood and tried to help Ally get up. She was like dead weight, then lunged toward him, almost toppling them both over. They were both giggling as they stumbled down the sidewalk toward the entrance of the DanZe building. As they approached the first planter Ally tripped and fell. Adam turned and placed his hand against the tree trunk to steady himself and laughed at Ally. He reached down and almost fell but got them both to their feet and walking again. As they were passing the second planter, Ally steadied herself on the tree as they continued past. Adam whispered, "You're good at this. Is there something that you need to tell me?" He said laughing. They continued down the street until they were out of sight of the DanZe building. They threw their bottles in a trash can a started walking normally and took a roundabout path back to the marina.

Back on the boat, Ally said. "I get the shower first."

Adam agreed and stayed in the cockpit until she returned for her watch with a fresh cup of coffee.

"Go shower and get some sleep. I will see you in the morning," she said and winked at him.

Adam hesitated, then said, "Okay," and headed to the shower.

CHAPTER TWENTY

NORTHERN MONTANA

Early in the morning, just before the sunrise, Johnny's cabin was aglow with light pouring from every window. There was a cold breeze, and the brightly colored aspen leaves were fluttering through the beams of light coming from the cabin windows creating sparkling yellow flashes. Johnny had been so busy for the last thirty-six hours that he forgot to sleep and close the curtains. Johnny was exhausted and needed to get some rest. He set his computer to record everything and told Mary that he needed some sleep and to wake him if anything happened. So far, it was business as usual with both Stevens and Wentworth.

Johnny awoke six hours later to the smell of fresh coffee. He hadn't awakened to that smell in many years since his wife passed away. He padded into the kitchen and found Mary sitting at the kitchen table with papers scattered about and a plate with a large cinnamon roll on it. She looked up as Johnny entered the kitchen and took a sip of coffee. "There is fresh coffee in the pot and cinnamon rolls on the stove. You look like you slept well. Are you ready to take on this conspiracy?"

"Good morning, Mary. Thank you for the coffee and rolls, they will start the day off right," Johnny said. "Let's get to work. Tell me what you have found, then you can get some rest."

As Johnny was pouring coffee and warming a large cinnamon roll, Mary began. "Not too much happened overnight. Wentworth arrived back in his office at 7:30 a.m. local time. Most of his work seemed to be normal, but there was one phone call that he made that was suspicious. He made a call on what appeared to be a burner phone and said to someone to schedule a meeting for tonight at 7:00 p.m. in his office. We are tracking calls from his cell phone and desk phone, but they weren't from them. The call was only twenty seconds long. We were able to locate the cell phone signal, but it went dark right after the call ended. I have a transcript of the call here." She handed him the transcript and said, "That is about it, I suspect that there will be more activity today. I need to run home and take care of a few things. I will come back later this afternoon so that we can continue."

Johnny took a bite of his cinnamon roll and looked at Mary. "Thank you, Mary. I really needed the rest. When you are at home get some sleep. Thanks again for your help."

Mary picked up her dishes and washed them in the kitchen sink. "I made some sandwiches for your lunch. They are in the refrigerator." She picked up her jacket and headed toward the front door. "See you this afternoon," she said as she walked out the front door.

"Bye, Mary," Johnny said as she was leaving.

Johnny picked up the transcript of the call that Wentworth made and read it again. *Something is going down soon. What is it?* Johnny thought. He reviewed the rest of the documentation and then decided that he needed to check the email account to control the terrorist activity. He logged in and checked both accounts. There was a reply from the terrorist contact with the information that he requested and the acknowledgment of the one-week delay for the bombings. He agreed to keep the cells on standby. He also received acknowledgment from Wentworth that all plans were on track and the date that the attacks were scheduled.

The attacks were scheduled for one week from that day in ten major cities across the United States: San Francisco, Los Angeles, Las Vegas, Denver, Dallas, Kansas City, Miami, Boston, Chicago, and Atlanta. It was going to take a large group effort to take down simultaneously. He was going to need some help. Johnny decided he needed to call Ian.

"Hey Johnny," Ian answered. "Where to next? We're waiting here in Bern for Adam and Ally to return. The jet is fueled and ready to go."

"Hi Ian. A lot has happened since we spoke. Tuck and Beck have trackers and bugs on Stevens. Nothing major to report there. Adam and Ally have trackers and bugs in Wentworth's office and home. All has gone according to plan so far. The information coming from Wentworth's office is troubling. He has been in contact with a terrorist group from Yemen and is planning on a series of coordinated bombings in ten cities across the United States. I have confirmed the dates and times. I also have the sleeper cell locations. I have spoofed the email account that they use and am controlling the communication. I have confirmed with the terrorist contact that there will be a one-week delay for the bombings, but Wentworth still thinks that they are going down when planned."

"Whoa, this is getting huge, and we need some help. What are your thoughts?" Ian asked.

"In addition to the planned terrorist attacks, Wentworth made a call from a burner phone to someone telling them to schedule a meeting tonight at his office. The meeting is after-hours, and we don't know who will be there. Adam has bugs in the office and his personal conference room. We will know more later. Adam and Ally also placed cameras near the door to the DanZe building so that we can run facial recognition on whoever comes in. There may be more to this than just the terrorist attacks."

"I agree. Let's continue with the surveillance, but we need to get a team in place to take out the terrorist cells. Since these attacks appear to be coordinated, we should coordinate the take downs to be simultaneous or we risk the other cells finding out and going to ground."

"That is what I was thinking. Do we have a trusted contact with Homeland Security or the FBI that can help us? There can't be any leaks, or it will blow the takedown. It appears that the Deputy Director of the CIA and the president may be involved at least somewhat with Wentworth. We need this to stay dark."

"Hmm. I think so, let me make a call and feel him out. I will get back with you. Thanks Johnny," Ian said as he ended the call.

Ian turned to David and said, "What do you think?"

"I agree, we need help taking this down. My question is why the specific date and time to coordinate the attacks? Is it just to show their advanced skills or is it some kind of distraction for a bigger attack or event. I suggest that we get eyes on each cell as soon as possible and then take them down, just before the planned attack. That way we can hopefully eliminate any backup attacks that we don't know about," David said.

Ian nodded his head in agreement. "I'm going to make a phone call to my contact in the FBI to see if he can help. Can you grab me a burner phone?"

David handed Ian a burner phone from the bag and said, "I'll go get some take-out food and bring it back while you make the call."

"Perfect, I love their meatballs at that restaurant down the street," Ian said as David was leaving the hotel room.

Ian powered on the burner phone and dialed a number from memory. The call took a moment to connect. It was answered with a "Hello."

Ian responded with "Have you ever hiked the Bright Angel trail? It's beautiful in September." The phrase was for security and only he and his friend knew the passphrase. They agreed that they wouldn't use names during the calls.

"I'm glad you called. I have been wondering what you were doing these days. Since you are calling from a burner, I would guess that this is a business call."

"When we spoke six months ago, I told you about a new business that I was starting with some colleagues. We are working on our first project and could use some help. This should be considered totally black. In the interest of security, can you meet Johnny at the ranch tomorrow so he can fill you in?"

"Sure, I can be there. I will fly into Bozeman and Johnny can pick me up."

"That will work. Text him your arrival time and I will let him know the plans. Thanks, talk to you tomorrow," Ian said as he ended the call. He removed the battery and SIM card from the phone and placed it in a sealed foil pouch.

Ian called Johnny on his encrypted phone.

"Hi Ian, what did you find out?" Johnny asked as he answered the phone.

"Okay, I spoke with Ben, and he is going to fly to Bozeman in the morning. You need to pick him up and take him to the ranch and we will have an encrypted video conference with the team."

"Do you think that he will be able to help us? It is a big job to coordinate and keep quiet," Johnny said.

"I think so, he knows a lot of people and I think he is the one that can pull it off," Ian replied.

"I will set up a meeting for tomorrow afternoon and let everyone know to be ready," Johnny said.

"Thanks Johnny. Are you going to need some help? There is a lot of data coming at you from all sides."

"Mary is coming over to help me. She is good and secure. We may need to think about bringing someone in to assist in the handling of the team and data analysis. We can address that once we finish this mission."

"I'm glad you have some help; I was worried about you," Ian said. "See you tomorrow on the conference call."

CHAPTER TWENTY-ONE

GENEVA, SWITZERLAND

Adam and Ally were sitting on the bow of the sailboat enjoying the sunny weather. They occasionally picked up the binoculars and looked around, specifically at the top floor of the DanZe building. They saw Wentworth working in his office and look out the window periodically. Ally picked up her iced soda and took a sip from the straw and looked at Adam. He looked back at her and smiled, then his cell phone rang.

He picked up the phone and looked at the screen and showed it to Ally. Adam answered the call as he was standing up. "Hello Johnny, give us a second to go below deck." They walked down the companionway and closed the door. "Okay Johnny, we are in the main salon and can talk."

"Hi Adam and Ally. We are working the terrorist issue and will be getting some help with this tomorrow. We will have a team conference call tomorrow at 3:00 p.m. at the ranch to plan this action. In the meantime, Wentworth is having a hush-hush meeting tonight at 7:00 p.m. local time. We don't know what it is, but he requested the meeting to be in his office with a burner phone. I have a feeling that this will be connected to the planned terrorist attacks. You have cameras on the entrance to the building. You should probably see if you can watch the parking garage and have eyes through the windows. I suspect that they will shut the curtains before the meeting."

"We scouted the parking garage earlier today. There is a parking attendant at the gate, but no other security. I think that we can enter the garage from the back, but we will have to go now and time our entrance so that we are not seen," Adam said.

"Adam, you go to the parking garage with a camera and trackers. I will stay here and see if I can tell who is in the meeting. I put a remote camera on top of the mast last night to get a better view of the office."

Johnny replied, "That is a good plan. Put comms in and I will hack into the local security cameras to help. There is not enough time to get a satellite into place."

"Time to go. Thanks Johnny," Adam said as he ended the call. He stepped into his berth and changed into dark clothing. Adam grabbed a handful of trackers and the high-resolution zoom camera and stepped back into the main salon. "Ally, I'm ready. Are you ready?"

Ally was sitting at the table and was watching the window through the mast-mounted camera. Adam stood beside her and felt the heat between them. He looked over her shoulder and saw a high-resolution image of the window. Ally turned toward him and smiled. "I have software that can reduce reflections, thermal imaging and it records in 120 feet per second at 'eight K' resolution. If we can see their faces, we should be able to run facial recognition on them."

"When did you install this camera?" Adam asked.

She leaned into him and said, "When you were sleeping last night."

"Good thinking," Adam said as he patted her on the shoulder. "I'll head out and keep an eye on the garage."

"Be safe, see you soon," Ally said as she winked at him.

Adam walked out and closed the companionway door behind him. He shouldered his backpack and stopped to get an iced soda on the way to the parking garage. He walked past the entrance and continued his walk. He walked around several blocks checking his back for a tail. Finding none, he said, "Johnny how is the back of the garage looking?"

Johnny replied, "Looks clear right now. Take the alley on the left, take cover, and wait by the back of the adjacent building. I'll give you the all clear. This will put you near the elevator so that you won't need to move around the garage much."

"Roger," Adam said as he turned into the alley. Adam stopped and leaned against the building to check for anyone following him. Seeing that it was clear he hustled down the alley and took cover behind some discarded cardboard boxes. "In place," Adam said.

"Standby," Johnny said. It was quiet for a couple of minutes. "Okay, it's clear. You should see the elevator to the right when you enter the garage."

Adam didn't need to respond; he checked all directions and ran to the wall that he needed to scale to enter the garage. It was approximately eight feet tall. Adam jumped as he was running and grabbed the top of the wall. It was rough on his fingers, and he wished he had put gloves on. He put the pain out of his mind and pulled himself up to the top of the wall. He peeked over it. It was clear and he threw one leg on the top of the wall and rolled over it. Adam landed in front of a parked car.

"I'm in the garage and making my way to the elevator."

No response was required. Adam peeked around the car as he was catching his breath. He quickly spotted a likely location to conceal himself and still have a view of the elevator. He looked all around and made his way to the location that he identified. He hid behind a car that was parked in a corner space. The car had been there for a long time. It had cobwebs under it and the tires were nearly flat. Adam made himself comfortable and said, "I am in position and watching the elevator." The meeting wasn't scheduled to start for two and a half hours. Adam made himself comfortable for the long wait.

At 5:00 p.m., the workers began flooding out of the elevators and making their way to their cars. There was a small traffic jam as the garage began to empty out. By 6:00 p.m. the garage was nearly empty. There were a few stragglers leaving late. *Workaholics,* Adam thought. No one had gone up in over an hour.

Johnny found the security camera for the entrance of the garage and monitored it for anyone entering the garage. One car, a black Mercedes E350 sedan entered at 6:15 p.m. Johnny said, "I have a black Mercedes entering the garage. I have the plate number and am running it now."

Adam waited and said, "I have the Mercedes in sight." He snapped pictures of the car as it parked. The lone occupant sat in the driver's seat for a moment and looked around. He reached over to the passenger's seat and exited the vehicle with a briefcase. He looked around again and pressed the lock button on the key fob. A short beep and flashing lights indicated that the car was locked and secured. While he was looking around, Adam got several good photos that were good for facial recognition. He continued snapping photos as he made his way to the elevator. As the doors were closing, he pressed the button for the top floor.

Adam waited and asked, "Any more cars?"

"Nothing yet," Johnny said.

"I can still see inside the office," Ally said. "Hold on... He is entering the office. He and Wentworth are chatting. The elevator is opening again. There are two people coming in. They must have been in the building already. They greeted each other and are moving to the conference room." "I have pictures of all their faces and am sending them to you now, Johnny."

CHAPTER TWENTY-TWO

GENEVA, SWITZERLAND

The elevator door opened on the top floor of the DanZe building. Qi Limpon, the head of the Chinese Peoples State, stepped off the elevator and walked directly toward Liam Wentworth. Limpon had a face with a permanent scowl and never showed emotion. He walked with purposeful quick steps. His black hair had shots of white beginning to show and was perfectly styled. As he neared Wentworth, he raised his arm to shake hands in the western greeting style.

"It is good to see you, Liam. How are you doing?" Limpon said.

"Qi, thanks for coming. I am doing well. The plans are coming together, and I look forward to reporting the status," Wentworth said. The elevator door opened again, and two men stepped out of the elevator. Wentworth turned toward the elevator as the doors were opening. "Tomas, Alex, thanks for coming. Let's go to the conference room."

They each took a seat at the table and Wentworth poured drinks for each man from his well-stocked minibar. He served each of them their drinks then took his seat at the head of the table. He picked up the remote and pressed a few buttons and the screens in front of them activated.

"Gentlemen, thank you for coming. Our plans are set and confirmed for the release of the virus next week," Wentworth said as he pressed a few keys on his laptop. "This is a map of the United States. The map showed red stars over ten locations. There will be simultaneous bombings across the country in the following cities: San Francisco, Los Angeles, Las Vegas, Denver, Dallas, Kansas City, Miami, Boston, Chicago, and Atlanta. The bombings will act as a distraction for the release of the virus. I have instructed the president of the United States to focus all military and law enforcement on the bombings. He will appoint CIA Deputy Director Stevens to head up this task force. They are both on our payroll and will keep the focus away from the balloons that will be launched just after the bombings have taken place. The Chinese ships that will launch the balloons are in route to their launch positions in the Pacific off the western coast of the United States and Canada. Qi, do you have anything to add about the fleet in the Pacific?"

Limpon nodded and said, "You are correct. The balloons with the distribution systems are on the ships. The virus has been pre-loaded and pressurized in the distribution systems. My teams on board each ship are well trained in the launch of the balloons and have communication with each of the other ships. There are six ships, and they will release the balloons just after the bombings are scheduled to occur."

"Thank you, Qi. I have confirmed with the group that will coordinate the bombings. They are in place and ready to begin this phase of the operation. I met with President Grange two days ago in Texas. He will command all resources from the FBI, Homeland Security, Secret Service, US Marshalls, and local law enforcements to work together to bring the terrorists to justice.

He requested that we try to minimize the casualties so that he looks good to the American people. I have agreed to those terms, although my idea and his idea of minimal casualties may be different. I have instructed the bombing group on the exact locations and time for the coordinated attack."

Wentworth turned to Tomas, his head of security, and asked, "Tomas, do you have any concerns with operational security?"

"No, we have kept a tight ship. No one outside of our group is aware of the operation. Will President Grange instruct CIA Deputy Director Stevens to manage the law enforcement from his side?" Tomas Finn said.

"Yes. We will call Stevens at the end of our meeting and give him the instructions; President Grange will also give the same instructions to Stevens. Alex, is the production plan in place for the vaccine?" Wentworth said.

"Yes, it is. The timing of this part of the operation will be controlled by the FDA approval of the vaccine. We must give enough time after the virus has reached pandemic levels to give the impression that we need to develop the vaccine. The scientists think that their research and testing has been for developmental purposes. They have also been paid a great deal of money with binding contracts that forbid them to speak to anyone outside of their team about this development. They will research and test the virus and determine that they can quickly produce a working vaccine. They will look like the heroes," Alex Giovanni said.

"Excellent," Wentworth said with a smile. "Let's call Stevens and fill him in on the operation. I already let him know that I would be calling him. You all can listen but keep quiet. He must only know that he is speaking with me. Everyone nodded in agreement. Wentworth placed a new burner phone on the table and initiated the call to Deputy Director Stevens using the speaker phone option.

After two rings, Stevens pressed the "accept call" button on the screen of his burner phone saying simply, "Yes."

"Stevens, the operation is approved to go on the original date and time. Grange will put you in charge of the multi-organization response. Your job is to keep the country focused on the terrorist investigation and delay the release of findings to the media. We must have several days to allow the distribution of the virus and pin it on the bombers," Wentworth said.

"Everything is in place on my side. Will you send me the locations where the bombings will take place? It will help to make sure that there won't be any accidental discovery of any of the cells," Stevens said.

"Yes, I will send you the locations in the email account draft. Did you handle the situation with your agent that we discussed a few days ago?" Wentworth asked.

"Still working on it. He went to ground, and we are still looking for leads to his whereabouts," Stevens said.

"We have noted on multiple occasions a man matching his description and an unknown woman around the DanZe building recently. Is there any chance that they know of your connection to me?" Wentworth asked.

"No chance. I have been very careful not to be followed and always used a new burner phone. Send me pictures of those people and I will run them through our database," Stevens said.

"Hopefully it is not him. I will send photos and check them out on our end. Any other questions?" Wentworth asked.

"Just one more. I expect that the agreed upon payment will be transferred into my numbered account before I take any action," Stevens said.

Wentworth sighed. "The payment will be transferred tomorrow. By the way, don't threaten me. We agreed on the price and timing, and it will take place as agreed." Wentworth didn't give Stevens a chance to respond and disconnected the call. Immediately, Wentworth removed the battery and SIM card and handed the pieces to Tomas to dispose of in the building's incinerator.

Wentworth looked around the room and acknowledged each man by holding eye contact a moment. "As we move forward with this plan, keep in mind that besides being rich beyond your wildest dreams it is paramount that not a word of this operation is to be spoken or written. I trust each one of you to know that if one goes down, we all go down. Shall we have another drink to toast our future?"

Wentworth refreshed each man's drink, and they stood in a circle and clinked their glasses together. The anticipation and excitement about their future was in each man's thoughts. It was indeed a monumental day.

CHAPTER TWENTY-THREE

GENEVA, SWITZERLAND

Adam continued to wait in the parking garage, knowing that all members of the meeting were upstairs. He had already placed a tracker on the black Mercedes. Adam was crouching down behind the car where he had been hiding when Johnny said, "I successfully ran facial recognition on each of the photos that Ally sent me. Adam, I have identified the make, model and license plates for the two men that joined the meeting from the building. I sent them to you. Check around and see if they are parked in the garage and place trackers on them. Once we are done, I will fill you in on the rest of what we learned."

Adam acknowledged and found the two cars: one Peugeot and one BMW. He took photos of the cars and placed trackers on them. They were locked so no listening devices could be placed inside. They would be able to track each car's location. Adam said over the communication devices, "Trackers placed. Is there anything else that I should do before leaving?"

"No. I am watching the cameras out back and you are clear to leave the way you came," Johnny said.

"Roger, I am leaving now," Adam said as he slipped over the wall. He hung by his fingers for a moment and then dropped, squatted down and checked the area. Seeing no one, he hustled back to the alley and made his way back to the yacht.

Back at the yacht, Adam descended the companionway stairs and greeted Ally. They disconnected and removed their comms. "I'm glad you made it back safely," Ally said.

"We need to chat with Johnny. Afterward, would you like to get dinner in the marina restaurant?" Adam asked.

"Sure, you will need to change first." She grinned.

Adam retreated to his berth and quickly changed clothes. When he emerged, Ally had just called Johnny and placed him on speaker.

"Hi Adam and Ally," Johnny said as he answered the phone.

"Hi Johnny. Adam and I are back in the yacht," Ally said.

"We have a lot to discuss. I will send you a report later, but I will tell you the basics now and we can discuss more details tomorrow in our meeting. We were right, this conspiracy is much bigger than just coordinated terrorist bombings. First, the players at the meeting were Qi Limpon, the head of the Chinese Peoples State. He was the guy that came to the meeting in the black Mercedes. The Mercedes is registered to the Chinese embassy in Bern, Switzerland. Limpon left the meeting and stopped at a bar. The two men that came to the meeting from the building are Alex Giovanni, the vice president of DanZe and Tomas Finn, the head of security for DanZe. Their trackers showed them heading towards their local homes. Also, Wentworth is still in the office," Johnny said.

"What was the head of CPS doing there?" Ally asked.

Johnny took a deep breath and blew it out slowly as he said, "Based on what was said in the meeting, it appears that the bombings are a distraction for the real attack. We know that

Stevens has been in communication with Wentworth, and he made a call to Stevens during the meeting. Remember when we thought that there might be someone higher up in the United States that is involved. President Grange is also part of this conspiracy."

"Are these all the players that we know of?" Adam asked.

"Yes, from what I can tell so far. Here is where it gets interesting. This isn't about political ideology or making a statement. It is about making money, a lot of money. It sounds like the Chinese have developed a virus that they are going to distribute over the United States using some kind of balloon-based distribution system. Six balloons will be launched from ships in international waters of the Pacific Ocean off the western coast of the United States and Canada. They will be launched at the same time as the terrorist attacks. While the United States is reeling from the attacks, the balloons will go unnoticed. The president is going to command that all military and law enforcement agencies work on the investigation into the terrorist bombings and Stevens is going to be tapped to lead the task force. His job will be to keep the areas clear around the bombing locations to reduce the risk of someone seeing something. He will also keep the focus of the country's law enforcement on the terrorist attacks. Meanwhile, this virus will be released and make people very sick and an untold number of deaths," Johnny said.

"You mentioned earlier that this was about money. Where does that come into play with these attacks?" Ally asked.

"Another interesting piece of information is that DanZe has already developed a vaccine for the virus and tested it. They will pretend that they have research that will give them a leading edge in finding an effective vaccine. The president will push the FDA into fast-tracking the approval of the vaccine and DanZe will be the sole provider of the vaccine worldwide. They already have production in place to handle the demand."

"We have to stop this insane plan, but we don't have enough resources," Adam exclaimed.

"That is what the meeting tomorrow is about. Ian has some contacts that should be able to help. One is coming here tomorrow for our meeting. I will call Ian next and let him know that we will likely need military resources as well. One more thing, your cover may be blown. They mentioned in the meeting that a man matching your description with an unknown woman have been seen around the building. Be careful out there and stay vigilant. That's it for now. Tomorrow, you will head back to Bern after our meeting. Talk to you tomorrow," Johnny said before disconnecting the call.

Adam turned to Ally and said, "Well, I didn't expect that. This is just getting deeper and deeper."

Ally's look of concern caused Adam to pause. He opened his arms and she slid into his embrace. They held each other for a few moments that felt much longer. They parted slightly and Adam stared into Ally's eyes and knew without a doubt that she was the one for him. He softly spoke. "Ally, we will be able to stop this. We have the element of surprise and Johnny is controlling some of the communication. It will need to be a large, coordinated effort, but I think that we can pull it off."

Ally slid her head against Adam's shoulder and said, "I am scared, but I am also hopeful. Being with you these last few days have felt so reassuring to me. We have learned so much that we didn't know a few days ago. Most of all, I am glad that I am with you."

Adam held Ally tight against his body and met her lips with his. The kiss was short but full of meaning. They needed to stay focused on the job at hand. Adam held her shoulders and looked her in the eye and said, "I feel the same way. We need to stay focused now, so let's go get dinner so that we can clear our minds and think about the next steps later."

They held hands as they headed up the companionway and strolled down the dock to the marina restaurant.

CHAPTER TWENTY-FOUR

The morning sun was bright and shining past the edge of the curtain of Adam's berth and directly into his eyes. He groaned as he rubbed his eyes with the heels of his hands. Blinking rapidly, he fumbled around to find his phone plugged into the charger on the bedside stand in his berth on the sailboat. He picked it up and squinted to read the time. It was much later than he expected, but he closed his eyes again for a moment before swinging his legs out of the bed and onto the sole of the boat. He sat there and looked around the small area of his berth. Being in the front of the boat the V-berth was quite small with not much room to move around. He stood, crouching some, due to the lack of headroom and put on a shirt and pants.

Ally had been up for a couple of hours and was working on the plan for their next steps. She stood and stepped over to the galley and started a pot of coffee. It had just finished brewing when the door to Adam's berth opened, and he stepped out. His hair was tousled, and he was still rubbing his eyes.

"Good morning," Ally said as she held up a cup of coffee, which he accepted gratefully.

"Thank you, Ally. How did you sleep?" Adam asked groggily.

"I tossed and turned. I couldn't stop thinking about what could happen if we fail. I finally got up a couple of hours ago and started working on our next steps. We can go over those later. I didn't want to wake you earlier with the smell of coffee."

"Did Johnny send us the meeting time?"

"Yes, the meeting will be in two hours. He also said that the security team at DanZe reported seeing a man and woman around the building several times. We need to watch our backs and wrap up this mission."

"Okay, we need to be careful and get out of here after the meeting. We should always take our essentials with us in case we need to evacuate."

"That is a good idea. Grab your backpack. We have time before the meeting to get breakfast if we go now."

"Great, I'm starving. Let me comb my hair and brush my teeth and we can go," Adam said. He smiled at Ally and gave her a gentle hug and stepped into the bathroom to get ready.

After breakfast, they walked back to the sailboat. They were about to board the sailboat when Adam put his arm in front of Ally and stopped her. He pointed at the companionway door and whispered, "Looks like we had company while we were out." The sailboat rocked unnaturally just as Adam was about to step onto the deck. Adam stepped back, pushing Ally behind him as he reached around to his lower back and slowly removed his Sig Sauer P938 compact nine millimeter handgun. Ally also smoothly removed her Beretta Nano nine millimeter handgun from her purse. Just then, a long thick black barrel of a silenced handgun appeared in the companionway door and fired three blind shots in their direction. They both jumped over the side of the dock into the dark water of the marina. They quickly swam under the dock and came up for air. They heard a man running down the dock. "Another attack. They must be on to us; we need to get out of here quickly," Adam said as they swam away from the sailboat to the ladder a couple of slips away.

As they approached the ladder, they were slammed in the back by an explosive force knocking them into the piers, causing their ears to ring. Adam grabbed Ally and looked her in the eye and asked, "Are you hurt?"

Ally shook her head and blinked a few times. "Just bruised and my ears are ringing. What happened?"

Adam turned and pointed toward their sailboat—or what was left of it. Smoke was rising from where the sailboat once floated. There was debris floating in the water and a piece of the dock was missing. "It looks like they were trying to kill us by blowing us up. We just surprised the assassin."

"Let's get out of here before the authorities arrive," Ally said as she climbed the dock ladder.

Once on the dock, Adam took the lead and Ally watched their backs. They moved quickly toward the marina parking lot.

Adam started the car, and they exited the parking lot and said, "We need to get another car. Call Johnny and see if he can arrange one."

"On it," Ally said as she pulled her phone out of her purse. She dialed Johnny's number and put it on speaker phone.

"Hi Ally," Johnny answered on the second ring.

"Hi Johnny. Someone broke into the sailboat while we were at breakfast. We surprised the intruder, and he took some shots at us. We dove into the water, and he ran off. As we swam to the dock ladder, the sailboat exploded. It was another attempt on us, and we must guess that they know we survived. We are driving in the rental car now and Adam is doing counter surveillance. We will need another car. Can you arrange that?" Ally said as she tried to catch her breath.

"Yes, I will take care of that. Head in the general direction of the Geneva airport. You will be able to get a rental car there. Once you think you are clear of any tail, ditch the car you are in and get an Uber to take you to the airport. I will text you the rental car confirmation details."

"Thanks, Johnny. We'll call once we get the new rental car and are on the road."

"Head to the airport in Bern once you get the rental car. We will postpone the meeting until you arrive in the Bern hangar. Drive safely. I will keep an eye on the satellite feeds and watch your back."

"Thanks again," Adam and Ally said simultaneously.

"Talk to you soon," Johnny said as he ended the call.

"I'm going to double back and see if we have a tail. Keep an eye out for any suspicious cars," Adam said.

They drove all over Geneva for an hour before they felt comfortable that they were not being followed. Ally consulted the maps on her phone and found a shopping center nearby. She logged into the Uber app and hailed a car to that location. They parked in the middle of the lot amongst the many cars and walked to the pickup location for their ride. They arrived with a couple minutes to spare and continued to scan their surroundings for anyone watching them. They did not see anyone, so they got in the backseat of the car.

The driver had soft music playing and kept to himself as he navigated traffic to Geneva International Airport. They requested to be dropped off at the international terminal and kept to their cover story. The driver dropped them off and Ally left a tip for the driver on the app. As soon as they exited the car, the driver said, "Have a nice trip home." He drove away without waiting for a reply.

They walked into the terminal and wandered around for a while before merging into a large group of people heading for the rental car transportation. They quickly located the bus stop for the rental car agency that Johnny provided and climbed aboard the next bus that arrived. The bus was full, and they entered and exited in the middle of the crowd of people. If anyone were following them at a distance, they would be hard to keep track of. They spoke to each other while glancing around the bus. No one on the bus appeared to pay any attention to them.

Adam signed for the blue Peugeot 208 rental car with the backup identification that they had with them and picked up their car from the parking lot. As they exited the lot, Ally was entering their destination into her phone's map app: the Bern executive terminal. Adam maintained vigilance by taking many unnecessary turns to shake any potential tail. As they neared the edge of Geneva, he felt more confident that they hadn't been followed, but one could never be too sure.

They headed southeast out of Geneva. The imposing rugged snow-capped peaks of the Alps were visible in the distance against the deep blue sky. Mont Blanc was clearly visible as the highest peak at 15,766 feet high. Adam was struck by the mountain's magnificence. As the road climbed, they were starting to feel that they were in the clear.

They passed through several small towns and turned at Cluses. The road was smaller and started to climb as they left the town. Adam kept looking in the rear-view mirror and had a look of concern on his face. Ally noticed and asked, "What is it? Do you see something?"

"I'm not sure. There is a silver car that has been behind us for a while. It is way back, but I have a bad feeling."

The road was climbing and there were many curves and switchbacks. It was hard to navigate the road and keep an eye on the car behind them. Ally grabbed the backpacks from the back seat and removed both handguns. She put the backpacks on the floor in the back seat and made sure that Adam could easily access his handgun. She kept hers at the ready. "Can you see them?" Ally asked.

"I keep seeing glimpses of them and it looks like they are getting closer. Look back and see if you can see them."

Ally removed her seatbelt and twisted around in the seat. "I see them. They are speeding up. It looks like a sports car and they are really moving now. You better speed up."

Adam pressed the accelerator to the floor and the engine screamed as it downshifted and gained precious speed. Adam was holding the wheel with both hands. His knuckles were white and his eyes wide as he piloted the car around the sharp corners with tires squealing in protest. "*Where are they?*" Adam yelled.

"*They are coming up fast and should catch up at the next corner,*" Ally yelled as she tried to maintain her upright posture. She spun around and pulled back the moon roof shade and pressed the button to open the moon roof. The noise of the wind was loud, and they had to yell louder to be heard. "*I could pop up through the moon roof to take some shots at them if I need to,*" Ally yelled as she double checked that there was a round chambered in her nine millimeter.

Ally turned again and the car was right behind them. The car was a Porsche 911 and could take the corners much faster than they could. There were two men in the car. The passenger was holding a large handgun. *"They are on us and they are going to shoot."* Ally yelled when the back window shattered. They both instinctually ducked. Ally dove into the back seat and aimed out where the back window once was. She took a couple of shots and ducked back down.

Adam was swerving back and forth to make it harder to hit him. He entered the next corner on the inside and was sliding sideways as he drifted around the corner. The Porsche 911 was a superior car in every way. The driver accelerated and pulled alongside of Adam. The passenger of the Porsche aimed his handgun at Adam. Just as he fired, Adam slammed on the brakes. The Porsche was instantly in front of them. Ally was trying to regain her balance when the next corner approached.

"Hang on!" Adam yelled. Ally fell into the back seat and grabbed onto the headrest in front of her. Instead of slowing for the corner, Adam sped up. The Porsche was in front, and Adam was aiming for the rear of the car. The Porsche tried to speed up, but the back end was starting to slide. The driver was correcting the skid when Adam bumped the back of the Porsche. Adam immediately braked hard, and Ally fell to the floor in the back seat. Adam felt the car skidding toward the edge of the road. Just before the tires left the road surface, Adam let off the brake, turned the wheel, and stomped on the accelerator. The car responded and tires gripped the asphalt. Time stood still as they watched the edge of the road and the open air of the long drop off the cliff they were headed toward.

The outside tires were in the dirt when their car abruptly caught and swerved back on the asphalt. Adam slammed on the brakes and came to a stop in the middle of the road. Smoke and dust hung in the air around the car for a moment before blowing away in the ever-present cold wind of the mountains. "Ally, are you okay?" Adam asked.

"Yes, I am fine. I lost my gun somewhere in the car. Maybe it flew out of the window, not sure. Where is the Porsche?"

"I don't know. I lost sight of them right after I bumped them," Adam said.

They both looked around and Adam got out of the car. His legs were shaking, and he could barely stand. He put one hand on top of the car to steady himself. He looked up and down the road and didn't see the car. Ally got out of the back seat and stood next to Adam. She grabbed his hand and she was shaking. Together, they slowly walked to the edge of the road and looked over the edge of the cliff. It was a long way down. The cliff was sheer and the cold wind was blowing up the cliff face. They both shivered and held each other close as they scanned the bottom. Adam saw it first and pointed to the small plume of dust and smoke. The Porsche didn't make it. Relief swept over them and they embraced. "We need to get to Bern as soon as possible," Adam said as he guided her back to the car.

They got in the car and continued their drive to Bern. Adam turned to Ally and said, "We need to call Ian and have him be ready to fly as soon as we get there. Also, call Johnny and have him postpone the meeting until we are airborne. We need to get out of Switzerland as soon as possible."

"You're right. I'm scared that we might not make it back to the airport. Keep an eye out for more bad guys. I'll call Ian and Johnny."

The rest of the drive to Bern was uneventful and they arrived at the hangar late in the afternoon. The door opened and they parked inside the hangar. The Learjet was outside the hangar and the door was open. Ian and David walked to the car as Adam and Ally were getting out.

"Adam, Ally, glad you made it back. The plane is ready. Grab your stuff and load up. Leave the keys in the car. It will be taken care of," Ian said as they walked toward the Learjet. "Johnny postponed the meeting, and we will initiate it once we are airborne and can talk. In the meantime, sit down and relax. You need some decompression time before we meet."

Ian and David were in the cockpit starting the engines and preparing for takeoff. Adam and Ally leaned back in their soft leather chairs and closed their eyes. The stress was starting to abate with the feeling of safety knowing that they were getting out of Switzerland.

They both dozed off moments after takeoff. Two hours later, Ian came back to the cabin and gently awakened them. "We need to have that meeting with Johnny now. I have set up the screen in front of you for a video conference with our secure satellite data link. We will start in fifteen minutes. Get a drink and go to the lavatory if you need. David and I will join from the cockpit."

Fifteen minutes later, Johnny's face appeared on the screen, and he said, "Hi team, Tuck and Beck are joining now. We will be ready to start soon." They were all quiet while everyone connected into the meeting. Everyone's image was tiled on the screen and Johnny said, "Okay, we are all here."

Johnny gave an update to the team on the information gathered from Geneva. "I did pick up some email traffic that Wentworth sent to Stevens with photos of Ally and Adam. Based on the attempts on your lives, I'd say that they identified you. If the intruder took your laptops, the hard drives and memory cards only had vacation photos and work-related content to your covers. No data was compromised."

"It seems clear that there are two areas that we need to focus on to stop this attack on the United States. One, the bombings must be stopped simultaneously just prior to the planned detonation time. Two, we need to stop the balloons before they distribute the virus. After this is complete, we can move on to the apprehension of the conspirators," Adam said.

"I have invited my good friend Ben Walters to this meeting. Ben works for the FBI and has considerable knowledge and contacts that we can use to take down the bombing suspects. The important thing about this operation is that it needs to be kept secret from all the upper levels of the FBI. At this point, we only know of Deputy Director Stevens and President Grange being involved. That might be it, but we need to err on the side of caution. We know in which cities and targets the bombings will take place. Ben, what are your thoughts on this take down?" Ian said.

Ben answered. "Hi team, it is good to meet you all and work with you. I know the agents in charge in each of these cities. I will work with them on the operation and coordination of the raids for each location. The raids will happen simultaneously just before the scheduled bombing. Remember that Johnny has infiltrated the communication link between Wentworth and the terrorist contact. The terrorists think that the bombing was postponed a week, so they will be waiting and hopefully less vigilant.

Operational security will be very tight with the minimum number of people knowing what is happening and when."

"That sounds great. I am glad that you agreed to help us in this capacity. I know that you are going out on a limb with your career," Ian said.

Ben chuckled and said, "I'm retiring next year, and I am sworn to do what is best for our country to protect it. Maybe I will join up with you all after I retire."

"I'm sure that we will have a place for you," Ian said.

"Okay, now we need to figure out what to do about the second problem of the virus distribution. How are we going to stop the balloons after they are launched or before they are launched?" Adam asked.

"The Chinese spy balloon that traversed the United States a while back was shot down after it crossed the country. We know that there will be a virus distribution system on board these balloons that will sicken and kill untold numbers of people. We need to stop them before they reach the United States," Ally said.

"Can we board the ships that are carrying the balloons and stop the launch?" Beck asked.

"It sounds like we only have two options. One, board each ship and commandeer the vessels to stop the launch. This would require a coordinated effort by the Coast Guard and may take more time than we have available. The second option would be to shoot down each of the balloons after launch. We would need to get the Air Force involved to shoot down these balloons. Either way, these are resources we don't have immediately at our disposal," Adam said.

"I have an idea that might work. I am good friends with General Andy Fitzgerald. He is a three-star general in charge of the Pacific Air Forces. The balloons will be launched in his operational theater. He is as patriotic as they come. We have been good friends since attending the United States Air Force Academy. We meet up at fly-ins a couple of times a year, and once a year we fly together to go fishing in remote regions of Alaska and Canada in our STOL planes. Anyway, that is a topic that I can discuss all day, but that doesn't serve us well right now," Ian said.

"The Air Force shot down the Chinese spy balloon once it was over the Atlantic to protect the America people from any type of fallout from the debris. I want to suggest to Andy to have his planes ready to shoot down these balloons over the Pacific Ocean before they reach the west coast. What do you all think?" Ian asked.

"I like this plan. How soon do you think you can meet with General Fitzgerald? Are there any other ideas?" Adam said.

"I have already spoken to Andy; he is in Washington, DC through the end of the week. We need to stop in Virginia to pick up Tuck and Beck. I already scheduled a time to meet with him in Virginia," Ian said.

"I have another idea. I have been working on long-range attack drones. They are large and have a range of one hundred miles and are each armed with two small missiles that have optical laser and infrared targeting systems. The missiles each have a small plastic explosive war head. They would be more than capable of shooting down a balloon. I have tested them and they work, but I have not fully completed the testing," Johnny said.

"How many drones do we have?" Adam asked.

"I have one that I have been experimenting with, but I have ten more due to be delivered by the end of the week. I just need to build up more missiles. That would take me a couple of days, but

I have been swamped with all the data coming in from the mission," Johnny said.

Ally leaned forward and said, "I can help, Johnny."

"Johnny, do you think that Merlin could help us put the missiles and drones together?" Ian asked. Merlin was the quintessential tinkerer. He invented things and made things work better. He was in his seventies and was balding. He regularly forgot to get his hair cut. He was brilliant but looked like a homeless person.

"That's a good idea. He is always ready to work on some tech project. That is what he lives for. I'll text him right now," Johnny said.

"Do we have the resources to put the drones in place across the west coast for launch?" Adam asked.

"I have done the calculations and have approximate launch locations for the Chinese ships. We would need to have the drones ready to launch from four locations to intercept all six balloons," Johnny said.

"David and I can each fly someone and drones to one location and we can take the other location," Ian said.

"I like this plan and it is more operationally secure. We should still meet with General Fitzgerald and have him on standby as a backup in case there is a problem with one of the drones," Adam said.

"I agree," Ian said.

"I just heard from Merlin, he will be in the lab at the ranch tomorrow," Johnny said.

"How are we going to take out the conspirators? That may prove to be more difficult. Any ideas?" Adam said.

"You are correct. I think that we can work with the Swiss to arrest Wentworth, Finn, and Giovanni. President Grange and Deputy Director Stevens will be more difficult. The evidence that we have is not admissible in court, so we need to pursue this through the FBI. Ben, can you help with this as well?" Ian said.

"Yes, I can, but as you said, this will be the most difficult part. Taking down a sitting president is very difficult. Let me think on how we can achieve this. I have some ideas that I need to work through," Ben said.

"I may be able to help you, Ben. I have many contacts in Washington, DC, including Vice President Powers. Let's talk after the meeting," Beck said.

"The next two will be difficult in other ways. We won't be able to work with the Chinese government to arrest Qi Limpon. I have thought about this one quite a bit. I would like to propose that we send a team to assassinate Limpon. It will take some time and tracking him will prove difficult, but it seems like the only way to eliminate him," Adam said.

"Johnny has been working on locating the terrorist organization that has been hired to do the bombing. It will take some investigation and intelligence gathering to figure this one out. They will probably go into hiding after the raids. Hopefully, we will get some actionable intelligence out of the terrorists that we capture in the raids," Ian said.

"That is a good assessment of that situation. We need to focus on the elimination of the threat first. We will land in Virginia, meet with General Fitzgerald, and pick up Tuck and Beck. Once we are back at the ranch, we will work on our next steps. Ben, you will immediately begin planning the raids for next week. We will meet again tomorrow after dinner at the ranch," Adam said.

Ian took over. "Any other questions?" No questions were asked. "Okay, see you all tomorrow," Ian said and ended the meeting.

Ian stepped out of the Learjet cockpit and stood next to Adam and Ally. He looked down at Adam. "Good meeting. You handled the pressure and priorities well and drove a good planning session. Try to get some rest on the flight back."

"Thank you, Ian. I hope it all works out. There are a lot of moving pieces and so many things can go wrong. You know what they say: The best plans are only good until they start," Adam said. He could feel the pressure mounting with the next steps of the mission. *Will we succeed or will many people die?*

Ally was watching Adam. She felt a deepening respect for him. She could see the weight that he was feeling of the impending attacks and the pressure of stopping them. As Ian returned to the cockpit, Ally put her hand on Adam's arm. He looked at her and she said, "If anyone can pull this off it is you and this team."

Adam held her hand. "Thank you for the encouragement," he said as he closed his eyes.

CHAPTER TWENTY-FIVE

SOMEWHERE OVER THE ATLANTIC OCEAN

Adam awoke and squinted as he looked out the window. The sun was bright, and the dark blue water of the Atlantic Ocean was sparkling. There were only a few clouds in the sky and flight was smooth. Adam stood and stretched as he walked to the lavatory.

Adam had just returned to his seat when he heard the lowering of the landing gear. He looked at his watch. Nearly eight hours had passed. He looked out the window and saw that they were on approach to Ronald Reagan Washington National Airport in Washington, DC. He looked over at Ally, who was still asleep. *She is beautiful when she is sleeping.* He debated waking her since they were minutes from landing. He gently rubbed her shoulder and awakened her.

Ally feeling Adam's hand on her shoulder kept her eyes closed a little longer than necessary, relishing his touch and feeling of completeness that she was experiencing in that moment. She slowly opened her eyes and smiled at Adam. "We're about to land in DC," he gently whispered in her ear. His breath brushing against her ear caused her to shiver and a flash of heat to radiate through her body.

Ian touched down with only the slightest bump as the wheels met the runway. He taxied to the private aviation area and shut down the engines. He and David completed the shutdown check-list. David ordered a fuel truck to fill the jet's tanks. Ian called General Fitzgerald and confirmed their meeting in the conference room of the private aviation terminal in thirty minutes.

Ian stepped out of the cockpit and stretched as he stepped into the main cabin. He stopped in the galley and filled up a to-go cup with steaming coffee. After filling his coffee cup, he turned to the main cabin and said, "Good morning. It looks like you two slept the entire flight. Are you ready to meet with Andy?"

"I'm ready, but I really need to brush my teeth," Ally said as she stood and headed to the lavatory with a small toiletry kit.

"Great flight, Ian. Must have been smooth, I didn't wake until a few minutes ago," Adam said as he stood and stretched.

Ian opened the door and extended the stairs. The cool morning air with the smell of jet fuel and humidity from the Potomac River rushed in. Ian stepped out and did some stretches on the tarmac. Adam stepped out and looked around as Ally joined him. "Beautiful morning. I love Autumn on the eastern seaboard," she said.

"Let's go meet Andy. David will join us in a few minutes after fueling is complete. Tuck and Beck are in the terminal already," Ian said.

They began walking toward the terminal and met Tuck and Beck inside. They greeted each other and Ian led them to the conference room that they booked in the terminal building. They all took seats around the table and talked about their experiences of the last few days. A quick two knocks on the conference room door caused everyone to turn. The door opened and General Andy Fitzgerald stepped inside. He was a tall, fit man, standing six feet, six inches tall. His eyes were a piercing blue and his hair was gray and cut in a military flat top. Everyone stood and Ian stepped forward and embraced his longtime friend with strong back slaps. Ian stepped to the side and introduced the team. "Please take your seats. We only have thirty minutes, so we need to jump right in."

"Andy, thanks for coming. As you know from our previous hypothetical discussions, we have started a private intelligence organization to investigate and contain threats against the United States and its citizens. We can do things that governmental entities can't do. We have strong financial backing and are developing the team. Our first mission fell into our laps when Adam stumbled out of the woods and found his way to Mary's house. I will tell you the story later, since our time is short today. When this is over, you should join me at the ranch for a long weekend."

"Sounds good, Ian. How can I help you?" General Fitzgerald asked.

Ian went on to tell General Fitzgerald what they knew about the plot to bomb the US across ten cities and then to simultaneously distribute a virus across the nation via Chinese spy balloons. General Fitzgerald's face got redder and the muscles in his jaw were flexing. He interrupted and said, "How sure are you of this intelligence?"

"Very sure, we have identified the ships moving into position and have Ben Walters from the FBI heading the surveillance and raids of the terrorist's cells," Ian said.

"Last time a balloon traversed the United States, the president would not allow us to shoot it down until it was over the Atlantic. We should have stopped it as soon as it hit our airspace. Although the president is my commander in chief, I disagreed with his order but couldn't do anything about it. What do you suggest that we do to get approval for shooting them down over the Pacific?" General Fitzgerald asked.

"I'm sure that you know Ian's brother, Johnny. He is a technical genius. He has developed a long-range armed attack drone with a range of one hundred miles. The drones are armed with small missiles that are more than capable of taking down these balloons. He has calculated that we can deploy the drones from four locations along the west coast. The drones have been successful in their initial testing but haven't been fully tested yet. We are confident that these drones can accomplish this task. If there is a failure, we need backup. That is where you come in," Adam said,

"We have been discussing this part of the operation on the flight over." Ian paused as the door opened and David walked in. Ian introduced David to General Fitzgerald and then continued presenting his plan. "David and I agreed that Vice President Powers should be brought in and hopefully he would authorize the action. If not, then it would be up to you to risk your career to do this."

"I know the vice president. I can talk to him. I think he would be willing to help," Beck said.

"I was just thinking—I can plan a live training exercise to provide backup for your drones. That might work. I also think that we should bring Vice President Powers into the fold. He will need to know what is happening with this mission. He will also be instrumental in the plan to confront and hopefully remove President Grange from office. Anything else? I need to get this in the works. Ian, please have Johnny send me the information on the ships and the launch window for the balloons," General Fitzgerald said.

"Will do, Andy. Thanks for your help. I feel better about being able to stop this attack with you on our side," Ian said.

They all stood and said goodbye as General Fitzgerald left the conference room.

"Let's get back to the ranch," Ian said.

They all filed out of the conference room and headed to the jet.

"I ordered sandwiches for us, I will pick them up and be there in a few minutes," David said.

"I'll help you carry them," Tuck said.

They were all waiting in the plane and had their gear stowed. Ian closed and latched the door and stepped into the cockpit. "David, why don't you take her up this time?"

"Be glad to," David said as he began the startup sequence. Once they had clearance for takeoff, they were speeding down the runway and headed to Montana.

CHAPTER TWENTY-SIX

SKIES OVER UNITED STATES

Adam, Ally, Tuck, and Beck were sitting in the main cabin of the Learjet on the flight from Washington, DC to Montana. Once they reached their cruising altitude of forty-two thousand feet, Beck got up and stepped into the galley. He came back with a tray of sandwiches and chips and set it on the table between the four seats. He picked up another tray with cups of ice and various bottles of soda and placed it on the table.

They were all hungry and ate all the sandwiches and chips. Adam cleaned up the table and they sat back in their leather chairs. They discussed their latest missions and talked about their pasts. The bonding time in the aircraft helped solidify their team. They each felt comfortable working with each other and knew each other's expertise.

Ally directed the conversation to how they were going to get evidence of the conspiracy on President Grange and Deputy Director Stevens.

"I have been thinking about this and it will be difficult to pull off. We either need to get the FBI or NSA to issue a warrant for a wiretap to listen to their calls. It's probably too late for that. Not to mention that it would be extremely difficult to get this against either of these two men. My suggestion is to get Johnny to initiate a search for offshore accounts for both Grange and Stevens and watch for deposits coming from Wentworth. If we can prove that they received large sums of money from Wentworth, we should be able to back track their involvement in the conspiracy," Adam said.

"I think that is the best approach, Adam. We need to treat this as a financial crime for now. Once we establish that, we can move to other crimes against the United States, maybe even treason," Beck said.

"Could there be a way to get one or both of them to admit to what they are doing?" Ally asked.

"I'd doubt that we could get Grange to talk unless we catch him on a hot mic sometime. That seems like a long shot to me. We should keep it in mind if we can come up with a plan. Stevens on the other hand may be easier to get to. He isn't surrounded by Secret Service twenty-four seven. Beck, you were able to talk to him and place a bug on his jacket, right?" Adam said.

"Yes, I did. I sat down next to him in a bar near his house. He is not married and is by himself a lot of the time. I think it is very plausible to get him to admit something given the right circumstances. Maybe a honeytrap?" Beck said.

"Not with me! He knows me and was the one who sent me to watch over Adam's parents. Adam and I also need to be very careful not to be exposed, especially in the United States. I would guess that Stevens is behind the assassination attempts on us and isn't too happy about the rescue of Adam's parents," Ally said.

"You are right, Ally. I don't think that I told you this detail, but when I was trying to get back to civilization, I called Stevens, and he was supposed to send an agent with a car to pick me up at some small town in Montana and then fly me back to DC. I had a weird feeling and decided to watch from a distance before meeting the agent picking me up. It turns out that he was a hired assassin, and he tried to kill me. I was able to take him out. That is how I got connected with Ian. I called Johnny to come get me and he took me to the ranch. After hearing my story, they decided to help," Adam said.

"That is good information. We should not underestimate Stevens. He knows espionage and has spent his life in the field. There is probably not much he doesn't know about. I agree with Ally's assessment that there are probably hit men looking for her and Adam," Tuck said.

Just then, a clunking sound was heard as the landing gear was lowered. They each tugged their seatbelts to make sure that they were fastened and prepared to land.

From the cockpit, the sky was almost dark as they began their descent. The lights from a few houses spread across the miles and a couple of cars were seen. When they were a few miles out, the lights of the runway illuminated, and David guided the jet to the runway for a smooth landing. He taxied to the hangar and shutdown the engines.

Ian stepped out of the cockpit, immediately opened the door of the aircraft, and lowered the stairs. They each stood and stepped down to the tarmac. The sun had just set, and the sky was darkening quickly. The air was cold in northern Montana and Ally shivered without a coat. Adam put his arm around her, and she snuggled into his side as they walked to the waiting ATVs and loaded their luggage. Inside the hangar, they found coats that would fit to keep out the chill as they motored their ATVs back to their cabins.

Adam and Ally got in one of the ATVs and Adam said, "Do you mind if we stop and check in with my parents before going back to the rooms?"

"I'd love to. I really enjoyed being with your parents when I was tasked to guard them. They treated me very lovingly," Ally said.

"That sounds like Mom and Dad. I'm glad they are safe here. Hang on, let's go," Adam said.

In a few minutes, they pulled up in front of Adam's parent's cabin and Adam shut down the ATV. They walked up the steps side by side and Adam knocked on the door. Adam's father, Ken, answered the door. "Welcome back, you two." Adam's mother, Susie, was peeking out the curtain and quickly sat down on the couch just before Ken opened the door.

A cold draft of air entered the cabin and Susie shivered a little. She was also smiling, not only at seeing their son home safely but knowing, as only a mother knows, that her son was in love. She could tell the moment that they pulled up on the ATV. There was a radiance coming from their faces that they couldn't hide.

Susie smiled and Adam gave her a big hug. Ken put his arm around Ally and pulled her into a tight side hug.

"Well, you two look tired. Was your trip a success?" Ken asked.

Susie said, "Ken, get them something to drink. They can tell us about their trip in a few minutes."

Ken shrugged and headed for the kitchen. He started a kettle of water on the stove and got out four mugs. A few minutes later, he brought a tray with a teapot, mugs, and teabags. He sat the tray on the coffee table and took his seat in the recliner near the fire-place. Susie was sitting in the chair next to him. Ken poured a cup of tea for Susie and handed it to her. Adam and Ally each made a cup of tea and told them about their trip.

After visiting for a couple of hours, Adam stood and said, "I need to get some sleep. Ally, are you ready to go?"

Ally stood, yawned, and said, "Yes, I am. Ken and Susie, thank you so much for the tea and company. We will see you tomorrow."

Susie stood and Ally moved toward her. They embraced and Susie whispered in Ally's ear. "He really likes you... And so do we."

As Adam and Ally were driving to their rooms in the bunkhouse, Susie said to Ken, "They are going to get married. I can see it in their eyes when they look at each other."

Ken smiled as he watched the ATV navigate the path and disappear around the corner. He turned to his wife and said, "I think you're right. I've never seen such contentment on Adam's face."

CHAPTER TWENTY-SEVEN

NORTHERN MONTANA

The sun had just shown itself over the eastern horizon in the cold Autumn morning of northern Montana. Adam was awake, lying in bed and was thinking about seeing Ally again. *I could get used to seeing her every day.* He threw back the blankets and headed for the bathroom. He dressed in a pair of shorts and a long-sleeved t-shirt to go for a run. He stepped out the front door and shivered in the morning chill. The view from the porch was of the huge meadows and the runway. The morning sun cast a golden glow across the landscape. The aspen groves were golden and trembling in the cold morning breeze created by the warming air. Adam stared at the view for a moment and thought that was just what he needed to wake up for the day. He took off at a slow jog down to the runway for a three-mile run.

As he ran, his mind went from Ally to the mission that they were on. He went over and over what they knew and tried to anticipate the next steps. The biggest unknown that he decided to focus on was the terrorist organization that was behind the bombing plot. Even though they were being contracted for the bombing, he knew that the terrorist organization would be benefiting from the bombing of the "infidels" and, most of all, the influx of cash from Wentworth.

Even though he didn't know the exact amount of the payment to the terrorist organization, he was sure that it was a very large sum. This cash would allow the terrorist organization, whoever they may be, to purchase weapons, explosives, to infiltrate, and attack the United States and its allies.

He knew that the contact for the terrorist organization was in Yemen—at least that was where the computer was located that accessed the email account. The assumption was that the terrorist organization was an Islamic-based organization. However, he needed to remember that it may only be a front to cover up the actual identity of the organization.

Adam finished his run and was walking back the short distance to his room as he thought, *I will probably be going to Yemen soon.*

The entire team assembled in the dining room of the main house for breakfast before their planning session started. Ian welcomed each person and directed them to sit at the dining room table. His kitchen staff began serving a large breakfast. The aroma of freshly cooked bacon and fresh pancakes were filling the room. Ian blessed the food and everyone plated what they wanted. The breakfast discussions were lively as everyone got to know one another and discussed aspects of the mission.

After the staff cleared the table, Ian stood and said, "Thank you, everyone, for your contributions to the team so far. As you know we have uncovered a conspiracy that is driven by greed. It is putting many innocent people at risk of death or injury and needs to be stopped. I want to start this meeting by asking a question to the team.

"As you all know, this is the first mission for this team. We moved up our start timeline when we connected, quite by accident, with Adam and heard his story. It started out as just helping him get back to his life, but quickly turned into a global conspiracy. I consider each one you to be members of the team and I hope that you will consider staying on the team permanently. We have funding to last longer than our lifetimes. We do, however, need a name. The name should be generic and would be reminiscent of a think tank, not a clandestine organization. Please think about it and we will discuss later, perhaps after we finish this mission."

Everyone agreed and Ian continued. "Adam, will you brief everyone on the mission status and the next steps?"

Adam stood and said, "Everyone knows the status of the mission as of yesterday. Wentworth is planning to distribute a virus in the United States to start a global pandemic using Chinese spy balloons outfitted with a distribution system to release the virus in the air over the United States. He has contracted with a terrorist organization to coordinate synchronized bombings in ten locations across the United States as a distraction or diversion from the virus distribution. For this to work, Wentworth has conspired with CIA Deputy Director Stevens and President Grange to focus the military and law enforcement on the terrorist bombing and to ignore the spy balloons distributing the virus. That is the overview of the mission. There are several things that need to happen and the timing is critical. First, we need to prevent the bombings by raiding the terrorist cells just before the designated bombing time. Second, we need to destroy the spy balloons immediately after launch. We have plans for these two aspects of the mission that we will detail in a few minutes. The next two items are just as critical, will take more planning, and will require much more time. The end result will be not just stopping the attacks but apprehending those behind it. We need to assemble the evidence needed to remove and prosecute Stevens and Grange in the United States, Wentworth, Finn, and Giovanni in Switzerland. Finally, we need to track down and remove Qi Limpon in China and determine the identity of the terrorist organization and take them out. Ben, can you review your plans to raid the terrorist cells?"

"Sure," Ben said. "First of all, it has been a pleasure to meet everyone on this team. I look forward to working with you all on this mission and future missions. Due to the connection of Stevens in this conspiracy, we must maintain operational security by keeping knowledge of this operation to only those we trust; therefore, I have only contacted one known FBI agent-in-charge from each office near the locations that bombings are planned. We held a planning meeting yesterday and they now have surveillance on each cell. They have confirmed each cell location and that each location is occupied by men of middle eastern descent. We are maintaining round-the-clock surveillance. At the appropriate time, all locations will be raided simultaneously. Remember, Johnny has control of the email connection with the terrorist contact, and they think that the bombing was postponed one week."

"Thank you, Ben. We couldn't have done this without your help. The next operation will be to destroy the Chinese spy balloons. Johnny, can you detail your plans for the drones?" Adam said.

"Yes, I have my prototype drone and have tested its operation. My battery of tests is not complete but enough to feel confident that we can destroy all the balloons using the drones with their missile armament. I received ten more drones, and my friend

Merlin is currently in the lab assembling all the drones and missiles. They will be ready to deploy in two days," Johnny said.

"There are four launch locations. David and I will each pilot a jet with the drones and their launch crews to the designated launch locations. David and I will crew the remaining two drone launches," Ian said

"We met with General Andy Fitzgerald of the Pacific Air Force. He has an armed training mission planned that will send up F-22 fighters from Vandenberg Air Force Base in California as a backup for our drones. If for some reason our drones fail to intercept the balloons and shoot them down, the F-22 pilots will be instructed to intercept them and shoot them down with a Sidewinder missile. The Air Force will think it is a routine training mission until they are needed.

"The drones will intercept the balloons over the Pacific Ocean before the distribution systems have been armed. The payload should end up harmlessly sitting on the bottom of the ocean. General Fitzgerald will ask the Coast Guard have vessels attempt recovery of the balloons with their distribution apparatus and to intercept the launch ships after they detect the spy balloon launches. Johnny and I will coordinate the drone attacks from the computer lab here at the ranch. Ben and General Fitzgerald will be in the loop to help coordinate the rest of the operations. Any concerns with these plans or does anyone have any additional information on these operations?" Adam said.

"Wentworth and his crew will know that their plans were disrupted when the bombings don't happen. They will probably go to ground. Do we have any plans in place to apprehend them so we don't lose them when the attacks are thwarted?" Ally asked.

"Good question, Ally. This is something that we need to work on in this meeting. Now is as good of time as any. Does anyone have any ideas on how we approach this?" Adam asked.

"When we met with General Fitzgerald in DC, we discussed the need to bring in Vice President Powers to facilitate the political aspects of this mission. He will need to be prepared to take the presidency from Grange when he is taken into custody and removed from office. It would be best if he is not blindsided by this. Maybe he can contact the Swiss to have them apprehend Wentworth, Finn, and Giovanni. Vice President Powers is a friend. We went to high school together. I would be happy to meet with him and plan the operation with the Swiss to apprehend those in Switzerland," Beck said.

The team all looked at Beck with faces showing their amazement that he and Vice President Jack Powers were high school friends. Ian said, "I think that is a great idea. Please contact the vice president right after the meeting. If you need to fly out to DC to meet him, I will take you."

"Beck, do you think that we should include the entire investigation or just the investigation into Grange and Stevens in this discussion with the vice president?" Adam asked.

"I think that he needs to be briefed on the entire investigation. This operation will be extremely difficult and will take precise planning and execution to bring to fruition. It will help our case to be working with Vice President Powers and having his oversight. Removing a sitting president from power is not something to be taken lightly. There are exact rules that need to be followed that will involve all branches of government. The vice president is the right man to direct this effort. The best option will be to apprehend President Grange and get him to resign from office immediately so that the transition of the presidency from Grange to Powers can happen smoothly. This is a political minefield and must be navigated from within. In addition, it will be a shock to the United States citizens and the world. There will be repercussions throughout the world no matter how it happens," Beck said.

"You are right, Beck. We have been fighting crime and when the criminal is the most powerful leader in the world. We can't afford to make any mistakes. Now, that leaves Qi Limpon in China. Ideas?" Adam said.

"I think I can help with this one. I speak fluent Mandarin. I learned to speak and read Mandarin from my wife who is of Chinese descent. Should this be an assassination or apprehension? If we apprehend Limpon and bring him back to the United States, we may be able to get additional information out of him regarding Chinese state secrets. I would suggest that we attempt apprehension but allow assassination if that doesn't work," David said.

"This can also get very political. We must be careful. If we do take him out, make sure that it doesn't look like an assassination but an accident. Our relations with China are tenuous at best, so proceed with caution," Ian said.

"I agree with Ian's assessment regarding China. Johnny, do you have any information regarding Limpon's location?" Adam said.

"I have been trying to locate him. Just before the meeting, I found that Limpon is planning a vacation to the Caribbean on the Island of Aruba. I think that he is planning on disappearing there. Aruba is very close to Venezuela who has close ties to China. He is scheduled to fly to Aruba the day after the attack is scheduled to happen in the United States. My guess is that he will stay in Aruba or travel to Venezuela by fishing boat to disappear. It will be easier for him to disappear in Venezuela. Hopefully we can catch him in Aruba," Johnny said.

"Aruba sounds like a nicer trip than China," David said.

"A lot closer as well. You can take the Cirrus Vision jet and be there in a few hours," Ian said.

"The last item is determining the identity of the terrorist group. What do we know about them, Johnny?" Adam asked.

"The source IP address that accessed the email account that is being used for communication with the terrorist organization is an internet café in Al Hudaydah, Yemen. The website for the internet café shows that they have several computers available for customers to use. The contact always appears to use the same computer since the IP address is the same. Either they are not a sophisticated computer user or they are very sophisticated and are using this IP address to spoof the actual IP address. My guess is that they are not that sophisticated. I searched for closed circuit cameras nearby, but there are not many in Yemen. We need to get eyes on the ground to identify the contact. It is also time sensitive, since this email account will not be used after the go signal is given for the bombing. When we have someone watching, we can send a message and wait till we get visual confirmation," Johnny said.

"I will go to Yemen and watch the internet café. I will see if I can place a camera on the computer or in the café so that we can get good images of the users. It is a long flight, so we should plan on leaving as soon as possible to give us the best chance to identify the contact," Adam said.

"Ally, can you help me with the logistics and communication for these operations?" "It will be difficult to manage on my own," Johnny said.

"Sure, I can do that," Ally said.

"Alright everyone, we have a lot to do in the next few hours. Beck, you will get in touch with the vice president. David, you and Beck can fly to DC to meet with the vice president. We can't fly directly into Yemen, so I will fly Adam and Tuck to Saudi Arabia, and they can slip into Yemen. Al Hudaydah is on the coast, so sneaking in via water will probably be easiest. I have some friends in Saudi Arabia that can help us with transportation. I will contact them right away and file a flight plan. Wheels up right after lunch," Ian said.

"We will deal with the conspirators when we conclude the operations to apprehend the terrorist cells and eliminate the balloons," Adam said. "Alright everyone, let's get moving."

CHAPTER TWENTY-EIGHT

NORTHERN MONTANA

After the meeting ended, Beck stepped out on the front porch of the ranch house. The sun was high in the sky. Although the temperatures were cool, the intense sun made it feel warmer. Beck unzipped his jacket and gazed at the meadows and pond in the distance. He took a deep breath and dialed the personal cell phone of Vice President Powers. After three rings, Powers answered the phone.

"Hi Beck!"

"Hi Jack. It's good to hear your voice. Do you have a few minutes? I know that you are a busy man," Beck said.

"I have five minutes; I am walking to my next meeting. What's up?"

"I am working for a new organization, and we have some information that I need to share with you in person. Would you be able to meet for thirty minutes tomorrow? The timing is critical."

"Yes, I am free for lunch. We can meet at my residence at noon. It is secure and private. Does that work for you?"

"I'll be there. Thanks for taking the time to meet with me. See you tomorrow," Beck said has he ended the call.

Beck found David sitting on the back deck looking over the mountains in the distance while he was working on the flight plan. Beck sat down next to David and said, "I just spoke with the vice president, and I have a lunch meeting scheduled at his residence at noon tomorrow."

David looked over at Beck and said, "That sounds good and fits with my plan. I think we should leave this afternoon and spend the night in DC. While you are meeting with the veep, I will prepare the plane for our flight back."

"Good plan, what time do you want to be wheels up?" Beck asked.

"If we leave at 1:30 p.m., that will give us time to meet with Johnny to work on the discussion plan. Shall we head over to see Johnny now?" David said.

"Yes, let's go," Beck said as he stood. They walked back inside and walked down the stairs to the basement level where Johnny had his state-of-the-art computer lab. Beck knocked on the door and Johnny said, "Come in."

"Hey guys," Ally said as she and Johnny turned in their chairs. "Isn't this place amazing?"

The lights were dimmed in the room and there were screens covering one wall. There were two workstations with three monitors each. The place was humming with energy.

Johnny motioned around the room with his hand and said, "Welcome to the Nerve Center. This is where we do all the magic. The servers are in the adjacent room and the satellite antennas are hidden out back from any overhead imagery. What can we do for you?"

"I have a meeting scheduled with the vice president tomorrow at noon. We plan on leaving for DC this afternoon. Can you print a summary of the evidence that we have? It will be useful to leave with the vice president," Beck said.

"You got it. What time are you flying out?" Johnny asked.

"We're leaving at 1:30 p.m. this afternoon," David said.

"Okay, come back in an hour and we can review the document," Johnny said as he turned to his computer and began typing.

An hour later, Beck and David returned to the computer lab. Johnny turned and handed a short document to Beck and said, "Look this over and let me know if you have any questions or need anything else."

Beck read through the document, closed it, and looked at Johnny. "This is perfect. How did you write this so quickly?"

"I have a proprietary AI tool that can process all the data that we collected and summarize. I just had to point it in the right direction. It was done in ten minutes," Johnny said with a smile.

Beck and David shook their heads in amazement and said in unison, "Thanks, Johnny."

"One more thing, I have been thinking that we should begin to plan the trip to Aruba so Adam and I can leave as soon as he returns from Yemen. We will need a place to park the Cirrus and accommodations. We expect to be there a couple of days early and set up our grab of Limpon. What can you tell us about his plans," David said.

"Limpon's flight is scheduled to arrive in Aruba a week from now. I will text you the details and photos of Limpon. He has rented a villa on the beach for three months, although I don't expect him to be there the whole time, but I do expect him to be there a week or two for the sake of appearances. He has two bodyguards trained in the Chinese special forces called Dragons of the East. He also may be traveling with his mistress. I would expect his bodyguards to be heavily armed and vigilant."

"The bodyguards will make this operation more difficult, but we should be able to handle it. We will have the element of surprise and should be able to place bugs in the house before they arrive," David said.

"I was going to suggest that. There should be a car in the garage that comes with the house. Be sure to place a tracker on that. Oh, there is also a boat moored at the private dock. You should add a tracker there as well. I will send you pictures and floor plans of the property," Johnny said.

"Thanks, that will help a lot. We will use the next couple of days to finalize our plans," David said.

"We'll get to work on the Aruba planning. Have a great trip," Johnny said.

"Bye guys, see you soon," Ally said.

Beck and David turned for the door, walked out, and back to their rooms to quickly pack. After packing, they took an ATV down to the hangar. They accessed the armory to pick out their equipment. It was not a trip they expected any violence, so they each just packed a compact Sig Sauer P938 and two magazines. They took the handguns and their bags and stowed them in the cargo area of the Cirrus Vision jet. David did his flight pre-check and walk around of the sleek aircraft. He was always excited before takeoff, especially in an aircraft like this one. It would be like flying a sports car, small but nimble and fast. After he verified all flight surfaces were free and clear and the tanks were full, he asked the ground crew to move the jet out of the hangar. David stood next to Beck as they watched the aircraft being pushed out to the tarmac in front of the hangar.

As it was rolling out of the door, Ian walked into the hangar with a smile on his face. He walked up to David and Beck and pointed over his shoulder with his thumb and said, "It sure is a beautiful aircraft isn't it?"

"Yes, it is. I am looking forward to flying it," David said.

"Do you have everything that you need?" Ian asked.

"Yes, it's already stowed. By the way, I will be meeting with Powers tomorrow at noon, then we return to the ranch," Beck said.

"Great. Stay safe and Godspeed," Ian said.

The jet was in position and ready for their trip. They began walking to the aircraft and David did a final walk around as Beck opened the door and sat in the co-pilot seat. David opened his door and sat in the pilot's seat. He went through the startup sequence and fired up the single jet engine. As the engine was coming up to operating temperature, David completed the rest of his pre-flight checklist and familiarized himself with the controls of the Cirrus Vision jet.

In less than half a mile, the jet was airborne and heading to their final cruising altitude of twenty-seven thousand feet. Heading east they enjoyed the view of the clear skies through the large windshield. David flew the jet through several different maneuvers to get a feel for the capabilities of the jet. They stopped in Wisconsin to fuel up and continued to Ronald Reagan Washington National Airport in Washington, DC. They taxied to the private terminal and parked the plane in the designated parking spot. David completed the shutdown of the plane.

David and Beck exited the aircraft and worked together to tie down the plane for the night. They got their overnight bags from the cargo area and David locked the plane. They walked to the private terminal, picked up their rental car, and drove to their hotel near the capitol building.

The next morning, Beck prepared for his discussion with Vice President Powers. Even though they were close friends, he was still nervous about discussing the latest matters with him. It would show a shocking conspiracy at the highest level and would be difficult to believe. Johnny provided Beck with all the material that he would need to prove to the vice president the clear and present danger.

Beck arrived at the vice president's residence thirty minutes early. He cleared through security and was instructed to wait for the vice president in the sitting room. He sat in an antique wing back chair and waited. Twenty-five minutes later, the vice president stepped into the room and Beck jumped to his feet. The two men shook hands and embraced in a back-slapping man hug.

"It is good to see you, Beck," Vice President Powers said as he directed Beck to follow him to the veranda.

The two men sat at a small table across from each other and spoke of old times as the staff served their lunch. Once the servers were gone and the door closed, Vice President Powers said, "Since we are limited on time, and you indicated that you have some important information for me. Let's hear it."

Beck took a drink of water and began telling the tale of the conspiracy and planned attacks on the United States. As he was speaking, neither man ate, and anger began welling up in the vice president. When Beck had finished the story, the vice president said, "How do you know that this isn't just a theory and is actually planned?" He then took a bite of his food.

Beck took a bite and told him about the surveillance of the terrorist cells, the Chinese ships moving into position, and how Johnny had commandeered the email communications between Wentworth and the terrorist organization.

"This is hard to swallow, Beck. I trust you and know that you wouldn't be here if this were not happening. What do you need from me to help you with this investigation."

"As you know, I am now retired from the CIA. I have started working with a private organization that just started. We haven't even decided on a name yet. The name will be reminiscent of a think-tank name, but we will be doing covert work." Beck went on to tell the vice president about Adam and how he stumbled upon Johnny and how helping him revealed this conspiracy.

"That is a wild story. I heard about losing an agent in Ottawa. I didn't know that he survived. We need an organization like yours to do things that the governmental organizations can't do. Plausible deniability is the term that is thrown around this town. Okay, I support your plans. I will do what I can to help your team and prepare to handle the fallout of this investigation. Keep me informed of your actions and I will personally contact the Swiss government and direct Ben Walters to report directly to me regarding the attacks and investigation into Grange and Stevens."

They both took a deep breath and finished their lunches. "Beck, thank you for bringing this to my attention. Even though the conversation subject was difficult, I enjoyed seeing you and sharing lunch with you. It has been too long."

"Yes, Jack, it has been too long. Once this operation is over, I would like to invite you to the ranch that we use as our headquarters. You may even be President Powers then," Beck said as he raised his eyebrows.

"Let's not get ahead of ourselves. No matter what happens, this will be difficult for the citizens of the United States. They will feel betrayal and anger and I will be their focus. This could be the most difficult transition ever. They have overlooked Grange's problems and greed. That will bite them, and I may be bitten due to my connection to him. I will have to work diligently to distance myself from him. Oh, by the way, I will call General Fitzgerald and authorize his mission as well."

Both men stood and Beck said, "Thank you for lunch and meeting with me."

Vice President Powers walked Beck to the front door, and they shook hands as Beck left. He got in the car headed to the airport.

David had taken an Uber to the airport earlier to get the jet ready for their next flight.

Beck returned the rental car, grabbed his bag, and headed to the jet. David was already there and had the jet untied and fueled up. They greeted each other and climbed into the jet. When they were cleared for takeoff, David throttled up and they rocketed down the runway and were airborne within seconds heading back to the ranch.

CHAPTER TWENTY-NINE

NORTHERN MONTANA

Ian watched David pilot the Cirrus Vision jet away from the hangar and take off. He was still impressed with the little jet. He loved the way it looked and sounded. As they faded from view, he turned his attention to the Learjet. It was going to be a long flight and he wished he had a co-pilot for the flight. The autopilot was superb on the Learjet, but he always preferred to have eyes open all the time; he figured he may have to get Adam or Tuck to spend some time in the cockpit while he rested.

The ground crew had already filled the fuel tanks and added the custom, long-range auxiliary tanks. They would be at maximum weight taking off, but they should be able to make the non-stop flight to Saudi Arabia. He planned to land at the King Abdullah International Airport in Jazan, Saudi Arabia. It was the closest airport to the Yemeni border. His contact would be waiting for them at the airport and transport them across the desert to a fishing vessel that would transport them to the Yemeni coast.

As he was completing his pre-flight inspection of the aircraft, the kitchen staff arrived with food and beverages to stock the galley. They went aboard and loaded the galley.

Adam packed and loaded his gear into the ATV. He stopped at the main house and went downstairs to say goodbye to Ally.

She stepped out of the computer lab and quickly gave Adam a long hug.

"I'm missing you already," Ally said as she gazed into his eyes. "Come back soon. I don't want to be away from you long," she said with a smile on her face. "Come in for a second. Johnny may have some information for you."

They entered the computer lab and Adam said, "Hi Johnny."

Johnny turned his chair. "Hey Adam, I've done some more searching and found a low-resolution, closed-circuit camera in the internet café. Unfortunately it is not connected to the internet. I saw it in an online photo of the internet café that was posted on social media. I don't have much more information about that. I did plan for an asset to meet you at the coast of Yemen. His name is Joshua. I have sent you the coordinates. He will have local clothing for you if you need it and drive you to Al Hudaydah. He has procured an apartment in the building across the street from the internet café. There will be a car available there for your use. We will plan your exfiltration once you have collected the intelligence that we need. You may need to follow the contact to learn more. Be careful over there. They don't like Americans and we don't have any assets there to help."

"Thank you, Johnny. We'll check in when we arrive in Saudi," Adam said as he turned to leave.

"I'll walk you out. Be right back, Johnny," Ally said.

They walked out the door. As soon as the door latched, they hugged again and held hands while walking to the ATV. At the ATV, Adam leaned toward Ally and kissed her. It was a long kiss that promised his return to her.

"I miss you already. I'll talk to you on the comms and hope-fully, I'll be back in a few days," Adam said as he moved his hand to the key. He really didn't want to leave Ally, and it felt like he would be incomplete when he was away. His heart was pounding, and he reached over to her and pulled her to him for another passionate kiss, then said, "I'll be back soon."

"You better," she exclaimed as she playfully pushed his shoulder.

Adam fired up the ATV, kissed the back of her hand and said, "Goodbye beautiful." He put the ATV into gear and drove away waving until he couldn't see her in the rearview mirror.

Adam stopped at the bunkhouse, picked up Tuck and drove to the hangar. They found Ian making the final inspection of the Learjet. They passed the kitchen staff on their way back from the hangar, so they knew they were well stocked with food.

Adam and Tuck went straight to the armory to load up their gear bags. They picked their weapons, body armor, ammunition, electronics, and imaging devices. Their packs were heavy. They were glad that they had transportation arranged and they hoped they didn't have to walk far.

They lugged the packs to the Learjet and loaded them in the cabin so that they could get everything ready before landing. Ian stepped into the main cabin and greeted Adam and Tuck. "Ready?" Ian said.

Adam and Tuck both nodded and took their seats.

"This will be a very long flight. There is a bedroom in the back of the plane if one of you wants to lay down to sleep. I may need one of you to sit up front for a spell and watch the sky while I take a nap," Ian said.

"Anytime," Adam replied and Tuck nodded.

"Let's get airborne," Ian said as he moved to the cockpit. Once he was seated, the plane jerked a little as the tug pushed it back out of the hangar. Ian went through the pre-flight checklist and made sure everything was working as expected. When the tug was disconnected and the area was clear, Ian started both jet engines and waited until they came up to operating temperature.

The jet was airborne and at cruising altitude in a matter of minutes. Once they reached their cruising altitude of forty-four thousand feet, Adam said, "Tuck, would you like something to drink?"

"A bottle of water would be great," Tuck said.

Adam picked two cold water bottles from the refrigerator and sat back down. They were facing each other with a table between them. They discussed the plans and Adam shared what Johnny told him just before they left for the hangar. They reviewed the data package that Johnny sent them and felt comfortable with the plan so far.

"The kitchen stocked the galley. Are you hungry?" Tuck asked as he stood up. "I'll bring something from the galley for you."

"Thank you, I am," Adam said.

Tuck put together a hot dinner of pulled pork, mashed potatoes, and baked beans. He handed a plate to Ian in the cockpit and took the other two back to the main cabin. He and Adam ate their dinner and talked about sports and other items of interest. Anything to take their minds off of the mission.

After dinner, Tuck said, "I think that I'll try to get some sleep in the back." He stood and went to the bedroom in the back of the plane. He was asleep in moments. Being a Navy Seal prepared him to sleep when he could.

Adam wasn't tired, so he stood and walked to the cockpit. "Tuck is sleeping in the back; would you like some company?"

"I'd love some. It gets lonely up here, but I never get tired of seeing the sky in all its forms," Ian said.

Adam slid into the co-pilot's seat and looked around. "The sky looks even bigger from the front," he said.

"Yes, it is a completely different experience up here."

They talked for a long time about their pasts and their plans for the future. Adam felt completely comfortable with Ian, like he was his favorite uncle. Someone he felt that he could talk to and confide in. Adam was looking at the dark night sky and the multitude of stars when he noticed the aurora borealis to the north. The sky was clear, and the aurora was pulsating bright greens and dull reds.

"I've always wanted to see the aurora," Adam said as he gazed at the aurora in awe.

"There is nothing like it, especially from the air. You have a much larger perspective of it," Ian said.

Adam thought for a few minutes then turned and looked at Ian. "Can I ask you something?"

"Sure, anytime."

"First of all, I want to be a permanent member of this team if you all will have me."

"I have been watching you and your performance has been extraordinary, and you have proven your leadership and operational abilities. I haven't spoken with the rest of the team, but I think that they will agree with that assessment. I already consider you to be part of the team."

Adam hesitated a moment and asked, "Will Ally be offered a role as well?"

"She has proven herself also. Yes, if the rest of the team agrees and she wants it. I think that she does, and I think that you want her to be a part of the team. You two work very well together, both in the field and off."

Adam smiled and stared at the stars for a few minutes, then asked, "Were you ever married?"

"Yes, my wife passed away five years ago. She bravely fought ovarian cancer, but it was too much for her," Ian said quietly. "She was the love of my life and made me promise to do what I loved when she was gone. That is when I started this organization."

"I'm sorry, I didn't know," Adam said gently.

"It's OK, I'm focused on this project and flying is what I love. When I am flying and see all these stars, I know that she is looking down on me, smiling and saying, 'Way to go, flyboy!'" he said with a smile as the memories flooded through his mind.

"How did you know you were in love with her?"

"That's easy. I was in flight school, and she worked at the reception desk. The moment that I saw her, I was smitten. I was almost late to my first ground school class because I was talking to her. When class was over, she was preparing to leave, so I asked her out for a milkshake. She agreed and I felt complete with her. From that point on, no other woman caught my eye," Ian said as he fondly remembered that first date.

"I feel that way about Ally. We've only known each other a few days, but I feel like we've always been together," Adam said then asked. "Am I crazy?"

Ian laughed and said, "I think that you were the last one to figure it out. We saw the way you two looked at each other that first day and everyone knew you two would be together soon. You're not crazy. When the right one comes along, you just know. Don't fight it, embrace the journey. It may be difficult at times, but the difficulties are far outweighed by the love and connection that you will experience. Having the draw at home will also help you to make the best decisions when you are in the field. Your decisions will affect more than just yourself. A relationship like this will be strong, if you support and serve one another."

"It's just... I have never experienced feelings like this before. I have had girlfriends, but it wasn't like this."

"It's going to be okay. Ally looks at you the way Mae looked at me. When we get back, tell her how you feel. I guarantee you that she feels the same way. I spoke with your parents and your mom knew you two were right for each other when she was the guard watching over them. She didn't know how you two would meet, but she knew then. Moms are that way, and your dad agrees with your mom."

They looked at the stars for a while and Ian said, "I need to go to the lavatory and rest for an hour. Can you sit up here and watch the stars? I will be in the main cabin If you need me just yell. The autopilot will keep us going in the right direction."

"Sure, there is a lot to think about."

Ian returned to the cockpit ninety minutes later and said, "Tuck is up. Why don't you go to the back and get some sleep? There is some melatonin in the lavatory if you need some."

Adam yawned and said, "Thanks for talking to me earlier, that really helped clear my mind." Adam returned to the main cabin and told Tuck that he was going to get some sleep as he walked to the back of the cabin. He lay down on the bed and fell asleep instantly. He woke when the plane touched down in Saudi Arabia. He sat up on the edge of the bed and rubbed his eyes. When the plane came to a stop, he stepped back into the cabin and sat next to Tuck.

CHAPTER THIRTY

JAZAN, SAUDI ARABIA

Ian taxied the Learjet to the designated parking spot at the King Abdullah bin Abdulaziz International Airport in Jazan, Saudi Arabia and shut down the engines. As the engines spooled down, Ian finished the shutdown sequence. He started the auxiliary power unit and kept the air conditioner on. It was going to get hot. Jazan was considered one of the hottest cities on earth. It was a seaside city with a booming luxury tourism industry. The airport was modern with a beautiful interior design.

Ian opened the door of the Learjet and was engulfed in a wave of hot air that felt like he was stepping into an oven. It couldn't be more different from the cool brisk air of Montana. He took a deep breath of the hot air that was tinged with airplane exhaust and dust. As he stepped down to the tarmac, an old, sand-colored Toyota FJ60 Land Cruiser pulled up next to the aircraft. Ian smiled when he saw the driver. He walked down the stairs, stretched, and met the driver with a warm embrace and air cheek kisses.

"Muhammad, it is good to see you again, my friend," Ian said as they slapped each other's backs.

"Always good to see you, Ian. What has it been—ten years?" Muhammed said.

Muhammed looked over Ian's shoulder and Ian turned and said, "Let me introduce my colleagues. Adam and Tuck, this is Muhammed. He is an old friend. I've known him for nearly three decades. You are in good hands with him."

Adam and Tuck both shook hands with Muhammed and greeted him with warm smiles.

"We have a long way to go. Load your gear in the back of the Land Cruiser and we will get going," Muhammed said as he handed each of them a bag of clothes. "Put these on, it will help us not to be noticed."

Adam and Tuck stepped back aboard the aircraft and got their packs. They also picked up the soft cooler with food and beverages that were packed previously by the kitchen staff at the ranch and put everything by the door. They both changed into the clothes that Muhammed gave them and tied the scarf around their heads in the Arabian style.

They picked up their bags, stepped off the aircraft, and loaded everything into the Land Cruiser. Adam took the passenger seat and Tuck sat in the back seat. Muhammed patted Ian on the shoulder and climbed in the driver's seat. The diesel engine started with a rumble and they headed out of the airport.

Ian watched them leave and then tied down the Learjet. He expected to be there for a couple of days. He walked to the terminal and ordered a fuel truck. He purchased a soda from a vending machine and took a long pull of the cold fizzy beverage. *They always taste better here for some reason. Maybe I'll bring a case home.* He slowly walked back to the Learjet and walked around the outside for a while before the fuel truck showed up. He greeted the driver and made sure that all the tanks were full. He paid the driver and gave him a generous tip. The driver showed him that there was ground power and he could plug the Learjet in to the local power system. Ian thanked him and slipped him a little more cash. He plugged into the ground power, climbed aboard the Learjet, and closed the door. He shut down the auxiliary power unit and the ground power kicked in.

The cabin stayed cool. Ian called Johnny and Ally and let them know that they had arrived in Saudi Arabia and that Adam and Tuck were on their way with Muhammed. Johnny was already tracking them with their personal trackers.

Muhammed drove fast on the rough, dirt roads heading south across the desert. The heat was radiating off the desert floor and through the windows of the Land Cruiser creating wavy currents of air that looked ethereal. The air conditioning was running at full speed and just keeping the heat at bay. Muhammed pointed out some local landmarks and oil wells as they traveled south. The landscape was flat, dry, and dusty. There were occasional clumps of brush growing along low areas that would collect the minuscule amount of precipitation that area of the world received. There must have been water wells, because there were several plots of land that were irrigated and growing crops.

Two bone-jarring hours later, the very dusty Land Cruiser pulled into a fishing village near the border of Yemen. Muhammed drove down to the coast and stopped at a dilapidated fisherman's dock. There was one rough looking fishing boat tied up at the dock and no one else to be seen.

"Wait here," Muhammed said.

Adam and Tuck nervously watched Muhammed walk to the fishing boat. They both had their hands on their firearms. Adam asked Tuck, "Do you think everything is okay?"

"I hope so. This is something that happens in the middle east. They're not trusting, and Muhammed is probably doing the greeting and paying the fishermen. Good question though. We must be very vigilant from here on out. It will be even more essential once we reach Yemen. I can speak and understand Arabic, but we don't want them to know that. We will act like we only speak English. We want them to feel comfortable speaking in Arabic around us thinking that we don't understand. We may learn something or find out if something is amiss," Tuck said.

Thirty minutes later, Muhammed returned and spoke. "All is well. Ishmael is ready to take you to Yemen and will drop you at the coordinates that you will provide to him once you are out to sea." Muhammed opened the back of the Land Cruiser and said, "I will pick you up when you return."

Adam and Tuck thanked Muhammed and carried their bags to the fishing vessel. They greeted Captain Ishmael, boarded the vessel, and stowed their gear. They looked back to where the Land Cruiser was parked and only saw dust as Muhammed drove away.

Ishmael started the old diesel engines and motioned for Adam and Tuck to go below deck until they were clear of land. Adam and Tuck complied and watched through the small port windows as they moved away from shore.

The fishing boat was slow, and it took an hour before Ishmael called them up on deck. There was no air conditioning in the cabin; it was hot, and they were soaked with sweat. The sea breeze on the deck was a welcome relief to the stifling heat below deck. They stood and watched the swells and clouds. Adam handed a paper to Captain Ishmael with the handwritten coordinates to the meeting location. Ishmael entered the coordinates into his top-of-the-line chart plotter that didn't fit with the condition of the vessel.

Ishmael smiled as he noticed Adam's look of confusion at the mismatch of the chart plotter and boat condition. "The ship just looks old. Everything mechanical and electronic is new. She is much faster than she looks, but we must maintain our cover by going slowly."

The chart plotter showed a six-hour voyage to reach their destination. It would be near sundown when they arrived. Adam moved to the stern of the ship and called Johnny.

"Hey Adam, I have Ally here and she couldn't wait to talk to you," Johnny said laughing.

Adam smiled and said, "Hi Ally, Hi Johnny. We are on the fishing boat heading toward Yemen. The chart plotter estimates our arrival time at our destination around 7:00 p.m."

"We are following your personal trackers, so we have your location. I will let our contact in Yemen know to be waiting for you when you arrive," Johnny said.

"Thanks to both of you," Adam said.

"Stay safe and see you soon," Ally said and ended the call.

Ishmael handed fishing poles to Adam and Tuck. "Might as well try to catch some fish on the way," he said.

Adam and Tuck grinned and took the fishing poles. They were already rigged, and Ishmael pointed to the live well for bait. It only took a few minutes for Adam and Tuck to have their lines in the water. It wasn't long until they had their first bite. Tuck reeled in a nice mahi-mahi, then Adam caught a red snapper. They continued to fish and filled Ishmael's locker with fish. Ishmael smiled and said with a loud voice, "What a day, and I didn't have to work." They all laughed as Tuck handed out water bottles.

Ishmael picked up his binoculars and scanned the horizon in all directions. Not seeing any other vessels, he began his turn toward the Yemen coastline. As they approached the shore, Ishmael slowed the boat and said, "I will get you as close to shore as possible. You will need to wade some. Get you gear ready."

Adam and Tuck donned their backpacks and grabbed their gear bags. All the bags were waterproof, so getting wet wasn't a problem. It would probably feel good after the heat and sun all day. The engines reversed and the boat came to a stop. Adam and Tuck thanked Ishmael and leapt into the water. It was waist deep and cool. They waded to the shore as they heard Ishmael reverse and speed off into the darkness. They were alone in a hostile country.

CHAPTER THIRTY-ONE

YEMEN

Adam and Tuck hit the cool water with a large splash. They wiped the seawater out of their faces as they waded onto the beach and looked all around. Not seeing anyone, they quickly crossed the sandy beach and climbed a small dune to get to a better vantage point. At the edge of the dune, they lay down so that they wouldn't silhouette in the fading light. Tuck pulled his compact binoculars out of his pack and peered over the top of the hill. He scanned the area and, in the distance, saw the outline of a vehicle. He watched closely to see if there was anyone there. He didn't see anyone. It was almost dark, so he switched to infrared imaging and found that the engine block was glowing brightly indicating that it was warm and had been running recently.

Tuck ducked back down below the crest of the dune and looked at Adam and said, "There is a warm vehicle about one click to the southeast. I didn't see the driver. Call Johnny and have him confirm if this is our contact or not.

Adam pulled his phone out and called Johnny.

"Hi Adam, I see that you are on the coast. Do you have visibility of the contact?" Johnny asked.

"We have a visual on a vehicle one click southeast of our location. We don't see the driver. Is this our contact?" Adam asked.

"I'm pulling up the satellite imaging now and am calling the contact. Hold on," Johnny said and muted the call.

Adam was waiting for a couple of minutes and Tuck was continuing to scan the area. Johnny came back on the line. "Adam, I have the vehicle on the satellite, but our contact is still thirty minutes out. That is not your contact, repeat, that is *not* your contact. It is likely that they saw you or heard the boat. Keep your eyes open and switch to comms so we can all communicate," Johnny said and ended the call.

Adam pocketed his phone. He pulled his comm out of his pocket, turned it on, and placed it in his ear. He tapped Tuck and he slipped back down the dune. Adam reported that this was not the contact and that their contact was still thirty minutes out. He pointed as his ear to indicate for Tuck to put his communication device in.

Johnny said through the devices, "I have movement. There are two bogeys moving toward you. They have rifles and are staying hidden as they move. They may be bandits or assassins, either way be careful."

Adam and Tuck clicked an acknowledgment and they both quickly assembled their FN M4 Carbine rifles and installed their optics. They also added silencers to the rifles to reduce the chance of someone nearby hearing them and bringing more men to the area. Since it was getting dark, they both donned their night vision goggles.

Tuck said, "Stay here and watch over the top of the dune." He pointed and continued, "I will move to that dune over there. We should be able to catch them at the same time. They don't have night vision, so we have an advantage." Tuck slid down the hill and ran to the dune.

Adam put his night-vision optics over his eyes and peeked over the top of the hill, leading with his rifle. He watched carefully for the men when he heard Tuck say, "I'm in position, scanning the area now."

Johnny said, "They are about half a click from you now. They should be in range in a few minutes."

They were quiet as they waited. Tuck saw the man closest to him and whispered, "Contact with one."

Adam then acquired the second man and said, "I have the second one."

"Wait till they get closer... On my mark... Fire!" Tuck said. Both rifles fired with a muted thump.

Adam watched through his rifle optics as the man he was aiming at flew backward with a blooming crimson stain on his chest. Satisfied that he wasn't moving he marked the location in his mind and searched for Tuck's target. It took him a moment to find the body on the ground. He could only see part of the man, but the pool of blood soaking into the sandy soil under the man's head told him the answer to his question. Both adversaries were down.

"Johnny, both are down. Are we clear?" Adam said.

Adam and Tuck kept the men in their sites and waited for Johnny to reply. A moment later, Johnny said, "No other movement of heat signatures, the area looks clear."

Adam and Tuck kept their vigilance and followed their rifles towards the downed men. When they reached the men, they kicked their weapons away and searched the men. They were clearly militants looking for an easy target. Their searches only revealed a small amount of money and cigarettes. They took the money and guns and moved to the vehicle.

They found an old Toyota Hilux four-wheel-drive pickup that had seen better days. A quick search inside didn't reveal anything useful. They took the keys and pocketed them in case they needed transportation later.

"I have your contact in sight, two clicks out. Move to the coordinates now," Johnny said.

Tuck led the way, and they concealed themselves to watch the pickup location. They could hear the engine of the vehicle moving in their direction. A moment later, they saw the vehicle lights bouncing around as their contact drove to the meeting location.

The vehicle was a white, double-cab Toyota Hilux four-wheel drive pickup. It was very dirty and looked like it had never been washed. Tuck and Adam watched the truck approach and stop in a cloud of dust. The driver turned the headlights off and shut down the diesel engine. Only the clicking sounds of the engine cooling were heard. The driver opened all the doors of the truck and turned on the interior light. He walked around the outside of the truck with his hands in the air and slowly turned around revealing that he was peaceful and alone.

Tuck motioned for Adam to stay put and Tuck stood and slowly approached the man with his rifle in a ready position. The man watched Tuck and said, "Johnny sent me. My name is Joshua, and I am at your service."

"Turn around slowly," Tuck said. As Joshua turned around slowly, Tuck felt more confident that he was who he said he was.

Johnny spoke through the communications device. "Adam sent a photo. I confirm that this is your contact."

When Joshua completed his pirouette, Tuck said, "Thank you for helping us. My name is Tuck." Leaving out his last name for anonymity, Tuck motioned for Adam to join him. "This is Adam. How long will it take us to get to Al Hudaydah?"

Joshua lowered his hands and extended his right hand and said, "Tuck and Adam, nice to meet you." He shook both of their hands as he said, "It will take about four hours to reach Al Hudaydah. Load up, let's go. There are a lot of bandits in the region."

They threw their gear in the bed of the pickup. Tuck took the passenger seat and Adam sat in the back. Joshua fired up the truck, turned on the headlights and turned around. Once they were on their way, Adam reached into the bag next to him and removed three bottles of water and handed them to Tuck and Joshua and kept one for himself.

The roads, if they could call them that, were just paths through the desert. Even though the roads were rough in Saudi Arabia, the roads in Yemen were terrible. Not only were they rough and dusty, but they also sometimes disappeared beneath sand drifting with the desert wind across the roads like snow blowing in a blizzard. Unlike the landscape in Saudi Arabia, there were only sparse small bushes and no agriculture to be seen. Everywhere they looked it was brown dirt and rocks. Some of the most inhospitable land Adam had ever seen. It would be easy to get lost, especially at night. The air conditioner in the Toyota worked well and kept the dust and heat out. Even though it was night, the air outside was still sweltering. Their dark tactical clothing didn't help with the heat. As they passed through small villages they all donned their head coverings to reduce any chances of being noticed. Joshua knew the roads and moved fast over the rough landscape. There were times that Adam thought that they were lost as the truck bounded over and slid sideways through deep sand drifts. The darkness was complete and the stars abundant as they drove through the night stopping only once to fill up the Toyota's diesel tank.

It was midnight as they were approaching Al Hudaydah. The city lights were sparse. They made their way through town not encountering much traffic. Joshua pulled up behind a building, killed the engine, and turned off the headlights.

"This is the apartment that I rented for you. It is on the top floor at the end of the hallway overlooking the street. Immediately across the street is the internet café that you have identified," Joshua said as he reached into his shirt pocket and pulled out a business card. It only had a phone number printed on it. He handed a card each to Adam and Tuck. "Here is my number. Call me when you need something." He picked up a keyring with two keys from the console near the gear shifter and handed to Adam. "Top floor, end of the hallway overlooking the street. Take these exterior stairs up. Oh, and the other key is for that Isuzu Trooper," he said pointing to the dirty old white SUV in the parking lot.

Adam and Tuck thanked Joshua and exited the Toyota. They grabbed their gear from the back and shook off the dust before shouldering their backpacks. Tuck led the way up the stairs with his rifle at the ready. They quietly entered the building and made their way to the last door overlooking the street. They took a moment to listen. Not hearing anything, Tuck used the key to unlock the door without opening it. He pocketed the key and nodded at Adam to be ready. They set their gear bags next to the door and held their rifles at ready position. Adam squatted down while Tuck remained standing. Adam touched Tuck's leg letting him know he was ready. Tuck pushed the door open and peered inside over the business end of his rifle. Not seeing anything, he entered the apartment, and they systematically cleared the rooms. The apartment was clear.

Adam stepped back to the hallway and grabbed their gear bags and closed and locked the door. The apartment was furnished but sparse: a couple of threadbare chairs and an old Formica kitchen table with three mis-matched chairs. The two bedrooms had old mattresses on the floor. Tuck looked out the window and, as promised, the internet café was just across the street. "We should get some rest. I will take first watch and will wake you in three hours," Tuck said.

Adam nodded and said as he headed to one of the bedrooms. "See you in three." Adam didn't bother to undress but lay on the old lumpy mattress fully clothed. He fell asleep immediately after a long stressful day.

Tuck pulled a chair up to the window and watched the street. Only one car drove by. The hours watching were long and dull. Tuck awakened Adam three hours later. It was still a couple of hours before sunrise. Adam awoke with a yawn and rubbed his eyes. He sat up and Tuck reported that nothing happened other than the one car driving down the street. Adam grabbed a thermos of coffee from his backpack and moved to the seat by the window.

Tuck lay down in the same room that Adam had used and closed his eyes and instantly fell asleep.

Early in the morning before the sun rose in the east, the first Muslim prayer chants of the day were heard across the city. There were men walking the streets preparing for the days' work. Adam concealed his chair to make it more difficult for anyone outside to see him.

The sun rose and the inside of the apartment was slowly illuminated. Tuck woke up before Adam came to awaken him. He came out of the room and said, "Good morning, Adam."

Adam turned to him and said, "Good morning. The city is coming to life. Now that you are up, we should call Johnny."

Tuck agreed and pulled out his phone. He placed a chair near Adam, and he dialed Johnny. He answered after two rings. "Hi Tuck and Adam."

"We are in the apartment that Joshua provided. It is in the perfect location to watch the internet café," Tuck said.

"Great. The internet café's website shows that they open at 9:00 a.m. local time. Can you see through the windows and see the layout of the café?" Johnny asked.

"Yes, it is dark inside, but it looks like the computers are setup near the windows and along one wall. I'll send you a photo," Adam said as he took a photo with his phone and sent it to Johnny.

"Use your high-power optics and see if you can read the stickers on the back of the computers," Johnny said.

Tuck opened the gear bag and removed high power binoculars and a small tripod. He moved a small table over and put the binoculars and tripod on the table. He checked each computer that he could see and read off the IP addresses. The computer in the corner matched the IP address that Johnny had identified earlier.

"Great, we won't need to place cameras, you should be able to watch from the apartment. I will create the email draft now. Keep watching the computer. I'll tell you when he reads the draft," Johnny said.

"Copy that," Tuck said. Adam and Tuck took turns watching the internet café. It was late afternoon when the contact appeared.

"We have a connection to the email account," Johnny said.

"Photos taken and are uploading now," Adam said as Tuck stood and began gathering some items to begin following the target.

"I am going downstairs to start following him. Adam, grab all the rest of our gear and take it to the car once I start following him. Keep your trackers and comms active," Tuck said.

Adam didn't take his eyes off the man at the computer as he said, "Copy."

"I received the photos, running facial recognition now," Johnny said.

Tuck waited at street level out of the target's sight line. Adam watched as the target one finger typed a message into the email draft. "He left a message in the draft folder and logged out of the email account. Standby, let me read it." A moment later, Johnny said, "They have confirmed the change in timeline and will send the order to activate the cells. No other activity on that computer. My guess is he is a go between. Follow him and see where he goes."

"He's leaving the café," Adam said as the target was walking to the door. "Opening the door now. Be ready Tuck. He turned right and is walking down the street at a normal pace."

"I have visual. Pack up, Adam, and I will keep you posted," Tuck said. Tuck was dressed in the common robes and head covering found in the Middle East. His darker hair, complexion, and beard helped him fit in with the locals better than Adam with his lighter skin tone and light brown hair.

Adam moved all their gear to the Isuzu Trooper that Joshua pointed out. He started the engine and turned the air conditioning to high while he waited for Tuck's next instruction. The interior of the Isuzu Trooper was like a sauna, and the air conditioner struggled to keep up. He was happy to see that the tank was full. The tracker showed Tuck's location several blocks away. He decided to move a little closer. He drove down the street and parked in front of an empty building and waited while monitoring Tuck's location. Twenty minutes later, Tuck stopped and said, "He just entered a building that looks like an abandoned store front. The windows are covered. Johnny, keep an eye on the front. I will check the back."

"On it," Johnny replied.

Adam moved to within a block of the location and waited for word from Tuck. Just then, Tuck said, "There is a large roll-up door in the back that was recently opened. There are fresh tire tracks in the dust going in. I'm going to peek through the door window. I don't see any cameras." Tuck carefully made his way to the side of the small door's window and listened for a moment. He could hear voices inside, but they didn't all sound Arabic. There was some other accent. It was hard to hear through the metal door.

He listened a moment longer. The discussion was still going on, so Tuck decided to take a quick peek using a small mirror. "He is inside discussing something with two other men. Their accents are not Middle Eastern." Tuck carefully placed his ear on the hot door and listened for a moment. He stood and moved back to a secluded position to watch the back door and said, "Okay, I didn't expect this. The other men are Eastern European, but I couldn't tell where they were from. I am watching the door."

"Tuck, can you slip a bug under the door? We should be able to make out what they are saying better," Johnny said.

"Copy," Tuck said as he pulled a paper-thin bug out of his pocket and activated it. He slipped up to the door again and slipped it under the door so that it adhered to the bottom of the door. They would never see it. He snuck back to his hiding spot and prepared his binoculars to digitally record and waited for the men to leave. "Done," he said.

"I have audio and am recording. The satellite view of the building shows a small, concealed satellite antenna. I will need you two to come back later and put a digital sniffer on the antenna and add bugs and cameras inside," Johnny said.

"Adam, be ready to follow the car when they leave," Tuck said.

"It sounds like their conversation is wrapping up," Johnny said. A few minutes later, the roll-up door opened and a man stepped out and looked up and down the alley.

Tuck got pictures of the man, including good close ups of his face. *Definitely Eastern European,* Tuck thought. The sound of a car starting broke the quietness. An older, black Mercedes sedan backed out of the building. There were two men in the front. The man who was driving was the man who opened the door. The other man was in the passenger's seat. Tuck had already set the camera to take continuous images and hit the "start" button. He got good images of the car and both occupants.

Tuck was concealed in a pile of boxes and trash that extended into the alley making a tight fit for a car to get through. He quickly prepared a tracker and waited inside a cardboard box that he prepared for that scenario. The car slowed down to a crawl as the driver threaded the car through the narrow opening. Tuck reached out and stuck a tracker on the rear bumper. The driver couldn't see him and they could then track the car much more easily. The Mercedes continued down the alley and Tuck said, "I was able to place a tracker on the car as it slowed near my position."

"I have the tracker and am watching the car's location. We should grab the man still inside and follow the other two men. Send me the images. Ally and I will get started on them. It may take a while to identify them," Johnny said.

"Uploading the photos now," Tuck said as Adam pulled into the alley and parked. Adam and Tuck stood on either side of the door and Tuck checked the doorknob. It was unlocked. Tuck slowly turned the knob trying not to make any noise. He kept his hand on the knob and looked at Adam in the eyes. They both nodded.

Tuck pushed the door open quickly and Adam rushed inside following his rifle. Adam saw the man sitting in a chair watching an action movie on the computer screen. He had on over-the-ear headphones and didn't hear them enter the building. Adam whispered in his communications device, "He doesn't hear us."

They quickly made their way to the man and Adam placed the end of his rifle barrel against the man's temple. The man didn't move but looked toward Adam.

Tuck knocked the headphones off his head and said in Arabic, "Put your hands on top of your head and lie face down on the floor."

The man complied and lay down. Adam pulled a pair of flex-cuffs out of his pocket and bound the man's arms behind his back. Adam searched the man and found an old .357 revolver in his waist band. Adam put the man back in the chair and zip tied his feet to the legs of the chair.

While Adam was securing their target, Tuck cleared the rest of the building and installed a couple of bugs and cameras. Seeing a staircase going to the roof access door, Tuck checked that the roof was clear, placed the digital sniffer on the satellite dish, and went back downstairs.

"Let's question him later. Bring him with us for now," Tuck said.

Adam placed the headphones back on the table next to the computer the man was using and closed the movie that he was watching. Adam opened the door to the alley and made sure it was clear before removing their prisoner. The alley was clear, so Adam and Tuck took their prisoner and put him in the cargo area of the Trooper. They secured his feet and threw an old blanket over him. They closed the doors and left the building. Adam had the tracker running on his phone when he started the Trooper. Tuck climbed in and they began making their way to the location of the other men in the Mercedes.

The man in the back of the Trooper was yelling and thrashing around. Adam looked over at Tuck and said, "Can you sedate him? It will be a while before we can question him and he might expose us."

"I agree. He sure is noisy," Tuck said has he climbed into the back seat. He opened the gear bag and opened the case with the hypodermic needles pre-filled with the sedative. He removed one and put the rest away. He looked around and leaned over the back seat, pulled back the blanket, and injected the man in the leg through his robes. The man's eyes opened wide, and he yelled in Arabic at Tuck. Tuck watched for a few moments as his eyelids began to droop. He was asleep in less than twenty seconds. "That's better," Tuck said as he climbed back into the passenger's seat.

Johnny came back on the communications device and said, "It looks like the car has stopped. The location is ten clicks away. They parked at a large house."

"Copy that. Let us know where we should park," Adam said.

"Looking at the satellite image now. In seven clicks turn right. There will be an alley on the left that looks secluded and abandoned," Johnny said.

Adam drove on and watched for the turn. He found it and turned right and then saw the alley on the left. He pulled in and parked the trooper in the shade of a building. "We're here," Adam said.

"He will be out for another hour or so. Let's take a look at the house," Tuck said as he grabbed his gear.

Adam opened the windows of the Trooper so that their prisoner wouldn't die in the heat. He grabbed his gear. They decided to tie the prisoner to the Trooper in case he woke up and tried to get out. There were tie downs in the back, so they zip-tied his arms and legs down. He wasn't going anywhere. They also duct taped his mouth shut to keep him quiet.

"Ready," Adam said. They took off in the direction of the house where the car stopped. When they had it in sight, they found that it was more like a compound. An eight-foot-high wall surrounded the property, and the guarded entrance was gated and locked. There wasn't much that they could see, but they could tell that it was much more secure than the neighboring buildings. They identified several cameras and headed back to the Trooper.

When they arrived back at the Trooper, they checked on their prisoner and he was still sleeping peacefully. They moved to the front of the Trooper and stood in the shade and Adam said, "Johnny, we don't have visibility into the compound. There is a high wall around the house with a gated and locked entrance. What can you see? We did see several cameras on the walls and a guard at the gate."

"I am watching but have only seen two guards patrolling the exterior. I will see what I can do to hack the closed-circuit cameras and security systems. It is harder in these places, since internet access is nearly non-existent. My suggestion is to wait 'til late tonight and see if you can get inside the wall. Joshua should be able to identify an interrogation location nearby," Johnny said.

"Okay, I will call him," Adam said as he pulled his phone out and dialed the number on the card.

"Hello," Joshua answered.

"Joshua, this is Adam. We captured our target and need to question him. We followed secondary targets to the location that I just sent you. Do you have a nearby location that we can question this man?" Adam asked.

"Let me look at the location. Yes, I know it. We need to talk. Meet me at the location that I just sent you," Joshua said and ended the call immediately.

Adam looked at his phone and saw the message appear. He touched the link, and the location was only a few minutes away. He motioned Tuck over and told him about the short conversation with Joshua. "What do you make of it?" Adam asked.

"It sounds like the location of the compound spooked him. We may have uncovered something much bigger than we know. We should move to the vicinity of the safe house and watch for anything that may be wrong. This is starting to weird me out," Tuck said.

They climbed back in the Trooper and slowly drove past the safe house. "I didn't see anything. Make your way around back, but not directly," Tuck said.

Adam continued driving and they passed within visual distance from the back and didn't see anything. Adam found a place to park that had some shade from a palm tree and they could see the safe house. They only had to wait a short time before the familiar dirty white Toyota Hilux pulled up to the house. Joshua got out, unlocked the front door, and entered the house. Tuck got out and walked to the house and checked the house out on foot. Seeing nothing, he said through the communications device, "It looks clear Adam. Drive around the block, pick me up, and we will park in front."

Adam pulled into the driveway and parked such that they could easily remove their prisoner without being seen. They approached the front door and Adam held back watching their six. Tuck knocked on the door and Joshua motioned them in and closed the door.

"Where is your prisoner?" Joshua asked.

"In the back of the Trooper. He is sedated but will be waking up soon. Joshua, help me bring him in. Tuck, clear the house," Adam said.

Tuck nodded and went to work checking each room in the house. Adam and Joshua drug the inert body into the house and tied him to a chair in the middle of one of the bedrooms. They made sure that the windows were covered and left the prisoner to wake up.

Adam, Tuck, and Joshua met back in the main room of the safe house. Joshua handed each man a water bottle and said, "The compound is owned by a Russian mobster. They are lethal and I don't suggest trying to enter. The Russian is known around here as 'The Leopard.' We don't know his actual name. We do have images of him, but they don't show up in any facial recognition scans, neither do his lieutenants. It is rumored that they have ties to the terrorist organization, Al-Mumeet."

Just then, they heard noises coming from the room where they stashed their prisoner.

All three men made their way to the room and saw that their prisoner was waking up. Moving back to the main room, they discussed their plans to question their prisoner. Tuck, who spoke fluent Arabic, would do the questioning while Adam watched from behind. They also decided that Joshua should leave and come back in an hour with a plan for Adam and Tuck to leave Yemen. Joshua agreed and left through the front door.

The Toyota Hilux's diesel engine started with a rattle and faded as Joshua drove away. Adam turned to Tuck and said, "Are you ready?"

"Let's do this and get out of here. We should check in with Johnny and Ally to see if they have found anything," Tuck said.

They had turned their communicators off to charge the batteries, so Tuck pulled out his phone and called Johnny.

"Hi Tuck. We've missed your conversations," Johnny said as he answered the phone.

"Our comms are charging, and we are in a safe house provided by Joshua. We are about to start questioning the prisoner. Have you found anything about him or the other two men that we saw?" Tuck asked.

"Ally has been working furiously on this and, so far, we have not been able to identify any of the men. Ally, do you have any new info?" Johnny asked.

"Nothing yet, still looking," Ally said.

"Joshua gave us some local information on the compound that the men pulled into. He said that it is owned by a Russian mobster known only as 'The Leopard.' It is rumored that he has ties with the terrorist organization Al-Mumeet. He also told us that he did not recommend that we try to penetrate the compound. They are very dangerous and vigilant with their security. He also said that they don't show up on any facial recognition scans," Adam said.

"We have confirmed that they can't be identified by facial recognition. We have some more leads to follow up on. I am inclined to agree with Joshua on this one. We need more information before we make a move on them. If we go now, we will likely tip our hand that we are on to them," Johnny said.

"That is what we were thinking also. We are about to question the prisoner and see if we can get some names. Joshua is coming back in an hour with a plan for us to leave Yemen," Tuck said.

"That is a good plan. Put your comms back in when you are questioning the prisoner. We can verify information real time," Johnny said as he ended the call.

Adam and Tuck put their communicators back in their ears and went to question the prisoner. Tuck entered the room and stood in front of the prisoner. He had pulled up a sun-protection mask over his face so that only his eyes were exposed. The prisoner was groggy and somewhat incoherent. Adam handed Tuck a bowl of water and Tuck splashed all of it into the prisoner's face.

The prisoner's eyes opened wide, and he jerked alert. He quickly moved his head side to side to see where he was. The room was darkened with the window covered; no other identifying items could be seen. Tuck stared at the prisoner until the prisoner made eye contact with him. The prisoner's eyes were wide with fear and his body was trembling.

Tuck spoke in Arabic and asked quietly, "What is your name?"

The prisoner replied that his name was Assad Hasan.

"Thank you, Assad. I am going to ask you some questions and if you answer them truthfully, I will help you escape. Do you understand?" Tuck said.

Assad nodded as he watched Tuck through fearful eyes.

"We know that you are the contact person for a terrorist organization, but not the leader. Who do you work for?" Tuck asked.

Visibly shaken, Assad shook his head back and forth indicating that he didn't want to answer that question. "They will kill me if I tell you."

"If we let you go, they will think that you told us, and they will kill you anyway. Answer our questions and we will get you out of Yemen and keep you safe. Who do you work for?"

Shaking, Assad realized that he was going to die regardless and didn't like the Russians using his religion for their purposes. He decided to help the Arabic-speaking American.

"I send and receive messages through an email draft. The information that I receive is from an unknown source and that source is paying a lot of money to Al-Mumeet to bomb ten locations in the United States."

"That doesn't answer my question. Who do you work for?" Tuck asked more forcibly.

With a shaky voice, Assad said, "There are some Russians here that are using Al-Mumeet to further their agenda. They are using Al-Mumeet to make money. We don't have a choice. They take most of the money, but it is our only source of funding."

"Thank you, Assad. You have been a great help. What is Al-Mumeet's agenda?" Tuck asked.

Proudly, Assad answered, "We fight for the one true religion, Islam. Our agenda is to show the world that everyone should be following the great prophet, Muhammed."

"Do you kill the infidels to accomplish this?" Tuck asked.

"Sometimes, but mostly we try to show the world the benefit of following the one true religion," Assad answered.

"We saw you watching a movie that is not allowed in Islam. We can bring you back to the United States with us if you agree to continue helping our government stop terrorist organizations like Al-Mumeet. Do you want us to bring you with us or leave you here?" Tuck asked.

Assad closed his eyes to think. He thought of the things that he saw on the computer and the freedoms that he would have if he helped, but he was fearful that he would be killed. If he stayed, he would certainly be killed. If he left, he may have a chance to survive in the United States. He made his choice and said, "I will help, but you have to keep me safe."

"Once back in the United States we will turn you over to the CIA and they will provide you a new identity in exchange for you working with them to find and destroy Al-Mumeet and the Russians. We will leave soon," Tuck said.

Tuck turned and left the room. He and Adam went to the main room of the house. They spoke quietly about the logistics of transporting their prisoner. Johnny came on the communicator and said, "Nice work, Tuck. That went very well and gives us a bit more information to work with. I will make arrangements with a contact of mine in the CIA to turn this prisoner over to them. I will have Ian plan the correct stops to make that happen."

A few minutes later, Joshua arrived back at the safe house. "Ok, I have a plan for you. I assume that you are taking the prisoner with you. You will drive across the Saudi border in a remote location. I will lead you to an area near the border where you arrived by boat. You will cross at night, and I have made arrangements for the border crossing to be clear at the time of your crossing."

"That sounds good. When do we leave to make the crossing on time?" Tuck asked.

"We will leave as soon as you are ready. We will have to wait near the border a couple of hours for the correct timing. In this part of the world, there can be many delays," Joshua said as he handed a paper bag to Adam. "I brought some food. Eat before we leave."

The men ate the food that Joshua brought. It was some traditional Saltha and Fasha. Tuck said, "This is delicious."

"It is from one of the best restaurants in town. I thought you would like it," Joshua said.

When they were finished, they gave some food to Assad. While he was eating, they loaded their gear into the Trooper. They untied Assad from the chair but kept his hands cuffed. Adam drove and Tuck rode in the back seat along with Assad.

Joshua motioned for Adam to follow him. They left the safe house and started the long dusty drive to the border. Tuck was ready with his rifle if anything were to happen en route. The drive was hot and dusty. In the daytime, the drive back was even more forbidding. The brown cloud of dust that they were following obscured any view of the surrounding landscape. Joshua pulled off the road and drove across the desert and parked behind a small hill out of sight from the road. He turned off the engine and got out. Adam parked next to Joshua, and they all got out and stretched. Adam handed everyone a water bottle. Joshua said, "We will wait here until it is time for you to cross. From the top of this hill we can see the border crossing."

"Thank you for all your help while we have been in Yemen. We couldn't have done it without you," Adam said to Joshua.

"Johnny has always been there for me and mentored me. I will always be there to help him if it is at all possible," Joshua said.

Adam motioned to Tuck that he was going to call Johnny to give him an update. Tuck nodded as Adam walked out of earshot from the rest of the group. He pulled is phone out and called Johnny.

"Hi Adam, someone here is dying to speak to you," Johnny said with a chuckle.

Adam smiled and said, "Hi Johnny, we are with Joshua near the border. What are the plans on the other side of the border?"

"I will send you coordinates for you to meet with Muhammad. He will drive you back to the airport. I have spoken with him, and he knows that you have a prisoner. He has made arrangements to get the prisoner aboard the airplane without any questions. Getting back in the middle of the night will help," Johnny said.

"Great, looking forward to getting out of here," Adam said.

"Hold on, Adam, someone wants to talk to you," Johnny said as he handed the phone to Ally. Johnny stepped out of the room to let them talk privately.

When the call ended, Adam came back to the group with a smile on his face. While Joshua kept an eye on Assad, Tuck and Adam climbed the small hill with their binoculars and watched the border crossing for a few minutes. Adam relayed the information from Johnny. The sun had set, and they were due to cross within the hour.

They said their goodbyes to Joshua and loaded up the Trooper. Joshua had verified that the crossing was clear, and they drove off in a cloud of dust. They were hyper vigilant as they approached the border. Seeing no one around, Adam didn't slow but maintained his speed as he crossed into Saudi Arabia. Their adrenalin was spiked as they were expecting gunshots when they hit the border. Thirty minutes later, they arrived at their destination. Muhammed was waiting for them in the same Toyota FJ60 Land Cruiser.

Muhammed greeted the men and loaded their gear into his Land Cruiser. They were to head back to the King Abdullah bin Abdulaziz International Airport. In the dark of night, Muhammed pulled into the private aviation area of the airport and stopped next to the Learjet. Ian already had the jet prepared for takeoff. They quickly loaded their gear and prisoner into the aircraft and took off for Raleigh, North Carolina.

CHAPTER THIRTY-TWO

NORTHERN MONTANA

Ally awoke after a fitful night's sleep. She had been working on the financial investigation of President Grange and Deputy Director Stevens. She needed a lead but hadn't been able to find one and that kept her from falling asleep.

She lay in bed staring at the ceiling thinking about the next steps. It was still dark outside, but the sky was beginning to lighten. She heard birds singing outside her window. As she relished the quiet peaceful dawn, she suddenly had a thought. *I wonder if Grange or Stevens owns a yacht or vacation home that they planned on escaping to when this was over?* If she could find that, maybe she could backtrack the money from there. She sat up fully awake. *That might work,* she thought.

She got up, dressed quickly and rushed to Johnny's computer lab. As she opened the door, she saw Johnny asleep on the couch that was placed on the side of the room. He had been up for many hours and needed some sleep. She quietly sat down at her workstation, logged into her computer, and began her search.

Johnny woke to the sound of soft clicking on the keyboard and, without moving, opened his eyes. He saw Ally totally focused on the screen in front of her, so he said, "Good morning, Ally."

She jumped and turned toward Johnny.

"I'm sorry that I scared you," Johnny said.

"I didn't mean to wake you; I was trying to be quiet. I had an idea this morning to backtrack the financial history of Grange and Stevens. I was thinking that if we can locate any recently-purchased vacation homes or yachts that they may be planning an escape to, we may be able find their numbered accounts," Ally said excitedly.

"That's a good idea. There may be many shell corporations to filter through, but it is a place to start. We have Limpon's account number and there may be a common institution for ease of transactions. Keep digging, I will get us some breakfast and bring it back," Johnny said as he sat up on the couch and put his shoes back on.

A few minutes later, Johnny returned with a platter of pastries and a carafe of coffee. They ate while they worked, and the time flew by. Johnny leaned back in his chair and rubbed his eyes and said, "What do we know about both Grange and Stevens that they have in common?" He looked at Ally.

Ally leaned back and turned her chair toward Johnny and thought for a moment, shrugged her shoulders and said, "I can't think of anything. They don't run in the same circles, they aren't affiliated with the same political party, no significant common friends, from different parts of the country. I'm haven't found anything in common."

"They're both divorced. Have you investigated their ex-spouses or mistresses? They may have used their identities or a mistress's identity," Johnny said.

"You're right! I didn't make that connection. I'll look into them right now," Ally said.

"No. You need a break to clear your head. We both do. Let's get some lunch and go for a walk. We have been sitting for days and we need to get some blood flowing through our bodies."

Johnny chuckled as he rose from his chair with a groan. Ally agreed, stood, and followed Johnny out the door and upstairs to the kitchen. The staff prepared sandwiches and lemonade, then served them on the deck. It was cool outside, but the fresh clean air was just what they needed. They ate in silence as they thought about what they needed to do next. When they finished lunch, Johnny said, "Let's take that walk." He stood and took the stairs from the second-level deck to the ground. Ally followed him and they walked side-by-side.

Johnny looked across the vast landscape and pointed to a small herd of elk grazing in the distance, then continued walking. "Most people combine their finances when they get married."

Ally's heart jumped at the comment—as she had been deep in thought, thinking about Adam.

"My wife passed away many years ago, but I still remember her social security number. Our finances were combined, and we always filed taxes jointly," Johnny said.

"That makes sense, but wouldn't the ex-spouses find out about someone messing with their identity? Most people have a credit report pulled for some reason or another," Ally said.

"True, but do you think that if your information were used in a small Caribbean Island nation that it would show on your credit report? It is also easy to bribe officials and many of those countries don't require any specific identification. You can buy citizenship. With a fake passport and enough cash, you could effectively disappear," Johnny said.

"You could be onto something. They could buy the property, bribe the officials to put it in the name of their ex-spouse, and then sell it to themselves to transfer ownership to their new identities. The ex-spouses would never be the wiser," Ally said.

They turned back toward the main house to get to work. There was a spring in their step as they entered the computer lab and sat down at their workstations.

"You take Grange and I will take Stevens," Ally said as she started pounding on the keyboard.

Several hours later, Ally let out a whoop and said, "I think that I found something."

Johnny rolled his chair over and said, "What have you found?"

Excitedly, Ally pointed at a map on her screen. "St. Vincent and the Grenadines is a group of small islands in the southern Caribbean. I found a property that has the name of Stevens' ex-wife on the deed. It is located on the island of Mustique. It is known for high-end properties and many celebrities have vacation homes there." She zoomed in on a home. "Here it is. It was sold to Stevens' ex-wife a month ago for five million dollars."

Johnny clapped his hands and said, "I think that you found it. Now, see what you can find out about the transaction and where the money came from. It sounds like more than Stevens could afford on a government salary and I would guess his ex-wife can't either."

Ally turned back to her computer and quickly typed on the keyboard and pulled up the information on Stevens' ex-spouse. They found out that she was remarried and worked at a local bank in Nebraska where she lived. She also found their latest tax return and said, "Nope, she can't afford a five-million-dollar vacation home!"

"After we track down the transaction information, we should contact her and let her know that Stevens bought her a vacation home in the Caribbean." Johnny said laughing, "I'm sure that will surprise her, and she should take possession of it."

"Good plan and great payback," Ally laughed.

Johnny spun his chair and rolled back to his computer and started typing on his keyboard. Ally started her search for the transaction details. Ally's search revealed that Mustique had a more-advanced database of properties and transactions than the rest of St. Vincent and the Grenadines. The cyber security was not so advanced, and it didn't take Ally long to hack into the system. She found out that the purchase funds were transferred to the previous owner of the property via an electronic transfer from a bank in Grand Cayman. The account number on the closing documents was partially redacted for security. It wasn't enough information, but it was a start and narrowed her search window.

Ally then started researching the bank and found it to be much more secure than any other system that she encountered. She turned to Johnny and said, "I found the bank in Grand Cayman that the funds were transferred from, but the bank has very advanced cyber security. Do you have any ideas how we can get access to the records that we need?"

"Hmm, what is the name of the bank?" Johnny asked.

"It is AFDS Bank, Limited," Ally answered.

"Hold on a minute, let me check," Johnny said as he turned back to his computer and began searching. After a few minutes, he said, "Here it is. I have a contact that works at that bank. We haven't talked in a couple of years. I'll give her a call and see if she can help us."

Johnny pulled out a burner phone from his desk drawer. He activated the phone and consulted his computer screen for the phone number, dialed his friend Emily, and put it on speaker so Ally could listen. He put his finger to his lips indicating for her to be quiet during the call.

The phone rang three times before it was answered by a voice that was breathing heavily.

"Hello," she said, panting.

"I hope I have the right number; I am looking for Emily, this is Johnny."

"Johnny!" Emily exclaimed. "Sorry, I'm out of breath. I was running when I heard the phone ringing. It is so good to hear from you. It's been years since we've seen each other."

"Yes, it is good to hear your voice and it's been far too long. After Martha passed away, I've been a recluse for a few years. I am back working and have a little matter that I need some help with," Johnny said.

"Sure, what do you need? You and your wife are like grandparents to me, and I always loved seeing you when you were down island," Emily said.

"I still have my place there and I will let you know next time I come down. I am doing some financial investigations and have a partial account number on a real estate transaction in Mustique that I need information about. I can't say much, but it is a high-level crime. We need to know how the account was funded and who the owner is," Johnny said.

"I can do that, but we need to be discreet. Can you meet me in person? I don't want anything documented," Emily said.

"Yes, I will fly down tomorrow," Johnny said.

"I'm looking forward to seeing you," Emily said.

Johnny smiled, turned to Ally, and said, "Looks like we are taking a little excursion to Grand Cayman. David can fly us down in the Cirrus Vision jet."

CHAPTER THIRTY-THREE

NORTHERN MONTANA

It was dark and cold when Ally's alarm awakened her from a deep sleep. She was bundled under several warm blankets and didn't want to get up. She pulled the blankets up under her chin and lay there a few minutes before she reluctantly climbed out of bed. The floor was cold on her bare feet as she padded to the bathroom. Twenty minutes later, she emerged from her room and stepped outside. It was cold that morning and the grass was covered in thick frost. She returned to her room and put on her down parka and gloves.

She sat in the ATV and snugged her scarf around her neck as the engine warmed up. She glanced to the bag on the seat next to her wondering if she forgot anything. She would only be gone overnight, so she thought it should be fine. She put the ATV in gear, drove to the hangar, parked, grabbed her bag, and entered the hangar. Johnny was already there, and David was doing the pre-flight check of the Cirrus Vision jet.

David looked over to Ally and Johnny, waved them over and asked. "Do you have all your gear?" They nodded and David said, "Let's load up then."

The ground crew pushed the small jet out to the tarmac while David was completing his pre-flight checklist. When the area around the jet was clear, David started the single jet engine and let it come up to operating temperature.

David turned to Ally who was seated in the co-pilot's seat and said, "Ready for wheels up?"

She nodded. David taxied to the end of the runway and after one final check pinned the throttles and they soared into the dark sky heading south.

It took five hours to reach Grand Cayman. Johnny slept in one of the back seats while Ally was fascinated with the views of the Gulf of Mexico and the various shades of blue in the tropical waters. She had never experienced a flight from the front seat before and thought to herself, *I should learn to fly. This is an amazing experience.*

"We are going to begin our descent to Grand Cayman. Do you see it down there?" David asked.

"Yes, I see it. It's hard to believe that I was freezing this morning and now I'm probably overdressed," Ally said with a chuckle.

"You won't need that parka on your lap, that is for sure." David said while chuckling.

Johnny felt the plane descending, woke up, and said, "Thanks for the smooth flight, David. I slept the whole way." David held up his thumb in acknowledgment.

A few minutes later, they touched down and taxied to the assigned parking spot and stopped the plane. They removed their headphones and exited the aircraft. They worked together to tie down the plane. When the plane was secure and locked, they walked to the private aviation terminal and checked in through customs. Keys for a rental car were waiting for them with the receptionist. She handed Johnny the keys and they walked out to the Toyota Raize SUV. Johnny drove them to his vacation home. It was a small home a couple of blocks from the beach.

"This is a nice place, Johnny," Ally said with a smile.

"It's been a while since I've been here. My wife and I used to come here often. After she died, it has been hard for me to experience things that we used to enjoy together. I'm not sure that I am going to keep it," Johnny said sadly as he walked slowly through the house looking in each room experiencing those memories that he was so fond of.

David and Ally looked at each other and, without saying anything, knew that Johnny needed some time alone. They set their bags down near the door and made their way to the front veranda and sat in rocking chairs overlooking the yard. The yard was well kept and had plenty of shade from the large trees. Between the houses, they could make out a bit of the deep blue ocean a few blocks away. They quietly talked about their lives and what their futures may hold. Ally thought about Adam and couldn't wait to see him tomorrow evening.

Thirty minutes later, Johnny opened the front door and brought out three ice cold bottles of water. He sat on the porch swing and said, "Thank you for giving me time to reminisce. My wife loved it here and always said that it was her happy place. As I walked through the house, I realized that I can't sell it. She would want me to continue to enjoy the peacefulness of this place. Winters in Montana can be tough. Maybe I should set up a remote working location here."

"I'm sorry for your loss, Johnny. Even though I didn't know your wife, I can feel her presence here as well. It is a lovely home and a great place to escape the cold winter," Ally said.

"Yes, it is. I had forgotten how wonderful it is here. I'm beginning to look forward to coming back for an extended period." Johnny paused with a faraway look in his eyes. "Now, down to business. Emily is taking a late lunch and will come by during her lunch hour. We can speak with her here. She will take the information we give her and check the records this afternoon. Then she will pick us up for dinner."

"Do you want me to be here or provide some overwatch?" David asked.

"I don't anticipate anything happening here, but we should always be vigilant. Thanks, David," Johnny said.

"No problem, I probably wouldn't understand all the technical lingo anyway," David said with a laugh.

"Why don't you each pick a bedroom and put your gear away? I will sit here and wait for Emily's call," Johnny said.

Ally and David both stood, went inside, and put their bags in their rooms. David stopped at Ally's door and said, "I am going to scout the neighborhood so I can keep an eye on the action."

"I'm going to take a quick nap," Ally said.

A while later, Emily called Johnny and said, "I'm on my way. I'll be there in ten minutes."

David had returned and was sitting with Johnny on the front porch and said, "That sounds like my cue." He stood and Johnny handed him the keys to the Toyota. David stepped down from the front porch, got in the car, and drove off.

Johnny knew that he was in good hands with David watching over them. He went inside and got the sandwiches out of the refrigerator that he had picked up earlier. He knocked on Ally's door and said, "Emily will be here in a few minutes."

Ally jumped out of bed and checked her hair in the bathroom mirror. She felt much better as she stepped out to the living room and saw Emily standing next to Johnny. She was a fit young woman with dark skin and thick, black, bouncy, curly hair that was as wide has her shoulders. She was extraordinarily beautiful and had a joyful countenance. Johnny turned to Ally and said, "Ally, this is Emily. She has been like a granddaughter to us since we have been coming down here. She was only five years old when we first met. I think she was at our house more than her own while we were here," Johnny said with a beaming smile on his face. "My wife and I are so proud of her!"

Emily blushed and put her arm around Johnny and laid her head on his shoulder. "I love you, Johnny, and I miss Martha so much."

"So do I, Emily, but life must go on. She would want us to continue with what we love. I have sandwiches that we can eat while we discuss what we are looking for." They all sat at the small kitchen table and served themselves sandwiches and lemonade. "Ally is a colleague of mine in our new investigative service that Ian and I formed. She will explain what we are looking for," Johnny said.

Ally had just taken a bite. She swallowed quickly and took a drink. She explained the situation without giving any operational details. "We have a partial account number and a time stamp of a funds transfer for a real estate transaction in Mustique. We need to know who the owner of the account is, who transferred money into the account, and the account number, if possible. I know that numbered accounts are private for a reason, but this is a high-level criminal conspiracy and had national security implications for the United States."

Emily looked at both Johnny and Ally and said, "I can find this information for you, but I will have to be very careful to cover my electronic tracks. I have a photographic memory and will memorize the information that you need. Banking rules have changed, and you can now request a warrant to get this information legally, but it requires a lot of evidence, and it takes at least six months to get. I will share this information with you because I know Johnny is doing this for his country and I want to help stop whatever is happening. You should be able to get the evidence you need to prosecute the owner of the account."

"Thank you. You don't know how much this helps." She showed Emily a printout of the property document with the amount, time stamp, and partial account number. Emily read the paper several times and set it down.

They finished their sandwiches and Emily said, "I should get back to work to see what I can find. I will stop by to pick you up for dinner at 6:00 p.m."

"See you then, Emily," Johnny said.

After Emily drove away, David pulled into the driveway. He walked in the house and said, "As expected, I didn't see anything." David saw the sandwiches and sat down to eat. He finished the sandwiches and leaned back in his chair and looked at Johnny and Ally. "What time do you want to leave tomorrow?"

Johnny looked at Ally and said, "How about we leave at 8:00 a.m.?"

"Works for me," David said.

"I'd like to stay forever." Ally said laughing. "8:00 a.m. is fine."

David looked around the kitchen and said, "I am going to get some food for dinner that I can eat in the car while you two are having dinner with Emily." He headed out the door, started the car, and drove off.

"Let's go for a walk while we wait for Emily. We have a few hours. I have something that I want to show you," Johnny said.

Ally stood and they locked the door as they stepped outside and walked a few blocks to Seven Mile Beach. The cerulean blue water of the ocean was stunning. They both removed their shoes to experience the warm, creamy coral sand that was smooth and soft under their feet. They walked along the sandy beach about a mile and turned inland at a cemetery that was located right off the beach. Johnny was suddenly quiet and focused on a shady spot amongst the array of headstones. Ally sensed that this was a pivotal time for Johnny and was quiet as she followed Johnny into the cemetery. He led them to a small headstone labeled "Martha Fox." Johnny knelt and swept some leaves off the grave. He quietly bowed his head. Ally stood respectfully back to give him space. His shoulders shook and she could tell that he was sobbing quietly. She stepped forward and knelt beside Johnny and put her arm across his shoulders. He continued to sob for a few moments. He tightly closed his eyes as his sobbing stopped. He wiped his eyes with the back of his hand and gently stroked the headstone.

Ally stayed by his side as he processed his grief. Johnny turned to Ally and said, "Thank you. I would like you to meet my wife. She is resting peacefully here in her happy place."

After a while, Johnny stood and wiped his eyes again and said, "I didn't expect to fall apart when I brought you here, but I am glad that you were here. I feel more at peace now than I have since she died. Let's head back so we don't miss Emily."

They turned and left the cemetery and walked back to the house. The beauty of the island took on a whole new meaning to Ally as she experienced the extraordinary love of a man for his wife. She hoped that Adam would be that way with her.

David was waiting for them when they returned and said, "Did you enjoy the walk?"

"We did. This is a beautiful place," Ally said, and Johnny nodded as he went to his room.

David pointed at Johnny and held his palms up as if asking, "What's up with him?"

Ally pointed to the front porch, and they sat outside. She spoke quietly and told him about the cemetery. David nodded in understanding. Just before 6:00 p.m., Johnny came out on the front porch with a sparkle in his eye and said, "Emily will be here in a few minutes." David stood, went inside to get his dinner, came back out, and drove off in the car.

A few minutes later, Emily arrived, and Johnny greeted her in the driveway. Ally came down from the front porch and got in the car. Johnny rode up front with Emily as she drove them to the restaurant. They were shown to a table on the deck overlooking the ocean. They ordered their food and Emily said, "Okay, I found out that the account is owned by a Dirk Stevens. There was a ten million US dollar deposit a month before the Mustique real estate transaction from a numbered account in Switzerland. I was able to get both account numbers but not the name on the account in Switzerland." She handed a handwritten note with two account numbers with the initials "DS" next to one of them.

"We found our connection," Ally said to Johnny. "Thank you so much for taking the time and risk getting us this information, Emily."

"Yes, thank you Emily," Johnny said as he thought, *Maybe Emily will be a good fit to work with me on the team. I will talk with Ian about it.*

After the business discussion, they enjoyed their dinner and conversation. Johnny and Emily were catching up and Ally enjoyed seeing Johnny so happy talking with Emily.

Emily dropped them off at 8:30 p.m. and said to Johnny, "I am so glad you came. I visit Martha regularly. Please come back soon so we can spend more time together."

"I will," Johnny said as he gave Emily a long hug. They both had tears in their eyes as Johnny turned toward the house.

Ally gave Emily a hug and thanked her again. Emily drove off and David returned.

CHAPTER THIRTY-FOUR

RALEIGH, NORTH CAROLINA

After the long flight from Saudi Arabia, Ian was on final approach to Raleigh-Durham International Airport. He was cleared to land. The Learjet touched down with a small puff of smoke from the tires as they immediately came up to speed. Ian taxied into the assigned parking space and shut down the engines. He ordered a fuel truck, stepped into the cabin and opened the door.

Adam and Ian exited the airplane and stood on the tarmac. They stretched as they waited for their CIA contact to arrive. A few minutes later, the fuel truck arrived and began filling the nearly empty tanks of the Learjet. Ian was talking to the fuel delivery driver when a new black Chevrolet Suburban approached on the tarmac and parked next to the Learjet. The driver, a man in his forties with blond hair wearing a tailored black suit with dark Ray-Ban Wayfarer sunglasses, exited the passenger door. The driver, also wearing dark sunglasses, stayed in the Suburban.

Ian waved and greeted the man with a firm handshake. "Good to see you, Miles. How has life been treating you?"

"Hey, Ian. I am doing well. What do you have for me?" Miles said.

"Miles, this is Adam, a colleague of mine and one of the men who apprehended the man we spoke about. Tuck will bring him out when you are ready. He is willing to talk and give information about the Yemenis terrorist group Al-Mumeet. We are investigating them and their connection to an attack that is supposed to take place in the United States tomorrow. We appreciate you keeping him stashed away and not telling anyone about him until we round up the terrorist cells," Ian said.

"Nice to meet you, Adam. I've heard about you and suspected something was not as it seemed. I would be interested in hearing your story sometime after this is all over. You have a lot to do, so let's get this prisoner loaded up and you can be on your way," Miles said.

"Thanks for helping us out, Miles. I suspect that we will talk again soon," Adam said.

Ian leaned in the door of the Learjet and asked Tuck to bring out the prisoner. Tuck came to the door and looked each direction than motioned for the prisoner to exit the aircraft.

Miles took a hold of the prisoner's arm and Adam said, "This is Asad Hassan. He only speaks Arabic and was a point of contact in Al-Mumeet. He has agreed to give information in exchange for a new identity in the United States."

Miles nodded and escorted Hassan to the back seat of the Suburban. He was seated inside, and Miles slid in next to him. Miles waved to Adam, Ian, and Tuck as he closed the door and the Suburban drove away.

"Let's get back to the ranch so that we can stop these attacks," Adam said.

A few hours later the Learjet touched down at the ranch in northern Montana. When Adam stepped outside, the air was noticeably colder than it was when he left a couple of days before. Adam noticed that the Cirrus Vision jet was being prepared for flight and the ground crew was busily checking the Learjet.

Adam and Tuck took one of the ATVs back to the ranch house. Ian stayed behind to give the ground crew instructions for their next flights and loaded three drones into the Learjet and three drones into the Cirrus Vision jet. They would need to fly the drones to the launch locations in a couple of hours. Ian stayed with the Learjet and took a nap in the bedroom on board.

Adam and Tuck entered the ranch house through the garage and Adam went directly to the computer lab. Ally and Johnny were working at their workstations and turned as the door opened. Ally squealed with delight, jumped out of her chair, and ran to embrace Adam. They hugged for a moment as Johnny watched with a knowing smile on his face.

Johnny cleared his throat. Adam and Ally turned to him. "I hate to stop this happy reunion, but we need to prepare for the drone launch. Adam, can you get the rest of the team to gather here in a few minutes?"

"Sure, they are upstairs. I'll go get them," Adam said as he hurried through the door.

A few moments later, Tuck, David and Beck accompanied Adam into the computer lab. "Ian is still at the hangar," Adam said.

"Thank you, Adam. Ian already knows what I am going to tell you. Each of you will have one or two drones to move into the launch positions that I give you. I have already secured the locations and they will be launched from rooftops. The drones are assembled and stored in large Pelican cases. When you reach your location, open the Pelican case and remove the drone. Each of the four rotors are folded in to reduce the case size. After you remove the drone, unfold each rotor. It will lock into place with an audible click. Make sure that each rotor arm is locked into place. Next, remove each missile from the case and latch one on each side of the drone landing skid. It is a positive latch system and colored red. Put one side of the bracket in the latch and turn to click. It will lock in place. There is also a magnetic electrical connector on a short wire coming from the drone. It is yellow and will attach to the missile in the corresponding yellow connector," Johnny said as he pointed to each location on the image of the drone on the large wall mounted monitor. "One minute before the launch schedule, you will press the green button on the top of the drone. This will power up the drone and it will automatically connect to our secure satellite link so that we can control each drone from the lab here."

"Where will we be going to launch the drones?" Tuck asked.

"Ian will have one drone in Los Angeles. Tuck, you will have two in San Francisco. Beck, you will have two in Portland. And David, you will have one in Seattle." Johnny said.

"Once the launch has happened, what do we do next?" Beck asked.

"After the drones are launched, pack up the cases and head back to the airport. This will be a one-way flight for the drones. The drones will self-destruct after the missiles are launched and the balloons are confirmed destroyed. Ian and David will return to pick up Tuck and Beck where they dropped them off. Tuck and Beck, you will have a few hours to enjoy some downtime while you wait. There will be rental cars waiting for you. I have assembled mission packets that are waiting for you on the planes," Johnny said.

"Thanks Johnny, I will be here interfacing with Ben as he conducts the raids on the terrorist cells and coordinates the drone strikes. General Fitzgerald will be online as well in case we need him as a backup. Ally and Johnny will control the drones and destroy the Chinese balloons. Any other questions?" Adam asked.

Tuck, David, and Beck headed to the hangar.

Ben was sitting in his FBI office with the blinds closed. He leaned his chair back and closed his eyes, and he thought about the logistics of the operation. He had received a call from Vice President Powers giving him the authority to run the operation, reporting directly to him. That eased his mind, but it was still going to be a logistical challenge to execute.

He initiated the online meeting five minutes early. The 65-inch TV in his office had a small video image of him in one corner. One-by-one over the next few minutes, Adam and ten other attendees joined the secure online meeting. The attendees were agents-in-charge in the cities that the terrorist attacks were scheduled to take place the following day.

Ben started the meeting and said, "Thank you all for your promptness. I would like to introduce Adam; he is the main coordinator of this mission. This is only one part of a multipoint operation."

"I would like to thank each of you in advance for your expertise and help with this operation. Ben will lead this portion of the operation. I will be listening in and coordinating with the other prongs of the operation," Adam said.

"I have spoken with each of you individually about this operation. Due to operational security, we don't say anything until I give the instructions. The raids must take place simultaneously. This is a coordinated attack and if any of the cells finds out about a raid, they may execute their bombing plan prematurely. Please give me an update on your surveillance of the cell in your city," Ben said.

There were no concerns reported. All cells were holed up in their safe houses and under surveillance twenty-four hours a day, seven days a week.

Ben thanked each person and said, "We will be on linked comms. The bombings are scheduled to happen at noon on the East Coast and 9:00 a.m. on the West Coast. We will initiate the raids one hour before the bombings are scheduled. We have hacked the communication with the terrorists, and they think that the bombing was delayed a week, so they won't be leaving early to plant the bombs. Any concerns with the timing?"

All the agents agreed and were ready to initiate their plan.

Ben closed the meeting and said, "Comms on and teams in place two hours before raid time."

Ben shut down the online meeting and leaned back in his chair and went through the plan in his head one more time. He sighed and called Adam and General Fitzgerald.

After three rings, General Fitzgerald answered. "Hello Ben."

"Hi Andy. Adam is on the line also. I just met with my team, and everything is in place and ready for tomorrow morning. I sent you a comm link so that you can monitor the situation in case we need you as a backup," Ben said.

"I received the comm link and will be ready. I will have twelve F-22 fighters in the air for a training flight. I received a call from Vice President Powers giving me authority to run backup on this mission. That helps cover my ass if anything goes sideways. I don't expect a problem though. No one knows about this but me," General Fitzgerald said.

"Thanks Andy. I also spoke with the vice president and am reporting directly to him. I will feel much better once this is over," Ben said.

Sensing the concern in Ben's voice, General Fitzgerald said, "There is a lot at stake with our respective operations and keeping them secure. We must remember that we are doing the right thing regardless of the possible outcome. If President Grange doesn't go down for this and he goes after us, we will know that we did the right thing. We can't let tyranny and greed harm the United States."

"You're right, but until the operation is over, it will weigh heavily on me," Ben said.

"That just shows that you are a man of integrity and loyalty. Keep up the good work, Ben. We will talk tomorrow and will be able to celebrate our success," Fitzgerald said as he ended the call.

Ben spent the rest of the day finalizing the operational plans. He was ready and left the office early to have a nice dinner and to get some sleep. It was going to be a long day tomorrow.

Ben lay in bed with his mind racing as he thought through all the scenarios over and over. He finally slept fitfully for a few hours and woke before his alarm went off. He showered quickly and left for the office. He stopped at a drive-through coffee shop and had to wait a few minutes for them to open. He was the first in line and ordered a large black coffee and a pastry.

He walked through the cubical farm toward his office. No one was there that early in the morning. He sat at his desk and turned the chair to look out the window. It was still dark, but the sky was beginning to lighten as the sun was getting closer to the horizon. He savored the coffee and pastry as he reviewed his plan for the day.

Two hours before the operation, Ben turned on his comms and waited for each of his key players to check in. Fifteen minutes later, everyone was online. His operation was ready to go.

Meanwhile, Tuck, Ian, Beck, and David were each in place on rooftops in Los Angeles, San Francisco, Portland and Seattle. They had already removed the drones from the cases and prepared them for flight. They all had comms in and were online with Johnny and Ally.

At one minute before launch time each man pressed the green button on each drone. The drones were silent as their advanced electronics and avionics booted up and connected to the satellite communication link. One by one, Johnny acknowledged each drone as it established its link and were communicating correctly.

There were twelve pilots in the Vandenberg Air Force base briefing room waiting for their commanding officer. A few minutes later their commanding officer and General Fitzgerald walked into the room, and everyone stood at attention and saluted their superiors. The commanding officer said, "At ease gentlemen, please be seated. Today's mission instructions will be given by General Fitzgerald. General, they are all yours."

General Fitzgerald looked at each of the pilots and said, "Today's mission was scheduled as a training mission for operational security. This is not, I repeat not a training mission. There is an immediate threat to the United States mainland and this mission is critical to the safety of the citizens of the United States. This mission is top secret for your eyes only. No one outside this room is to be privy to the mission parameters before or after the mission completion. Is that understood?"

All the men said, "Yes Sir!" in unison.

Fitzgerald nodded at the men. "Thank you for your understanding. There are six Chinese shipping vessels in the Pacific Ocean spread out along the Pacific Coast of the United States and Canada. These ships are sitting in international waters and there is actionable intelligence indicating that they will be releasing spy balloons like the one that traversed the United States last year. Each balloon will be carrying a payload of a virus that will be distributed across the country." He paused as each pilot digested the information and he could see the anger building in each pilot. "We will be on a backup mission to intercept each balloon and shoot it down with a Sidewinder missile if needed. Private armed drones are the primary operator for the destruction of the balloons. As a precaution, we will provide backup support. Each team will be given the ship's coordinates and for the balloon that they will be intercepting. Any questions?"

One pilot raised his hand and asked, "Sir, what about the shipping vessels? Will we be striking those also?"

"Good question, Major. We will not be intercepting the shipping vessels. Admiral Boswell of the Pacific Coast Guard has Heritage-class cutters with fast attack craft in place to intercept and commandeer the vessels after the balloons are destroyed. We will be also on standby in case they need support. I don't expect any problems. These are commercial shipping vessels and should not be armed with anything other than small arms. Any more questions?"

"No Sir!" the pilots said.

"Lieutenant Colonel, please distribute the details to the pilots. Gentlemen, good luck and Godspeed. You will be debriefed when this is over. Thank you for your service," the General said and then he left the room and returned to his office.

General Fitzgerald activated his comm device and joined the FBI operation to listen in.

Adam said through the comms, "The drones are ready for launch. Ben, General Fitzgerald, are your operations ready?"

Ben answered, "Yes, the teams are ready to execute the raids.

Fitzgerald answered, "Yes, the pilots are on the flight line now and are ready to take off. Admiral Boswell has his ships in place and is ready to intercept and commandeer the shipping vessels."

Adam, feeling the enormous weight of the operations, took a deep breath and squeezed his eyes closed. He opened his eyes, glanced at Ally, and she gave him a comforting smile. He sat straighter in his chair and said, "Thank you, gentlemen. Ben, please initiate the raids." Adam gripped the arms of his chair so tightly that his knuckles were white. His heart was hammering in his chest as he listened, waiting for the action to take place.

Each agent-in-charge for each city checked in and confirmed that their teams were in place and waiting the go signal. Ben took a deep breath and looked at his watch. One minute, and it was time. He watched the time and said, "Go!" When the minute changed. It was time to listen to the operation.

Adam muted his microphone and turned to Johnny and Ally. "Initiate the drone strike," he said.

Upon receiving the go-ahead, each team immediately breached the terrorist safe houses taking them completely off guard. The element of surprise worked, and no shots were fired. The terrorists were all apprehended and the bomb making supplies were found. Ben waited, his heart beating fast and his mouth dry. One-by-one, each agent reported back about the success of their individual mission. As each report of success was reported a feeling of relief washed over Ben. Ben thanked each agent-in-charge and allowed them to drop off the comms. They were going to hold the terrorists and process the scene throughout the day.

General Fitzgerald said, "The pilots have reported the launch of the balloons. They are on scene to confirm the drones have destroyed the balloons."

Adam, Ally and Johnny were watching the video feeds from the drones. "The drones are nearing missile launch range. Hold a moment. Balloon one destroyed... two... three... four... five... six. All six balloons have been destroyed and locations marked," Johnny said.

Adam's heart was pounding, and his breathing was fast. He swallowed trying to moisten his dry mouth. He took a deep breath and said, "Thank you, gentlemen. The attacks have been stopped. The immediate threat is over, and we can sleep well tonight. Please let me know when the shipping vessels are under the Coast Guard's control," Adam said.

"Will do. Talk to you soon, Adam and Ben," Fitzgerald said as he turned off his comm.

"We will debrief later. Thanks again," Adam said has he ended the communication link with Ben.

"Johnny, please connect us to the team," Adam said.

"Okay, we are all online now," Johnny said,

"Hi team. We just finished the operation. Ben and the FBI successfully raided each terrorist cell location without incident. Johnny's drones were one-hundred percent successful in destroying each of the Chinese balloons."

"That is good news, I just picked up Tuck and we are heading back to the ranch. We'll be there in a couple of hours," Ian said.

"David, what is your ETA?"

"I should be landing at the ranch in one hour," David said.

"Thank you all. See you in a few hours," Adam said as they all signed off the comms.

Adam called Ben, then added Vice President Powers to the call. While they waited to be connected, Adam leaned back in his chair and rubbed his eyes and took a drink of cold coffee and frowned. A few minutes lapsed and then Powers picked up the phone and said, "Hi Adam and Ben. How'd the operations go?"

"Mr. Vice President, the mission was a one-hundred percent success. All the terrorist cells were captured in the raids by Ben's teams and the explosives were contained as evidence. My team used small attack drones that we developed to shoot down and destroy all the balloons. General Fitzgerald's pilots confirmed each balloon's destruction. Admiral Boswell has the Coast Guard commandeering all the shipping vessels as we speak," Ben said.

The vice president let out a sigh and said, "Thank you, Adam and Ben. Your teams have done a great service to the United States and will not be forgotten."

"We'll keep you posted on the remaining items of the operation," Adam said.

"Talk to you soon. Thank you for calling, Adam and Ben," the vice president said as he ended the call.

CHAPTER THIRTY-FIVE

ISLAND OF ARUBA

Early in the morning the day after the attacks on the United States were thwarted, Adam loaded their gear into the Cirrus Vision jet while David did his pre-flight checklist. They took their seats in the small aircraft. David joined Adam a few minutes later and began the startup procedure. When the engine was at operating temperature, they rocketed down the runway and were airborne heading for Aruba.

After a short refueling stop in Jacksonville, Florida, they flew down the eastern coast of Florida and were over open ocean south of Miami. The cerulean, blue waters of the Caribbean islands became visible shortly afterward. The view was astonishing. Jewel-green tropical islands neighbored desert islands in a stunning array. The crystal-clear waters surrounding the islands in the dark blue of the deep water made Adam want to live the rest of his life with Ally in those beautiful islands. A few hours later with the tanks nearly empty they began their approach into Aruba.

Adam and David awoke instantly to their alarms going off at 2:30 a.m. They had arrived in Aruba the previous evening, well before the scheduled arrival of Limpon of the Chinese Peoples State. Their intelligence showed that Limpon was going into hiding after suppling DanZe Pharmaceuticals with a virus and distribution system that Liam Wentworth tried to release in the United States.

After spending time during the day before scouting out the villa that Limpon had rented, they decided it was time to go inside and place bugs, cameras, and trackers on the boat and vehicles. Johnny had confirmed that the security system was basic and there were no cameras installed.

Johnny reserved a vacation rental house a few blocks away making for easy access. Their rental was on the same beach, so they decided to access the rear of the house that faced the beach. Adam and David quickly dressed in black tactical clothing, blacked out their exposed skin, and met in the kitchen of the rental house. The coffee maker timer had been set and the pot was freshly brewed. They each poured a large mug of coffee to get them going at the early hour.

As they finished their coffee, Adam said, "Ready?"

"Ready as I'll ever be," David said as they headed for the back door. Each man donned their backpack with their gear and headed out the back door. The beach was deserted, and the moon was nearly full. The water was dark with small amounts of bioluminescence lighting the surf as it hit the beach. They stayed near the property lines and quickly made their way down the beach to the villa that was rented by Limpon. There were no lights on inside the house, but the light by the back door was lit. A fishing boat was moored to a small dock directly out from the house.

David said, "I will go attach the tracker and bugs on the boat. Wait here and watch my six."

Adam acknowledged with a pat on David's shoulder.

David hustled down the beach to the dock and slipped over the rail of the boat. Carefully, he picked the lock on the cabin door and cleared the vessel. He hid a tracker under the instrument panel at the helm. He placed bugs and cameras in discreet locations above and below deck. He locked the boat and met back up with Adam waiting at the edge of the property. He was only aboard the boat for five minutes.

"No movement," Adam reported through the comms. "Johnny, are we clear to enter?"

"Alarm bypassed. No traffic out front. You are clear," Johnny said.

"On our way," Adam said as they carefully made their way to the door at the back of the garage. It was a standard lock and was easy to pick. Adam had it open in less than thirty seconds. They slowly opened the door, expecting a piercing alarm and flashing lights. It was dark and quiet. They both had their handguns at the ready, slipped inside, and quietly closed the door. They turned on the flashlights mounted to their handguns and cleared the garage.

Inside the garage, there was a Land Rover Defender and two small Honda scooters. Adam placed trackers on the scooters and David placed one on the Land Rover. They then moved to the door and entered the house. They previously determined that the house was vacant and waiting for Limpon to arrive, so they were confident that no one was there. They remained vigilant though and led with the barrels of their guns. They systematically cleared every room of the house, then went to work placing bugs and cameras. Once they were all placed, they exited the way they came and locked up.

They were back in their rental house an hour later. It was still dark out and there was time to get a few more hours of sleep. They each went to their rooms, washed up, and fell asleep.

The next morning, knowing that they had time before Limpon was scheduled to arrive, they decided a little downtime would be nice. They drove into town and found a place to rent jet skis to tour around the island. The jet skis would be fun, but they also afforded them the opportunity to scout out a backup location to question Limpon. They were hoping to take him out to sea and question him there, but a backup plan was always prudent.

They rented the skis for the day, applied copious amounts of sunscreen, and headed out to sea. They raced each other across the crystal-clear water and had a good time all while watching for the best backup location. They passed the villa and toward the northern end of the island they found just the place. The water was rough and the shore rocky. Not a place to play. At night it would be as deserted as you would find on the small island. They spent the rest of the day playing in the water and racing the jet skis around. When they returned to the rental house in the afternoon, they were exhausted.

"Let's check in with Johnny," Adam said.

"Good idea. I'll call him," David said as he pulled out his phone and called Johnny.

"Hi David, are you sunburned?" Johnny said with a chuckle.

"A little, those jet skis sure are fun! Any updates?" David asked.

"No, everything appears to be on schedule for Limpon's departure. His plane should be leaving in a few hours. I'll let you know when it takes off and the estimated arrival time," Johnny said.

"Sounds good. We have all the trackers and bugs placed and activated," Adam said.

"I have verified that they are all working and transmitting. Have a good night. Get some rest, you're going to need it," Johnny said as he ended the call.

Adam looked around at the empty kitchen, and said, "How about we go get some food? I saw a restaurant on the beach on the way into town."

"I'm always ready to eat good food. We don't get the option for fresh seafood in Montana. Let's go," David said as he pulled the keys to their rental car out of his pocket.

While they were having dinner, they both received a text from Johnny indicating the Limpon was aboard the flight and would arrive early the following morning.

They awoke early to confirm that Limpon was on the plane that they expected him to be on. David volunteered to watch the airport while Adam watched Limpon's villa. David took a scooter from the garage of the rental house and made his way to the airport just before the sunrise. The air was cool and damp with the salty smell of the ocean. He savored the short ride to the airport. He found a secluded area in some trees near the airport fence to stash the scooter. He approached the fence and made sure that no one was around. It had barbed wire on top, so he pulled a Kevlar blanket from his pack and laid it over the barbed wire, then climbed over the fence. He retrieved the blanket and found a spot to hide with a clear view of the private jet parking area. There were several jets already parked there. He made himself comfortable and checked in through the comms. "I'm in place with a clear view of the tarmac."

"Copy, I am in place watching the front of the villa," Adam said.

"The plane's ETA is twenty-four minutes," Johnny said.

In exactly twenty-three minutes the plane touched down. It took a few minutes to taxi to the assigned parking space.

"I have eyes on the plane. It just parked and is shutting down. A black Mercedes car is driving up to the plane," David said.

It was a few minutes before the door opened and the pilot stepped down to the tarmac. David had the binoculars to his eyes and began snapping photos using the digital camera built into the binoculars. Two obvious bodyguards stepped down to the tarmac after the pilot and carefully looked all around and inspected the car. After they felt it was safe, one man stepped back into the aircraft and brought out Limpon. He was followed by two young women. They immediately walked toward the open back door of the Mercedes and got in. Just then another car pulled up and stopped behind the Mercedes. The driver got out and approached one of the bodyguards. He handed him the keys and quickly jogged back to the terminal building.

"Limpon and two young women are in the Mercedes and the two bodyguards are in the blue Suzuki hatchback. Wait, another man just stepped out of the plane. He is heading toward the Mercedes and getting in the front seat with the driver. He is carrying a satchel that looks like a computer bag. The cars are driving off now. I'll start the upload and head back," David said.

"The last guy is probably Limpon's personal assistant. His name is Chen Yang. I will verify with the photos," Johnny said.

David snuck back out of the airport and began the ride back on the scooter. The ride back was just as pleasant as the ride there—a great way to clear the mind and think about the next steps.

While David was on his way back, Adam reported that the Chinese arrived at the villa and had gone inside. The Mercedes left and the blue Suzuki was parked on the street in front of the house.

Adam and David reunited back at the house and Adam booted up the laptop. He connected to the bugs and cameras so that they could monitor what was happening at the villa.

The scene was as one would expect for someone on vacation seeing their accommodations for the first time. They looked around and unpacked. The bodyguards carefully searched the villa and property and thankfully did not find any of the bugs that they placed. The new technology was a game changer.

Limpon looked in the bedrooms that the young women chose and told them that they should put their bathing suits on and go to the pool in the back yard. They giggled and excitedly found their bikinis. A few moments later they were splashing in the pool. Limpon gestured for Yang to come into the office area of the villa. They sat down and Limpon said, "The rest of the money should have transferred into the numbered account. Have you confirmed with the Venezuelan fisherman when to pick us up?"

"Yes, it is confirmed. The money has already been transferred into the account," Yang replied.

"Good. Until then, let's have a good time with the girls," Limpon said with a lewd grin.

Yang smiled and nodded then said, "Should I have food delivered?"

"Yes, we should keep a low profile while we are here. I would like us to go fishing tomorrow. We can take the boat and leave the guards here. They won't like it, but we are on vacation, and nothing can happen with no one around," Limpon said.

"I will make the necessary arrangements. What time do you want to leave?" Yang asked.

"Let's not go too early, we may have a long night." Limpon chuckled. "Let's leave at 11:00 a.m."

Adam and David looked at each other and David shook his head as he said, "Those men are sickos. Did you see how young those girls were? I would guess that they are only fifteen or sixteen. Is there any way we can take them out now before they use those girls?"

"We have a great opportunity to intercept Limpon and Yang in the boat tomorrow. That is our best option. However, I have an idea, and we need Johnny's help," Adam said as he pulled out his phone and called Johnny.

"Hi Adam, how is life in paradise?" Johnny said as he answered the phone. "I heard what they said about the girls. What can we do to stop them?"

"Tomorrow is our best opportunity to question and eliminate Limpon and Yang when they go fishing, but that won't help those girls tonight. I have an idea and we need to work fast to accomplish it. Yang said he was going to order food in. I would guess that he would order from a local restaurant and have it delivered. I would like to intercept the delivery driver and place sedatives in the food so that they fall asleep and wake up in the morning. What sedatives can we use that will not knock them out immediately so that they think they drank too much alcohol?"

"That is a great idea. You should have what you need in the kit. Use the sedative with the red label. It is tasteless and won't take effect for thirty minutes. I suggest that you pay the driver well and wear a disguise. We don't want your descriptions anywhere. I will continue to monitor the bugs for the restaurant that is called. You two get ready," Johnny said.

"Thanks Johnny," Adam said and ended the call.

"I'm not much for playing dress up. This is your gig," David said with a laugh.

"Okay, I need to look local. You monitor the bugs, and I will go shopping. Be back soon," Adam said has he headed out the door. A moment later the scooter started up and zoomed down the street.

Adam was back in less than an hour with a couple of bags. David raised his eyebrows as Adam looked and smiled at him as he walked into the room. "I'm going to get ready now," Adam said. David laughed and continued to monitor the bugs on the laptop.

After an hour, David began to wonder if Adam was okay. He was about to check on him when Adam walked into the living room. David was shocked. He knew it was Adam, but didn't recognize him. His hair was different, the shape of his body was different, and his skin tone was different. Even his face looked different.

"How did you do that?" David asked.

Adam smiled and turned around. "I learned how to do this in the CIA. I always remember what the locals look like and listen to how their accents sound. I practice the accents under my breath so that I can mimic it if needed. I had to buy some local clothes and some supplies. I also always carry a makeup kit whenever I am working."

"I was right to have you take this part of the mission," David laughed. "It's truly amazing how different you look."

Just then, Johnny called and David answered. "Hey Johnny. You should see Adam. He transformed into a perfect islander."

"While you two were playing dress up, Yang ordered their dinner. It will be delivered from '*The Loco Parrot*'. Yang asked for it to be delivered at 7:00 p.m.," Johnny said.

"Thanks Johnny. I will watch for the driver and Adam will stop him when he is close," David said as he ended the call.

They looked at the map and identified the best location for the interception. David took the scooter and watched the restaurant. Adam took the car and found a place to park where he could block the road and intercept the delivery driver. They had their comms on so that they could communicate without their phones.

At the correct time, the delivery driver loaded a styrofoam box on the back of his scooter and tied it down. David started his scooter and followed the delivery driver at a distance. He would be easy to follow since there was only one route that made sense to take. The delivery driver zoomed down the expected route. "Delivery driver en route. I am following. ETA five minutes," David said.

"Copy." Adam said and watched in the direction he would be coming from.

"Thirty seconds. I am stopping," David said.

Adam saw the headlight heading in his direction. At the appropriate time, giving the delivery driver enough time to stop, he pulled the car across the road. The scooter came to an abrupt stop and the driver started yelling at Adam. He got out of his car with his hands in the air saying, "Sorry, bro. The car rolled and I can't get it started."

When the delivery driver saw that Adam was a local, he put the kick stand down and said, "Let me help you. Maybe we can get it started or moved to the side of the road." The delivery driver was surely on island time.

"Thanks, bro," Adam said as the delivery driver checked under the hood.

"I see the problem." the delivery driver said. The battery wire was loose. He wiggled it and said, "Try it again."

Adam turned the key and the car started. The delivery driver closed the hood and said, "Easy fix, bro."

Adam said, "Thank you. Can I finish your delivery? Here is one-hundred dollars for your trouble."

The delivery driver looked at the money and thought, *that's a good tip,* then said, "Sure, bro." He grabbed the bill from Adam's hand and turned to get the box. He handed the box to Adam, turned his scooter around, and sped back toward the restaurant.

"I have the food. He's gone," Adam said.

David started his scooter and met Adam at his car. He was already injecting each box of food. He finished as David arrived. He tied the box to the scooter, and they swapped vehicles. Adam sped toward the villa as David headed back to their rental house.

Adam arrived at the villa and carried the box to the front door and rang the bell. He stood there waiting for them to open the door. It took longer than expected, but then one of the bodyguards opened the door. Adam handed the box to the man and the man handed him some cash. Adam thanked him and jumped back on the scooter and sped down the road back to the rental house.

Adam opened the door to the rental house and walked in. David, turned to the door and said, "Well done. You should have been an actor."

Adam laughed and said, "It was fun, and I got a good tip. I put it in a baggie, we may be able to get fingerprints off it later." He turned toward the bedrooms and said, "I am going to change."

David continued his vigil of watching the laptop and listening to the bugs. Adam returned and sat down next to him. "Nothing to speak of yet. I picked up some food on the way home. I'll go get it and we can watch the main event," David said as he stood and stepped into the kitchen.

A few minutes later, David set down a plate of conch sandwiches and cans of soda on the table next to the laptop. They both sat back in their chairs and made short work of the sandwiches. As they watched the images on the laptop and listened into the audio, Limpon told the girls to go to their rooms and get ready for the evening activities. He then told the bodyguards that they could retire to their rooms for the night. Yang got up and prepared a strong drink for Limpon and served it to him. He then poured one for himself.

Limpon and Yang continued to drink, and each man appeared to be thinking of the upcoming pleasures awaiting them. As Adam and David watched, each man's eyes began to grow heavy, and they fell asleep where they sat. David navigated around on the computer and checked the rooms of the girls and the guards. They were all asleep. Adam and David did a high five. "The plan worked!"

Just then, Adam's phone rang. He pulled it from his pocket and saw that it was Johnny calling. He answered it and put it on speaker so David could hear and said, "Hi Johnny, I have David with me."

"Good job, they should be out about eight hours. I have an algorithm to monitor the cameras for movement. You both can get some rest. I will let you know if there is any movement," Johnny said.

"Thanks. It is always good to get some sleep on a mission," David said.

"Anything else, Johnny?" Adam asked.

"Nothing for now. Get some rest, we'll talk again tomorrow," Johnny said as he ended the call.

CHAPTER THIRTY-SIX

ISLAND OF ARUBA

Adam and David decided that they would intercept the fishing boat with jet skis. They were up early and at the rental shop when they opened. They rented the skis for the day and left their car at the rental shop. Taking off on the jet skis, Adam and David made their way back up the coast to their rental house and beached the jet skis there.

Adam and David had just finished packing the gear that they would need into their backpacks when Adam's phone rang. "Hi Johnny. What have you got for us?"

"Yang just finished loading the boat and went back inside. They both woke up with hangovers, laughed about drinking too much and missing out on their time with the girls. They both look ready to go fishing. Limpon is instructing the guards to watch over the girls and that he and Yang will be fine on the boat by themselves since they would each have a handgun. They will be armed, so be careful as you intercept," Johnny said.

"That makes it a bit more difficult. We may want to make an underwater approach. I have experience with this. I'll take my diving gear and the hydro scooter on my jet ski. I will leave Adam with the Jet Skis and approach under water when they stop to fish. I will subdue the men and call Adam over," David said.

"This should work. The Jet Skis are fast, so I can be there quickly if you need me," Adam said.

"This adds another level of difficulty. I will get a live satellite view and watch them. Your comms are waterproof to ten meters, so you can leave them activated as you are in the water if you aren't going deeper than ten meters. I will relay their whereabouts when your head exits the water. I won't be able to see you, since you will be under the edge of the boat, so let me know you are there with two clicks on the comms... Wait a minute," Johnny said and paused a few moments before continuing. "Yang and Limpon just boarded the boat and pushed off the dock. Yang is piloting the boat. You should go and get offshore so they don't see you. I will keep you updated on the comms." Johnny ended the call. Adam and David activated and inserted the comms into their ears as they hurried to the beached jet skis.

They were both wearing wet suits, so they just needed their masks and pony tanks. David also grabbed a hydro scooter. They ran across the sand loaded their gear on the jet skis and muscled them off the sand and into the water. Once they were floating, they boarded the jet skis and fired them up and headed out to sea.

"We are in position," Adam reported to Johnny through the comms.

"I am watching their boat, and the tracker shows them moving west at eight knots. They are less than two clicks north of you heading west. You should be out of sight so head west on a parallel path," Johnny said.

"Heading west," Adam said as they matched the speed of the boat heading west.

Twenty minutes later, Johnny said, "They stopped and have dropped anchor."

"Stopping and preparing to enter the water," David said as he and Adam stopped the jet skis and lashed them together. Adam prepared David's jet ski to be towed while David prepared the hydro scooter. He tied a line to it and placed it in the water floating it next to the Jet Ski. He then checked his regulator and mounted the pony tank to his buoyancy compensation vest. He cleaned his mask, spat in it, and rinsed it out. With the mask on the top of his head, he loaded the destination into his navigation watch and slipped off the jet ski into the water. He powered up the hydro scooter and checked the battery gauge. It indicated it was fully charged. With his mask over his eyes and the regulator in his mouth, he looked at Adam and gave him the ready signal by extending his thumb up. He untied the hydro scooter and let air out of his vest and sank to twenty feet.

It would take David twenty-five minutes to cover the distance to the fishing boat. The water was warm and crystal clear. David noted many fish and thought it would be a good day to be fishing or diving for pleasure. He thought, *Maybe we can catch a couple of fish before we head back.* He smiled at the thought. He monitored his progress on the navigation watch and slowed down when he got close to the boat. Since the water was so clear, he decided to dive another ten feet but not exceed the comms' waterproof depth. He hoped that the specification was accurate. He slowly made his way into the shadow of the boat. It was directly above him. Slowly ascending by adding air to his vest, he rose toward the bottom of the boat. Keeping in mind any decompression stops, even though he wasn't that deep, it was best to be careful.

A few minutes later, he surfaced under the bow of the boat. He tied off the hydro scooter and gave two clicks on the comms.

Johnny came on immediately and said, "They are doing more drinking than fishing. They didn't notice you. Right now, both men are on the stern of the boat each with a line in the water. I have an idea to distract them. Remember the remote operation of the hydro scooter? Tie a line to it and attach it to one of their fishing lines, then swim back to the boat. When you are in place and ready, tell the scooter to take off and they will think that they have caught a big fish. Both men will be focused on the fight. You can take them from behind and can recall the scooter to your location after you subdue the men."

David clicked the comms two times to acknowledge Johnny's instructions. He sank back down into the water and found one of the fishing lines. He attached a small line to the hook being careful not to move it enough to alert the man holding the rod. He left the scooter hovering near the end of the line. There was plenty of slack so that the hit would be quick.

David swam back and got into position. He removed his fins and mask and tied them to the boat. He pulled is handgun out of the waterproof bag and carefully chambered a round. He was ready. He took a deep breath and pressed the button on the remote for the hydro scooter. He waited.

Moments later, the boat was rocking as both men jumped up. They were both screaming with excitement and didn't notice David slip over the side of the boat. Limpon and Yang were standing side by side while Limpon was frantically trying to reel in the fish. His rod was bent, he was leaning back, and they were both focused on the line entering the water. David quietly stepped behind Yang and pistol-whipped him, knocking him unconscious. David silently lowered Yang to the deck and then pistol-whipped Limpon unconscious. His rod flew into the water and David pressed the "return" button on the remote.

David disarmed both men and zip-tied their hands with flex-cuffs. He then reported over the comms, "I have both men subdued and the boat is clear. Adam come on over."

Adam arrived in a few minutes.

"Adam, can you secure the hydro scooter to my Jet Ski? Can you also grab my mask and fins? They are tied to the port side."

Adam secured the items to David's jet ski and lashed both jet skis to the back of the boat. They dragged the men to opposite sides of the boat. They searched their pockets and took everything that they found and placed it into waterproof bags. They decided to question Limpon first since he was the main target.

Adam splashed a bucket of sea water in Limpon's face. He thrashed around and opened his eyes, blinking rapidly. He tried to raise his hands, but they were cuffed behind him. David said in Mandarin, "I need you to answer some questions. We know about the virus and the distribution system that you provided to DanZe for the attack on the United States. Who are you working with?"

Limpon looked at him and said, "I don't know what you are talking about. I am on vacation and fishing with my close friend."

David punched him in the face and his head snapped back and hit the side of the boat. Limpon's nose was bleeding, and his eyes were watering. "*Answer my question,*" David yelled more forcibly.

Limpon was shaking and said, "If you promise not to kill me, I will tell you what you want to know."

"*I will start by killing your friend if you don't tell me now,*" David yelled as he turned and pointed his gun at Yang who was awake and watching with fear in his eyes.

"*Tell them,*" Yang yelled to Limpon.

Limpon hesitated and David lowered his gun and pointed it at Yang's knee. "*Tell them, Qi,*" Yang yelled.

Limpon shook his head and said, "I can't."

David fired. Yang's right knee exploded in a mass of blood and bone. Yang screamed and passed out.

Limpon was shaking with fear. David pointed the gun at Limpon's knee. "Answer my question," David said quietly.

"I sold the virus and provided the distribution system to Liam Wentworth of DanZe Pharmaceuticals. It was not sanctioned by China. I am the head of the Chinese Peoples State intelligence services and have much authority. I received my final payment and am disappearing next week. No one will ever hear from me again. No one else is involved. I am a very rich man. I can pay you one million dollars just to let me go. I will disappear never to be seen again," Limpon said.

"What is your private account number?" David asked.

"I can't give you that. You will take everything," Limpon said.

Suddenly David fired another shot this time into Limpon's thigh. Limpon had a look of surprise and screamed in pain. He didn't pass out, and David pointed his gun at Limpon's other leg.

"What is the account number? And we will let you go," David said gently.

Limpon recited the account number and Adam typed it into his phone.

David turned and shot Yang in the forehead and then aimed his gun at Limpon and said, "Please repeat the account number."

Limpon did and it matched the one he gave earlier. David looked at Adam and he nodded indicating that Johnny verified the account number. David turned and shot Limpon in the forehead.

Both men were dead and bleeding on the deck of the boat. The intensity of the violent interrogation caused Adam to close his eyes and take a deep breath before he stepped into the cockpit, fired up the engines, and took the slack out of the anchor chain. David operated the winch that lifted the anchor. They headed west until they were over deep water and Adam pulled the throttles back to neutral. The boat was idling.

David tied the dive weights that they brought to each man, and they threw them over the side of the boat. The blood was sure to attract the multitude of sharks in that area.

David and Adam prepared to scuttle the boat. Adam found the hatch exposing the engine and fuel tank. He placed a block of C4 near the bottom of the fuel tank. If the wreck was ever found, as unlikely as it was, it would look like a fuel tank explosion. He set the timer for five minutes. He exited from below deck and David was waiting on his Jet Ski. Adam straddled his Jet Ski and they took off. Once they were far enough away, they stopped and turned to look back. The boat suddenly exploded in a fireball and smoke. What was left of the hull floated for a moment and quickly disappeared beneath the surface. The residual smoke left behind by the explosion disappeared on the breeze. The surface of the ocean roiled where the boat was a few moments before returning to its natural state as if nothing ever happened.

David grinned and looked at Adam and said, "Limpon said he was going to disappear, never to be seen again." They laughed and turned back toward the island.

They returned the jet skis after dropping off their gear at the rental house. On the drive back Adam said, "I have been thinking about the underage girls that Limpon brought with him. They are most likely his sex slaves or will be sold as sex slaves. Limpon and Yang were trafficking them one way or the other. We should anonymously report them to the authorities and make sure that happens before we leave."

"I have been thinking the same thing. Let's call the local police from a burner phone," David said as he pulled the car into a local market's parking lot. Adam went in to get some bottled water and a local burner phone.

Adam opened the car door and got in. David drove to a parking lot overlooking a beach. Adam installed the local SIM card and powered up the burner phone. When it connected, he called the local police and gave them the information about the girls and the two older, rough-looking Chinese men with them. The police thanked them for the tip and said that they would investigate it right away.

"We should watch the house to be sure that the police show up. Remember that pull out with those trees just down the road from the house. It has a good line of sight to watch from," Adam said.

David started the car and said, "Good idea. I remember the spot. I think that there may be a hiking trail there as well, so parking won't look out of place." They drove there and parked in a place where they could see the front of the villa that the Chinese were in. It took longer than they expected, but the country did run on what people referred to as "Island Time." Several police cars pulled up to the house with their lights on and sirens blaring.

"I hope the police don't get shot. Those bodyguards are armed and dangerous," David said.

When the police knocked on the door, one of the bodyguards opened the door and as soon as the door opened, he had a gun in his face and was yelled at to get on the ground. Other officers swarmed into the house and a couple of shots were fired.

David and Adam waited and watched hoping that the officers were safe. Soon an ambulance pulled up and a gurney was taken inside. A few minutes later a sheet covered body was removed. The body was a big man, so likely the other bodyguard. The bodyguard that opened the door was secured in the back of a police cruiser. The two women were escorted out gently by a female officer, taken to a SUV, and placed in the back seat. The officer climbed in with them. Another officer drove them away.

"That worked out well. Let's go pack and head back to the ranch now. We still have other conspirators to apprehend," Adam said.

CHAPTER THIRTY-SEVEN

GENEVA, SWITZERLAND

Liam Wentworth was in his office conference room with Tomas Finn and Alex Giovanni. They had all the cable news networks running and still had not seen any reports of the bombings. Wentworth slammed his fist on the table and yelled, *"Where are the bombing reports? Tomas, call Limpon and get the status of the balloon launch!"* Wentworth ignored Finn and typed the password for the email account and checked the draft folder. Nothing was there.

"His phone goes straight to voicemail. It's off or doesn't have a signal," Finn said.

"We'll have to wait and see what happens. Maybe the United States is censoring the media to prevent widespread panic. I could see that happening," Giovanni said.

Just then, the internal phone rang, and Wentworth picked it up. *"What?"*

His secretary said, "The lunch service that you ordered is here. Shall I bring it in?"

"Yes, deliver it to the conference room," Wentworth said as he slammed the phone down.

The door to the conference room opened and the men were silent as the secretary entered pushing a cart loaded with food.

She quietly prepared the cart and then left the conference room and closed the door behind her.

"We should have had cameras set up to view the bombing sites," Wentworth said as he paced the room and picked up a sandwich.

"Remember we talked about that and operationally it could have been traced back to us, so we chose not to," Finn said.

"You're right. I'm going to call Grange," Wentworth said as he picked up the phone and asked his secretary to call President Grange. He hung up without thanking her.

A few minutes later the phone rang and Wentworth picked it up and said, "Yes."

His secretary said, "The president will be on line one in a moment." She hung up.

Wentworth pressed the line one button, turned the speaker on, and waited.

A minute later President Grange's voice was on the speaker saying, "Hi Liam. What happened with your operation? I'm not happy about being in this position."

"That is why I called you. I'm trying to find out what happened," Wentworth said.

"Nothing! That's what happened. I haven't heard any reports, and I am always the first to know," Grange exclaimed.

"Mr. President, everything was in place and confirmed moments before the operation was to start. This problem is coming from your side. Does Stevens know anything?" Wentworth said.

"I haven't heard from him. Have you talked to your Chinese contact?" Grange asked.

"No, I can't reach him," Wentworth said.

"There is something wrong. Call Stevens and see if he knows anything. I still expect to be paid; I have fulfilled my end of the deal," Grange said.

"I'll call Stevens. No one is getting paid if the operation didn't happen," Wentworth said loudly as he hung up the phone. He walked out of the conference room to his desk to retrieve a burner phone to call Stevens. He fell into his chair at his desk while he waited for the phone to power up. He called Stevens.

Stevens was sitting at his desk watching the news shows wondering what happened when his personal cell phone rang. He didn't recognize the number, but knew it was Wentworth. He answered the call. "Hello."

Without any greeting, Wentworth said, "What is happening?"

"I don't know, I have been watching the networks trying to figure out why there has not been any coverage of the bombings. I have not heard any law enforcement reports of bombings either," Stevens said.

"It's your job to know what is happening in your country," Wentworth said.

"It was your job to plan and execute the operation! It looks like something failed in your operation. If I hear anything, I will let you know," Stevens said loudly as he ended the call.

Wentworth stormed back into the conference room, slammed the door and yelled. "*Something is wrong. It looks like nothing happened with the operation!*"

Just then the conference room door exploded open and armed Swiss police officers entered with their guns drawn and aimed at the men. They were yelling for them to raise their hands and to get on the floor. "*You have no right to be in here! Get out!*"

Wentworth said. One of the officers moved toward Wentworth, ready to pull the trigger. He yelled again for him to get on the floor.

Wentworth and his two men complied and lay on the floor. The officers cuffed all three men and hauled them to their feet. They were searched for weapons and perp-marched down to the awaiting police cars. The remaining police officers worked on securing the facility, gathering evidence and questioning employees.

CHAPTER THIRTY-EIGHT

NORTHERN MONTANA

The Cirrus Vison jet was on approach to the ranch when the runway lights suddenly turned on. David always felt a moment of relief when they turned on automatically as his aircraft approached at night. Although, he could land the plane in the dark with his advanced avionics, it was still nerve racking not to have any visual references. The Cirrus Vision jet floated down to the runway and touched down with little puffs of burnt rubber smoke as the tires came up to speed in an instant.

David slowed the plane and taxied to the front of the hangar. He powered down the engine and climbed out of the cockpit. They had been flying many hours and David's muscles were stiff. He stretched as his feet hit the tarmac.

"Nice landing, David," Adam said as they were walking to the hangar in the cold night air. Late September in northern Montana was more like winter in the southern climes. When they entered the hangar, Adam opened the coat closet and pulled his jacket from the hangar and shrugged it on. Outside on the tarmac, the ground crew was busy as they scurried around the aircraft preparing it to be moved into the hangar.

Adam walked out of the hangar, breathed in the cold air, and could see his breath in the lights as he looked around to see if Ally was waiting for him. He felt disappointed when he didn't see her. He turned and picked up his bag and started walking toward a parked ATV.

The sound of a racing ATV engine caused everyone to turn toward the roaring sound as the ATV skidded to a stop in front of the open hangar door. Adam smiled as he saw that Ally was driving and Johnny was grimacing and hanging on with both hands. Ally shut off the ATV and hurried over to greet the men, specifically Adam. She welcomed David back, then hugged Adam and welcomed him back with a firm squeeze. *I'd like to be greeted like this every time I return from somewhere,* Adam thought. He couldn't stop smiling.

Ian stepped out of the hangar and said, "Come on you two, we need to have a quick debrief."

Adam and Ally walked slowly bumping their arms and shoulders as they entered the hangar and stepped into the conference room. Everyone was there already. Adam pulled out a chair for Ally and sat down next to her.

"Let's make this quick we all need to get some rest. We'll go over all the details and next steps tomorrow. Johnny, please give us a status update," Ian said.

Johnny had bags under his eyes and yawned as he said, "Adam and David just returned from Aruba. They eliminated Limpon and his assistant Yang. They were able to acquire Limpon's private account number. I have already pulled the twenty million dollars from that account. He was also involved in the trafficking of underage girls. The local police were able to rescue the two girls that they brought with them.

"Ally and I have found financial evidence of Stevens accepting money from Wentworth and DanZe pharmaceuticals. Wentworth and his two associates, Finn and Giovanni, have been arrested by the Swiss Police, and DanZe has been shut down pending their investigation. Any questions?" Johnny asked.

Hearing none, Johnny continued. "Adam and Tuck apprehended the terrorist contact and brought back valuable intelligence that will help us track down those behind the terrorist organization Al-Mumeet."

"Thank you, Johnny. We are off to a good start, there are still some loose ends to tie up. We will meet tomorrow to detail the remaining items. Let's meet here at 10:00 a.m. Good job everyone! Get some rest," Ian said.

Everyone rose from their seats and walked out to the awaiting ATVs to head back to their rooms. Adam rode with Ally. She hesitated and waited for the others to go first, then she smiled and started the ATV. Adam held on as she turned suddenly and drove down a trail away from the cabins.

The lights on the ATV were bright and Adam had to hold on with both hands. Ally expertly drove the ATV over rises and up the winding trail. It kept climbing and soon they came to the top of a small hill. The trees thinned as they neared the edge. Ally parked the ATV facing a cliff at the edge of the hill. Without a word, she got out and pulled a blanket out of the back of the ATV and spread it on the ground overlooking the cliff.

She said to Adam with a smile, "We're going to look at the stars." She patted the blanket beside her.

Adam smiled and sat down next to her and said, "I was so happy when you met me at the plane. At first, I wasn't sure you would come, but I'm glad you did."

Ally leaned her head on Adam's shoulder and said, "I'm sorry that I was late, we were finishing our investigation into Stevens.

I missed you more than you know. I wanted to spend some time alone with you while we had a chance. Johnny showed me this place the other day and suggested that I bring you here."

Adam twisted and put his hand under Ally's chin and gently lifted it toward his face. He kissed her gently on the lips and knew, at that moment, they were going to be together for the rest of their lives. They hugged for a long time before looking into each other's eyes.

Ally said in a breathless whisper, "That was nice. You should come home to me more often."

Adam lay back on the blanket and stared at the sky while Ally sat next to him looking at every detail in his face by the light of the moon. Although it was cold, they didn't notice. Adam turned his head toward Ally and said, "When we met, I felt an instant attraction to you. You were guarding my parents who were being held by Stevens and I was very unsure of what I was feeling. Over the last couple of weeks, I have come to know that you are a remarkable woman and someone that I would like to spend the rest of my life getting to know."

Ally smiled and said, "I feel the same way. I so enjoyed being with you for those days on our trip to Switzerland. I know that we were working, but it felt like a preview of things to come."

"I thought so too but was afraid to admit it to myself. I had a long discussion with Ian on our flight to Saudi Arabia. He told me about his wife that he lost to cancer and how they loved each other. I realized then that what we have is special and he said that everyone saw it before I did," Adam said.

"David flew Johnny and me to Grand Cayman to get some financial information from one of Johnny's friends there. That is how we tied up the evidence on Stevens. Anyway, while we were waiting, Johnny took me for a walk and showed me his wife's final resting place. It is in the most beautiful cemetery overlooking the ocean. His grief showed me his love for his wife. It broke my heart to see him grieve and I knew at that point that I wanted to experience that deep love with you," Ally said with a look of undying love in her eyes. A look that was unmistakable in its gaze.

Adam knew he made the right choice and said, "Ally, I love you."

"I love you, too, Adam," Ally said as she leaned down and kissed Adam passionately.

Adam yawned and said, "My body doesn't know if it is day or night. I need to get some sleep. We better head back before we freeze to death." Ally had wrapped her arms around herself, and Adam held her hands as she stood. They hugged again and folded up the blanket.

Ally started the ATV, and they headed back down to their rooms at a more leisurely pace.

The next morning, Adam was up early and went for his morning run. He quickly showered, changed, and headed up to the main house hoping to find Ian. He walked in to the smell of bacon cooking and it made his stomach rumble. He found Ian and Johnny sipping coffee and talking in front the roaring fireplace.

Adam walked into the room and stood near the fireplace holding his hands to the warmth. He turned to Ian and Johnny and said, "Do you have a minute to talk?"

"Sure, have a seat," Ian said.

Adam sat down and raised his hand toward the fireplace and said, "This feels good. It sure gets cold early up here."

"It does, but I love the peaceful seclusion of the area, especially after an intense trip like the one to Saudi Arabia and Yemen. What was it that you wanted to talk about? Ally?" Ian said.

Adam's eyes got wide as he said, "How'd you know?"

"Adam, everyone can tell that you two were meant for each other. We're all older and know or have seen what love is like. The connection that you two share is easy to see," Ian said with a grin.

"I agree. While working with Ally, I have seen her side. She has been anxious for your return and mentions you all the time," Johnny said.

Adam was silent for a moment collecting his thoughts and building the nerve to ask the question that had been on his mind all night. Gazing into the dancing flames of the fireplace with his heart racing, Adam asked the men, "Is it too soon to ask Ally to marry me?"

Ian smiled and laughed. "Normally, I would say that it is too soon, but in your case, I think that you should. You two have done more together in the last couple of weeks than most couples do in their lifetimes. The stress and difficulties that you have faced alone and together have given you two a unique bond," Ian said.

Johnny stood and said, "I'll be right back. I have something that I want to show you." He walked out of the room and was gone for a few minutes. He returned and sat down in his chair and held out his hand to Adam. In it was a small black felt box. "I want you to have this," he said as Adam gently took it from his hand.

Adam opened the box revealing a wedding ring with a solitaire diamond perched on top. It was a stunning ring and Adam's mouth was gaping as he stared at it. "This is the ring that I gave

Martha when we married. Ally reminds me of her. We were never able to have children, so I have decided that you two should have it," Johnny said.

"I can't take this. It's too much," Adam said.

"Yes, you can, and you will. It is just collecting dust on my dresser and will be there when I die if you don't use it. Ally deserves it and so do you," Johnny said.

Adam was blinking away the emotions that he was feeling and said, "I don't know what to say. It's such a big gift. Thank you." He continued to stare at the jewel.

Ian was smiling and said, "Adam, you have had a lot of emotional upheaval over the last few weeks, but you are a strong man, and I know that you didn't expect to meet Ally, let alone be thinking of marrying her." Ian thought for a moment and then said, "I spoke with our benefactor, and we are going to offer you and Ally a position in the organization. It hasn't been announced yet, and the team must vote, but I want you to know so you can take it into consideration as you plan for your future."

Adam nodded and said, "Thank you. I have a lot to think over. I am going to go for a walk. I'll see you at the meeting."

CHAPTER THIRTY-NINE

NORTHERN MONTANA

The smell of breakfast cooking and coffee brewing wafted across the doorway as the team and Adam's parents entered the main house for breakfast and their meeting afterward. The smell of freshly brewed coffee and fresh-baked cinnamon rolls drew everyone toward the dining room. They served themselves and stood around talking as everyone gathered in the dining room. Ian was the last to enter and everyone found their seats. The staff began serving breakfast around the table family style. Talking gave way to the tinkling sound of utensils and dishes as everyone filled their plates. As they ate, the discussions continued ranging from mission ideas to sports.

When everyone finished, Ian signaled the staff to clear the table and said, "We should move to the conference room in the hangar."

Ian just started to stand when Adam said, "Before we go to the conference room, I have something to share." Adam stood up and said to the others, "Please be seated a moment."

Everyone sat back down and looked expectantly at Adam. Adam looked around the room at each member of the team and finished on Ally. "It has been a rollercoaster the last few weeks. I stumbled upon this wonderful group of people that I now consider my closest friends. I am honored and amazed that we have been able to work together for good without the red tape of government entities."

Adam turned to look at Ally as she turned toward him. He knelt in front of her and took her hands in his and said, "Ally, the moment that I saw you guarding my parents something happened in my heart. There has been a connection between us from that moment. Even though it has only been a few weeks, our connection has grown stronger, and I don't ever want that to end. Ally, I love you."

Ally was tearing up as she looked into Adam's eyes. She couldn't find her voice but mouthed, "I love you, too."

Adam reached into his pocket and removed a small black felt box and held it in front of him. As he opened the box, he said, "Ally, will you marry me?" Adam looked up at her face and was in awe of her beauty and his heart with pounding with anticipation of hearing her answer.

A moment later, through tears, Ally said, "Yes, Adam, I will marry you." They stood and embraced and had a quick kiss. Adam's parents, the entire team, and house staff jumped to their feet and cheered as Adam gently placed the ring on Ally's finger. It fit well and Ally couldn't stop staring at the ring.

"When did you have time to buy a ring?" Ally asked.

"I'll tell you the story later. It is a very special ring," Adam said.

Adam turned and held Ally by his side and said to everyone in the room, "Thank you for sharing this moment with us. I wouldn't have had it any other way. We should head to the conference room so we can get this mission behind us, and we can plan our wedding!"

Everyone filed out of the room to the ATVs waiting outside. A rumble of ATV engines starting preceded a cloud of dust as they headed through the cool morning air to the hangar. The team filed into the conference room a few minutes later and took their seats around the table.

Ian started the meeting. "First of all, I would like to say congratulations to Adam and Ally! We could all see this would happen sooner or later. I'm glad it happened sooner!" Everyone clapped and congratulated them again. Ian pressed the power button on the remote and turned on the screens while Johnny navigated the screen on the laptop to start the video meeting. Ben Walters from the FBI joined next and then a new face joined the meeting that most of the team didn't know.

Ian looked at the screen and said, "Welcome gentlemen. We all know Ben Walters. I would like to introduce James Reyes from Homeland Security. James is a friend of Beck and is totally trustworthy and has been briefed by Beck."

Everyone nodded and Johnny filled them in on the latest mission status.

"Thank you, Johnny. As you know the attack has been stopped and several of the conspirators have been apprehended or eliminated. The first priority will be to use the evidence that we have obtained to arrest Deputy Director Stevens and President Grange. The second priority will be investigating the terrorist group Al-Mumeet and who is behind them," Ian said.

From the screen, James spoke up and said, "I have reviewed the evidence that you have collected on Stevens, and it is enough to pursue an arrest warrant. However, I think that we need to hold off on the arrest for now but keep him under surveillance until we amass the evidence on President Grange. We should coordinate those arrests so that the other one doesn't run. If they think that they have gotten away with it, we may be able to collect additional evidence and apprehend them when their guard is down. We must have rock-solid evidence before we approach a judge for an arrest warrant. In this case, we must be sure to follow every letter of the law and the constitution in the case of the president."

"I agree, James. This also must be kept secure. If it leaks that we are investigating them they will run, and they both have the resources to do so immediately, and we will have little chance of catching them outside the United States," Ben said.

"Those are both really good points, and we will adhere to those. Our group, who has yet to be named, will assist and turn over all evidence or information that we collect. I would suggest that you two are our only contacts for this matter. Now, what is our next step in the investigation into Grange?" Ian said.

"We know the account that deposited money into Stevens' and Limpon's accounts is a numbered Swiss Bank account. We assume that it is attached to Wentworth or DanZe Pharmaceuticals. We could use some help from the FBI or Homeland to get the owner of the account number from the Swiss authorities so we can trace back the payments to the conspirators," Ally said.

"We can do that. I will contact them to share information and relay it to you," Ben said.

"Johnny, do you have anything else on this investigation?" Ian asked.

"Hold on a second." Johnny paused and he was focused on his screen. "Okay, while we have been in this meeting, we picked up a phone call from Grange to Wentworth. There was no answer of course, but it appears that Grange is getting nervous, so we need to find what we need as soon as possible."

"I am going to call the Swiss right now. I'll drop off the meeting and call Johnny later," Ben said as his picture disappeared from the screen.

"I will drop off also and get to work planning how we will arrest Stevens and Grange," James said. Just before he exited the meeting, Beck spoke up.

"Hold on James. I may have some information for you. I am high school friends with Vice President Powers. I met with him a few days ago and filled him in on the operation. We can call him, and he can help facilitate this since he will be taking over when the arrest comes, and he needs to know that it is coming down."

"Okay, Beck. That sounds good. Let's meet in an hour and call him," James said as he ended the call.

"That is the most critical part of the mission right now," Ian said and he surveyed the team members. "Should we adjourn now?"

"One more thing," Johnny said. "We will need some inside help for the banking transactions. I would like to suggest that my friend Emily in Grand Cayman be brought in as a consultant to help with the investigation."

"I second that proposal. She was a great help and knew how to keep what she was doing to help us operationally secure. She is trustworthy and would make a great addition to the team especially for the follow-the-money scenarios that we are bound to run into often," Ally said.

"How soon can she be here, Johnny? We can send a jet to pick her up, but it might be quicker to catch a commercial flight and pick her up here in the United States."

"I already checked. There is a flight out tonight from Grand Cayman to Chicago. We can send a plane to pick her up there and have her here in the morning. I did ask her if she would be interested in assisting in more of the investigation without giving her any details. She has two weeks leave and will take it immediately," Johnny said.

"Does everybody agree?" Ian asked and everyone agreed. "Get her here, Johnny. It will be good to see her again. I haven't seen her since she was twelve." Ian looked around and said, "Alright everyone, let's go catch a president."

Everyone stood and headed for the ATVs. David and Adam were walking together, and David said, "Since the others are working on the finance side of the equation, do you think that we should check in with the CIA to see if they have any actionable intelligence from the questioning of Hassan?"

"I was thinking about that. It probably wouldn't hurt. Let's talk to Ian since he knows them," Adam said.

They turned back to find Ian spending time going over everything on the Learjet. "Hey Ian, do you think that we should call your contact that we left Hassan with for questioning to find out if they have found anything?" Adam said.

"I can call him and ask. I have been thinking about how to approach this side of the investigation and I think that it will take much longer than we think. I am sure that the Russians are buried deep behind false identities and shell corporations. Let's keep thinking of ways to find and infiltrate this organization. Miles will let us know when they get enough information from Hassad," Ian said.

"Thanks, Ian. You are right. We must spend the effort to figure this out first before engaging so that we cut off the head not just poke them in the eye. It really bothers me that a ragtag terrorist group is being funded and used by the Russians to damage the United States," Adam said.

"This takes the religious zealotry of the terrorists and makes them more like a mercenary terrorist group. It is no longer based on their religious beliefs but on raising money to put the true believers on the front lines. The lives of zealots—for money. It's wrong on so many levels," David said.

CHAPTER FORTY

NORTHERN MONTANA

Adam dropped off David at the main house and he continued to his parents' cabin. He pulled up and stopped out front. Ken heard the ATV pull up and he opened the front door before Adam had time to get there.

"Hi Adam," he said with a smile.

Adam jogged up the three steps to the front porch and embraced his father in a strong hug with pats on the back. Ken held Adam at arm's length, looked him in the eyes, and said, "I am proud of you son and know that you did the right thing this morning. Your Mom and I are very happy for you and Ally." Ken kept his hand on Adam's back and guided him through the front door. He closed the door behind him and watched as Adam knelt in front of Susie. Ken felt such love for his wife and his son in that moment.

Susie turned toward Adam and put her trembling hands on each side of his face. With tears in her eyes, she said, "I love you, son. From the moment that I met Ally, when she was assigned to guard us, I knew that somehow you two were meant to be together. I didn't know how it would happen, but I knew that it would somewhere, somehow. Congratulations. I can't wait for the wedding."

Adam had tears in his eyes and couldn't believe that his parents were so loving and supportive. They had always been there for him, and he would be there for them. He looked back and forth between his parents and said, "I am so glad that you both could witness my proposal this morning. If you would have told me two weeks ago that this would happen, I wouldn't have believed it."

Susie looked to Ken and said, "I don't have the energy. Can you prepare lunch for us? Adam, you'll stay for lunch?"

As Ken stood and walked toward the kitchen, Adam said, "I think so. Let me text Ally." Adam pulled his cell phone from his pocket and quickly typed a message to Ally and received an immediate reply. "She said that they are busy tracking down a lead and were eating sandwiches at their computers. So, yes, I will stay for lunch."

Beck and Ian stepped into Ian's office in the main house and sat down in the plush leather chairs. Beck pulled out his phone and placed a call to James at Homeland Security. When James answered, Beck said, "Hold on while I call the vice president. It may take a few minutes to connect with him." Beck put James on hold and dialed the vice president's personal cell phone. After several rings, Beck began to think that he wouldn't answer, then the vice president's voice said, "Hi Beck, how's it going?"

"It's going well. I have Ian Fox and James Reyes from Homeland Security on the line with us, is that okay? We need to give you an update," Beck said.

"That is fine. I am walking to my office and will be there in a couple of minutes," Powers said.

"Okay. Let me get James on the call," Beck said as he added James to the call. "Hi James, are you with us?"

"Yes, I'm here," James said.

"Okay, Gentlemen, I am in my office, and we are secure for our discussion," Powers said.

"Let me introduce Ian Fox. He is the leader of the organization that I am working for. James Reyes is with Homeland Security, and we are working together with Ben Walters from the FBI on our investigation," Beck said.

"It's a pleasure to meet you gentlemen. I only have fifteen minutes, so let's get to it. What have you got?" Powers said.

Beck explained the evidence that was found linking Stevens with Wentworth and Wentworth's arrest and subsequent shutdown of DanZe Pharmaceuticals. He also detailed where they were on the investigation into Grange's connection.

"This is going to get ugly. I have been doing some research on how we should proceed with this unprecedented action. It is difficult to know exactly how this is going to work, but I am putting together a plan. At this point, I have a list of congressional leaders on both sides of the aisle that I need to work with before this happens. I will have a meeting with them. You will attend and present the evidence. We will give the go-ahead during the meeting for the actions to take place," Powers said.

"I think that is the right course of action. We will keep you updated. I expect this to happen in the next few days," Ian said.

"I'll be ready. James if you need anything approved for this action, let me know. Anything else?" Powers said.

"Nothing else, sir," James said.

"Thank you, Mr. Vice President," Beck said and ended the call.

Ian looked at Beck and said, "That went well. It helps to have friends in high places. Let's go get Adam and check in with Johnny to see if there is any new information."

Ally and Johnny were in the computer lab furiously typing away and focused on their screens. Ally leaned back in her chair and stretched. She looked over at Johnny and said, "Grange sure is a slippery guy. I have found all kinds of shady business dealings that he has been associated with. It's hard to believe that he could have been elected dog catcher let alone the president of the United States."

"I know what you mean. Most people don't dig into the candidate's past but just listen to what they are saying. He got elected because people are tired of the professional politicians and their perceived corruption. He is just as corrupt, perhaps more so, but isn't a professional politician. A businessman worth billions portrays someone who can handle the job. He won't go down easily, and it will be a media firestorm for months or even years. The presidency will be marred, and Vice President Powers will have his hands full trying to maintain order and will likely lose his re-election campaign," Johnny said.

"It will be a sad day for the United States, even if he is a greedy, egotistical, sorry excuse for a president. I don't relish seeing the fallout from his actions, but the citizens need to know," Ally said with a frown as she looked at the notification that just appeared on her computer screen.

"I just got an email from Ben, let's see what it says." She navigated to the email and read it, then turned back to Johnny. "Ben says that he spoke with the Swiss about the account information from Wentworth and that they will be forwarding the information to him tomorrow morning."

Johnny nodded and said, "That is good. Emily will be here, and she can help with the investigation into that account. We've been at this for hours. Let's take a break. That will help us think, and I know you want to check on Adam," Johnny said as he made air quote marks with his fingers.

"Is it that obvious?" Ally said while blushing and gazing at the ring on her left hand. She hoped Johnny didn't see the warm color in her cheeks. "My eyes could use a break," she said as she stood, stretched, and walked toward the door.

Adam finished lunch with his parents and left so his mom could take a nap. Ken walked him to the door and said goodbye. Adam started the ATV and headed back to the main house so he could check in with Ally and Johnny. As he parked the ATV, Ally walked out on the deck of the house and smiled as she looked down at Adam getting out of the ATV. She hurried down the stairs of the deck and flew into Adam's arms. Adam was laughing and said, "That is the way I like to be greeted!"

Ally gave him a quick kiss and leaned back in his arms as she said, "We're taking a break for an hour or so. Do you want to go for a ride?"

"Sounds good. Hop in," Adam said. He started the engine and drove on the trail back to the overlook where he made the decision to ask Ally for her hand. They arrived a few minutes later and sat in the ATV admiring the view. It was dark when they were there the night before, but during the day the views of the distant mountains were stunning. The mountains were beginning to show patches of snow and swaths of golden aspen leaves on the lower slopes. They leaned against each other and enjoyed the view for a few minutes.

"Did you have a nice time visiting with your parents?" Ally asked.

"Yes, I haven't had a chance to be with them for a long time," Adam said as he laughed. "You know, my mom says that she knew that we were meant for each other the moment she met you when you were guarding them."

"I instantly felt a connection with them that I couldn't explain. Little did I know that my world was going to be turned upside down in the best way possible," Ally said.

"I know we spoke briefly about your parents on the sail to Geneva. Do you have any other family?" Adam asked.

"As you know, I was an only child, and both of my parents were also, so no extended family either. I am so happy that I have your family now. And you, of course," she said.

Adam leaned over, embraced, and kissed her. They sat in the embrace for several minutes until it became uncomfortable being twisted in the ATV. They sat back and smiled. Adam reached forward and turned the key to start the ATV and said, "Time to get back to work."

When Adam and Ally returned to the main house, Ian was just coming out with his flight bag. Ally kissed Adam quickly, jumped out of the ATV, and headed back to the computer lab. Ian walked up to Adam and said, "Can I get a ride to the hangar?"

"Sure, hop in. Heading to Chicago to pick up Emily?" Adam asked.

"Yep, I'll be back late tonight. Do you want to fly with me to Chicago? We'll have a couple of hours before Emily's flight arrives. We can pick up a few things and get some hot dogs," Ian said.

Adam thought a moment and said, "Sure, that sounds great. Ally is busy and I would just be a distraction to her, since I probably wouldn't stay away from the lab for long. Let me send her a text and let her know."

When they parked at the hangar, Adam texted Ally.

Ally texted back immediately saying, "Please be careful, I love you."

"We aren't finished with this yet. There could still be people looking for you. Why don't you grab a handgun and some ammunition? Can't hurt to have it. Hopefully, we won't need it. I have mine in the Learjet," Ian said as he began his pre-flight check.

Adam stepped into the armory and picked his favorite Heckler & Koch HK45 compact. He loaded two magazine and made sure that the HK45 was clear before ramming a fully-loaded magazine into the base of the grip. He slipped the gun into his waistband and put a spare loaded magazine in his pocket. He locked up the armory and walked to the Learjet. Ian was just inside the door and said, "We're ready. Let's go."

Adam joined Ian in the cockpit as Ian finished the pre-flight checklist. The crew pushed the Learjet back onto the tarmac in front of the hangar. Ian started the engines and began the take-off procedure. Minutes later, they were airborne heading east to Chicago. The flight took less than two hours.

The landing at Chicago O'Hare was smooth and Ian taxied the Learjet to the private aviation terminal and parked in the assigned space. He shut down the engines, exited the aircraft, and tied it down. As they were walking to the terminal building to pick up a rental car, Adam noticed a man sitting at an outdoor picnic table, watching. He wasn't eating and it was a little too cool to be sitting outside. He noted the man's appearance and they continued into the terminal building.

After signing the rental agreement, they walked to the parking lot and found their car. It was a black Toyota RAV4 SUV. Ian drove and Adam got in the passenger's seat. He looked around the parking lot just before getting in the car and noticed the man—who was sitting outside when they arrived—walk out of the terminal into the parking lot.

Ian started the car and was backing out of the parking space. Adam told him about the guy that he saw. Ian said, "He may be another assassin. We must be careful; I'll watch for a tail. You keep an eye on the mirrors and see if you can tell what car he is getting into. I will turn the wrong direction and then turn around so maybe we can catch him off guard. It may just be a coincidence."

Adam watched the side mirror on his side of the car and kept glancing over his shoulders. It looked like the guy got into a car, but he couldn't see the make and model. Ian turned left out of the parking lot and drove for a few blocks, then made a U-turn and headed back the way they came. The man was about to pull out of the lot to follow them when they came back toward him. They could see him clearly as they passed. He was driving a white Ford Focus.

"We know what he is driving and what he looks like. Keep an eye on our tail and see if he is following us," Adam said.

"Got him behind us," Ian said as they were exiting the airport.

They headed north on I-294 and exited after a couple of exits. Ian picked a side street and turned into a neighborhood. The white Ford was still behind them several cars back. No other cars turned into the neighborhood and Ian noticed the car drive past. He made a quick U-turn and backtracked to the road he turned off and saw the Ford turn into the neighborhood on the next street.

Adam said, "I have an idea. Let's follow him and then let him find and follow us. Then lead him to a busy parking lot and drive around looking for a place to park. As we round a lane where he can't see me, I'll jump out and hide. You find a place to park and wait. I will sneak up behind him and apprehend him after he parks."

"Good idea," Ian said as he followed the Ford at a distance. When the Ford turned, he raced to the next street and made sure that they were seen. He continued at a normal pace as if he were taking a short cut through the neighborhood.

Adam was looking at the map on his phone and said, "Turn right, two streets up. That will take us out of the neighborhood."

Ian followed his directions and found his way to the edge of the neighborhood. Adam took another quick look at the phone and said, "Turn right. We will go a mile or so and there will be a large shopping center on the right."

"Got it," Ian said has he navigated according to Adam's instructions. They were both keeping an eye on the Ford. Ian turned into the shopping center. It was a huge home improvement store with a lot of work trucks and cars in the parking lot. Probably people getting supplies for their weekend projects. They drove up and down a couple of rows looking for a space to park in. "I have a silencer in my bag. We don't want to draw any attention," Ian said as he neared the end of the parking lane. Adam quickly screwed the silencer onto his HK45 and as they turned from one lane to the next, he opened his door and jumped out. He rolled once and hopped to his feet and hid behind a ratty construction truck loaded with all kinds of junk. Ian drove a little farther down the lane and pulled into a spot between a van and a pickup.

Adam watched as the Ford quickly pulled into a space on the opposite side of the lane from Ian. Keeping out of his line of sight, Adam ran in a crouch until he was behind the car next to the Ford. He snuck a quick look through the car's windows and saw the man. He was still in his car with the window down. Adam waited with his gun drawn keenly aware of how exposed he was. The man moved to get out of the car. When he reached the rear of the car, Adam placed the barrel of his gun in the man's side and said, "Keep walking to the RAV4." They walked across the lane and between the Toyota RAV4 and the van it was parked next to.

"Put your hands on the roof of the car," Adam said with a forceful push of the barrel into the man's kidney.

Ian jumped out of the car and joined Adam to search the man. The search revealed a handgun in his waistband, a knife on his belt, another knife on one ankle, and a compact backup handgun on the other ankle. They disarmed the man and bound his hands with a roll of duct tape that Ian always carried in his flight case. They put the man in the back seat of the RAV4 and drove away.

Adam rode in the back with the man who was following them and said to Ian, "Take us some place where nobody can hear us." Then he turned to the man that they just captured and said, "Who are you and who do you work for?"

The man stayed silent.

Adam pushed the gun into his side harder and said loudly, "*I asked you a question! It would be better for you if you answered it! Who are you and who are you working for?*"

The man turned and said, "If I tell you, will you let me go? It's just a job for me, no harm done."

Adam said, "Tell me and I will decide if I let you go and when."

"Fair enough. I am a contract assassin and there is a bounty on your head. Your name is Adam Darby, and the bounty was placed on the dark web by someone named 'DDS.' I don't know his identity other than that pseudonym. Maybe he is a disgruntled dentist, I don't know and don't care."

"How much is the bounty?" Adam asked.

"Half a million if I get you and the girl. Two-hundred-fifty-thousand dollars each," the man said.

"What is your name? Your real name. Answer correctly and we will let you go after I verify it," Adam said.

Just then, Ian pulled off the road onto a small dirt road. The man said, "My name is Bill—uh, William—Green."

"Thanks. Sounds pretty generic. You sure that is the truth?" Adam asked.

"It is the truth. I won't tell anyone that I saw you," the man said as the car came to a stop in some thick trees. Ian got out and opened the man's door and kept his pistol trained on him and motioned with the barrel of the gun to get out of the car. The man did and Adam slid across and followed him out of the car.

Ian led them into the woods a hundred yards or so and had the man lean against a large tree. They used the duct tape to tape his legs and chest to the tree. Adam said, "Keep an eye on him. I am going to verify his identity." Adam took a picture of his face and used a measuring app to determine his height. He stepped out of earshot and called Johnny.

"Hi Adam. How's The Windy City?" Johnny said as he answered the call.

"A little hot. We were found and followed by a contract assassin. I just sent you a picture. He says his name is William Green. If that is his name, we will leave him tied to a tree. If not, we'll shoot him."

"Hold a minute, let me check. I have the picture and am starting facial recognition. Let me do a search on his name. Just a minute... Okay, here it is. I have a match on the picture and the name. He was a sniper in the Army and has been doing security work in the Middle East. Sounds like he is telling the truth."

"Thanks Johnny. Can you please search the dark web for a hit on Ally and me posted with the pseudonym of 'DDS?' Remove it if you can."

"DDS? Sounds like Deputy Director Stevens, doesn't it? I'll take care of it," Johnny said as he ended the call.

Adam walked back to Ian and said, "His name and facial recognition check out. Looks like he is telling the truth."

Adam walked behind Green and nicked the duct tape so that he could eventually get out. They would be long gone by then. Adam said to Green, "We are keeping your weapons and phone. You should be able to get loose in a few hours. We kept our promise, and we expect you to keep yours. We know who you are and where to find you, so if I find out you talked, we will hunt you down."

Adam put the man's phone up to his face and unlocked the phone. He disabled the phone's facial recognition biometric security before walking away with Ian.

"*I won't say anything,*" the man yelled as Adam and Ian walked away.

Ian looked at his watch and said, "We need to get going if we are going to get a hot dog before picking up Emily."

Ian started the car, and they drove back the way they came. Ian said, "There is this restaurant called '*Luca's*' that has the most amazing hot dogs. It's on the way and it's quick."

"Sound great to me!" Adam said.

They enjoyed hot dogs at Luca's and drove to the airport to pick up Emily. They waited for Emily to exit Customs. Ian saw her and waved to get her attention. She saw Ian and waved back as she turned toward them. Ian and Emily greeted each other with a hug, then Ian introduced Adam. They helped her gather her bags and headed out to the rental car.

It was a short drive to the private aviation terminal. Ian parked and returned the car as Adam helped Emily carry her bags to the Learjet and stow them in the cargo area. Ian arrived and said, "It will be a few minutes while I do the pre-flight check." Ian unlocked and opened the door and lowered the stairs. He gestured for Emily to board the aircraft. "Make yourself comfortable. There are snacks and beverages in the galley. Adam, can you give me a hand getting the plane ready?"

"Thank you, Ian. I've never flown on a jet like this. I am so excited," Emily exclaimed as she climbed the stairs and began looking around the main cabin.

Adam stepped over to Ian and said, "What can I do to help?"

"Let's get the plane untied and the straps stowed in the cargo compartment," Ian said as he disconnected the tie-down straps and handed them to Adam. He rolled them and stowed them. Ian finished his pre-flight check by removing the engine covers, checking that the tanks had been filled and making sure all the flight surfaces were moving freely. "Time to load up," Ian said as he double checked that the cargo compartment was closed and latched.

They boarded the plane and found Emily sitting in one of the leather chairs with a soft drink in hand. Ian asked, "Do you like the Learjet?"

Emily had a smile from ear-to-ear and said, "Yes! This is so cool."

"Would you like to ride in the co-pilot seat?" Ian asked with a smile and gestured with his hand toward the cockpit. "You can bring your drink."

Emily nodded excitedly, jumped up, and followed Ian to the cockpit. Adam grabbed a soft drink and sat in the soft leather seat. He leaned back and closed his eyes.

Ian had Emily sit in the co-pilot's seat and continued his pre-flight checklist. He explained each step to Emily, and she was hanging on every word. Her eyes were wide with anticipation when he had her press the button to start the jet engines. Once the engines were up to operating temperature, Ian taxied to his place in line for take-off. There was one Airbus A330 and one Boeing 737 commercial passenger jets queued in front of them. The Learjet seemed so small next to those aircraft. When it was their turn and Air Traffic Control gave them clearance for takeoff, Ian pushed the throttles forward, and the Learjet jumped forward and soared into the sky in moments.

Emily was amazed at the experience of takeoff. The sun had set earlier, and the darkness revealed the diamond-like shimmer of the city lights below. Their flight path took them over the wide-open spaces of the northern states. The stars were abundant in the clear, dark sky. Emily admired the view of the stars and the occasional pinprick of light scattered in seemingly random patterns on the ground. In what seemed like only a few minutes to Emily, the plane began its descent. "It doesn't seem like two hours have passed from up here!" Emily exclaimed.

Ian explained the landing procedure as they descended in the darkness. He showed Emily the altimeter and how to read it. Emily said with a little concern, "It says that we are at five thousand feet. Where are we going to land? I don't see any lights."

"There is an automatic lighting system on my runway. When we get three miles out, the lights will turn on. There are sensors and cameras on the runway to monitor for animals. That way, I can see what is there before I land." Ian looked at the instruments and pushed a couple of buttons. "The lights should come on in a few seconds." No sooner than he said that, the lights turned on in a brilliant display in the pitch-black field. Ian pointed to the cameras displayed on the screen, and the runway was clear and no alarms were triggered by the sensors. "We are clear to land," Ian said.

Emily held onto the arm rests as the plane slowed and dropped to the ground. The wheels touched the runway with a short squeal, and they were suddenly rolling along and slowing rapidly. Ian looked over at Emily and smiled as he said, "How'd you like that?"

"It was amazing and makes me want to learn to fly," Emily said as Ian taxied the plane to the tarmac in front of the hangar and shut down the engines.

"We're here. Let's go meet the rest of the team and I'll show you to your room," Ian said.

When the Learjet door opened, Ally and Johnny were waiting on the tarmac. Johnny greeted Emily with a long hug and said, "I'm glad you could join us. I brought you a parka." He handed her a warm coat. She was shivering as she put it on and zipped it to her chin.

"Thank you, Johnny! It is so cold here. Ian let me ride in the co-pilot's seat all the way here. It was awesome!" Emily said beaming.

"I'll bet you want to learn to fly now. Am I right?" Johnny asked.

"I've never experienced anything like it. Yes, I'd love to learn to fly," Emily said.

Ally had just greeted Adam with a hug and kiss and was holding his hand. She turned and said to Emily, "I want to learn to fly also. Maybe we can take lessons together," she said.

"Sounds great to me," Emily said.

Ian had unloaded Emily's luggage and loaded it on the back of an ATV. He walked up to Emily and Johnny and said, "Johnny, do you want to show Emily to her room?"

Johnny led Emily to the ATV with her luggage and they drove off. Adam and Ally took another ATV leaving Ian with the jet and ground crew.

CHAPTER FORTY-ONE

NORTHERN MONTANA

The next morning, Adam and Ally showed Emily to the main house and gathered with the rest of the team in the dining room for breakfast. After meeting all the team members and having a filling breakfast, Johnny and Ally showed Emily to the computer lab. Before they got down to business, Johnny had Emily sign an NDA to cover them legally.

Johnny told Emily the details of their investigation and her eyes were wide. When they finished, Emily said, "This is serious business. I can help with the investigations, especially the financial side. Where do you want me to work?"

Johnny showed her to a workstation and showed her how to log in to the system. Once she was up and running, he gave her what she needed and let her get to it.

Ally was working at her workstation and Johnny logged in and went to work. They had a lot to do. After a few hours as it was nearing lunch time, Emily turned her chair toward Johnny and Ally. She stretched and watched them for a moment then she said, "I think that I may have found something."

Johnny and Ally turned almost simultaneously toward Emily. "What have you found?" Ally asked.

"Well, I started with the account number that credited Stevens' account. I was able to use the account number to locate the bank that it originated from in Switzerland. The banking systems have a very advanced cyber security system, so they are nearly impossible to penetrate or hack. There is a system to allow other banks to verify funds prior to making or requesting a transfer. I was able to use that system to verify that the account number belonged to Wentworth. I was also able to look at the history of debits and credits from the last thirty days. I found three similar transactions and the account numbers that they belong to. Does this correlate to what we know about the recipients?"

"Yes, that does. Other than Stevens, we also suspect President Grange, Qi Limpon, and an unknown name for a terrorist organization. It may be Russian, but we aren't sure yet," Ally said.

Johnny listened and said, "Focus first on finding the account number associated with Grange. He is our priority. We can work on the terrorist organization later."

"We can make an educated guess on the account number. Only one of the three accounts was in a Caribbean bank, and it happened to be the bank that I work at. The other two were Swiss banks. My guess is the one in my bank is Grange's account. I can remotely login to my work account and check," Emily said as she began banging away on her keyboard.

"Be careful to cover your tracks," Ally said.

"Got it. It will look like I am just checking my email. I will reply to some just to give it legitimacy," Emily said.

A few minutes later, she said in and excited voice, "Yes, I got it!" Ally and Johnny turned and looked at her. She was still typing for a few minutes as they watched. With a flourish she hit the "enter" key and spun her chair around to face them.

"What have you got?" Johnny said.

"I verified that the account belongs to Grange. He received a deposit of ten million dollars from Wentworth just prior to the planned attack date. He transferred just over five million dollars to an escrow account in South Africa the next day. My guess is he purchased a property there," Emily said proudly.

"That is great. This is the evidence we needed to arrest Grange. We need to follow the money to South Africa, so we know the property location. That was a successful morning, let's go upstairs, get lunch, and tell the others. We will need to have a meeting with Ben and James this afternoon. I will send them a meeting notice right now, then I will meet you upstairs," Johnny said as he turned back to his computer.

Ally and Emily hurriedly ascended the staircase to the main level and headed straight to the dining room. The rest of the team was already there eating lunch. Ally took her seat next to Adam and had Emily sit next to her. They both had smiles on their faces, and everyone looked at them for an explanation.

Ally said, "We have news, but we need to wait for Johnny. He'll be here in a couple of minutes."

Ally and Emily served themselves a plate of smoked brisket with sides and had just started eating when Johnny arrived and took his seat.

Everyone stopped and looked at Johnny and he said, "Okay everyone, Emily is a genius! She found the link from Wentworth to Grange. We have a little more work to do, but he received ten million dollars from Wentworth and then it looks like he bought a property in South Africa for a little over five million dollars the next day. I set a meeting at 3:00 p.m. with Ben Walters from the FBI and James Reyes from Homeland Security."

"Excellent work, Emily. We will meet in the conference room in the hangar. Enjoy your lunch," Ian said.

Everyone congratulated Emily on her find and welcomed her to the team again.

At 3:00 p.m., the team assembled in the hangar conference room. Johnny set up the meeting and soon Ben and James appeared on the screen.

"Hi Ben and James," said Ian. "Thank you for making time to meet today. Johnny has an update on the investigation into President Grange. Johnny?"

"We have been digging into the financials of Wentworth and any financial connections that we could find. Specifically looking for evidence of Grange's involvement. We brought in Emily Jackson as our financial forensics' expert. She was able to help us track down a ten-million-dollar transfer from Wentworth to Grange through a numbered account at a Grand Cayman bank. We also found that the next day there was a transfer from Grange's account to an escrow account in South Africa where he has purchased a large estate home in Cape Town," Johnny reported to the team. "We will have the finalized report to you within an hour of the end of this meeting."

"Good work. I think that this is enough for us to take to Vice President Powers to start the process to arrest Grange. Beck, can you facilitate a meeting with the vice president?" Ben said.

"Yes, I will call him now," Beck said as he stepped out of the conference room.

"I agree Ben. We need to move as soon as possible," James said.

"Ben, do we still have eyes on Stevens and know his whereabouts?" Adam asked.

"Yes, it is business as usual for him. No indication that he knows that we are on to him," Ben answered.

Beck came back into the room and said, "I just spoke with the vice president. He will meet with us at 9:00 p.m. at his home. He will have a federal judge and some other officials there to review the evidence we will present and to facilitate the arrests and removal from office."

"I will fly some of our team to DC as soon as the meeting is over. The jet is ready to go," Ian said.

"Okay everyone, you know what to do. Let's get these guys," Ian said as he ended the meeting. "Adam, Beck, Tuck, David, you four should come with me to DC. After the meeting, we will join the arrest team picking up Stevens and assist with Grange. Johnny, Ally, Emily, complete your report and get it to Ben and James. Please provide assistance as needed to help the teams with the arrests. Wheels up in twenty minutes."

Everyone filed out of the room. Adam and Ally stepped outside the hangar for a quick goodbye. They would only be gone overnight, but every moment apart was long for their young love. Adam gave Ally a long hug and kiss and Ally said, "Be careful, you need to get back to me as soon as possible. I love you."

"I love you too, Ally. See you soon," Adam said before going back in the hangar to get his gear from the armory.

They loaded up the Learjet and were flying east in less than thirty minutes. The Learjet touched down at Ronald Reagan

Washington National Airport at 7:30 p.m. The team rented three cars so they could go their separate ways following the meeting with the vice president. They arrived at his house at 8:30 p.m. and were invited to wait in the sitting room. Ben and James arrived a few minutes later just before the vice president walked in and said, "Gentlemen, thank you for coming. I have a conference room that we can meet in. Please follow me."

They walked into the conference room and five others were already seated. "Please take a seat everyone and I will make introductions," the vice president said as everyone was taking a seat. "Ian, please introduce your team."

Ian introduced everyone on his team and then the vice president said, as he pointed to the man immediately to his left, "This is Paul Scott, Director of the CIA. To his left is Nick Fredricks, Director of the Secret Service; Ginger Michaels, Senate Majority Leader; Anthony Rossi, Speaker of The House; and finally, Chief Justice of the Supreme Court, Kevin Roderick. Okay, time is of the essence. Ian, please present your findings."

"Thank you, Mr. Vice President. Gentlemen, thank you for attending this meeting." Ian went on to explain their findings, starting with a chronological summary of events that led to this meeting. He detailed the evidence that they have gathered against President Grange and Deputy Director Stevens. The men listened intently and waited until the end of his presentation to ask their questions.

CIA Director Scott, a slightly overweight balding man with white hair on the sides of his head, said, "Stevens has always been an exemplary employee and has been with the CIA his entire career. Although your evidence shows little doubt that he is taking a payoff and has put the American people at risk, it is still hard to think that someone like that can be turned. This investigation was very well done and warrants an immediate response by arresting Stevens and removing Grange from office."

Secret Service Director Nick Fredricks, a fit man with black hair wearing an impeccably tailored dark suit said, "I wholeheartedly agree. I will personally lead the team to confront Grange. Although, I shouldn't say this—I won't be sorry he's gone. He has a history of abusing his office staff and my agents."

Speaker of The House Anthony Rossi, a tall man of Italian heritage with short salt-and-pepper hair, said, "There are specific constitutional criteria that need to be followed for the removal of a sitting president from office. First, the house would hold impeachment proceedings, and if impeached by a simple majority, then the Senate will hold similar impeachment proceedings. Then the president would need to be found guilty of charges before being removed from office."

Senate Majority Leader Ginger Michaels, a stout no-nonsense woman with a thick waist and short gray hair, said, "Thank you for the confirmation of the process, Anthony. To expedite the removal of President Grange, we should confront him with our evidence against him and convince him to resign effective immediately. Once he has officially resigned from office, we can take him into custody and prosecute him for these crimes. What do you think, Kevin?"

Federal Judge Roderick was an older gentleman with gray hair on the sides of his head with a bald patch down the middle. He was reviewing the packet of evidence that was handed out at the beginning of the meeting. He set the packet down, removed his reading glasses, and looked around the room before he spoke. He was clearly a man with wisdom and common sense. "First of all, let me say that this is outstanding work and you all should be commended for the work that you have done. It pains me to see that there are people in the leadership of this country that will put themselves and greed in front of the American people. This will leave a stain on our country for years to come. It is imperative that we handle this with utmost professionalism. Do not let your disdain for these individuals cloud your judgement in doing your duty to bring them to justice."

Chief Justice Roderick paused and then said, "The vice president briefed me on this investigation a couple of days ago and forwarded me this packet of information earlier today. I have taken the liberty based on the evidence presented to have already prepared an arrest warrant for Stevens. This arrest should happen immediately following this meeting. Anthony and Ginger are correct; the removal of President Grange following the constitutional impeachments and prosecution to a guilty verdict will take a long time, even if we expedite the process. Ginger, you are correct; the resignation of the president is the best option. He is a man who craves power and will resist the idea of resignation. The vice president, speaker of the House, Senate majority leader, and I will join the Secret Service contingent and confront the president tonight. Mr. Fox, please send one or two of your agents to explain evidence as well. Once President Grange officially resigns, we can immediately transfer power from Grange to Powers. Good luck and Godspeed, gentlemen.

Vice President Powers looked directly at Ian and said, "Ian, you and your team did an outstanding job figuring this out. I look forward to working with your team in the future. When this is over and the smoke has cleared, we need to meet and form a working relationship for future concerns."

"I will call a press conference first thing tomorrow morning to explain to the American people what has taken place," said the vice president. "This will be a long night for all of us. Thank you all for coming," he said as he closed the meeting.

Adam and David followed Secret Service Director Fredericks out and Adam asked him, "May we join you as observers on the arrest team?"

Director Fredericks said, "Absolutely. Please follow me." Adam and David followed Fredericks to the White House a few blocks away. At the security checkpoint, Director Fredericks secured badges for them, and they were allowed to enter. They met with the agent-in-charge for that shift in the Secret Service White House office.

The agent-in-charge was shocked at what was happening on his shift. "This is something for the history books." He spoke quietly and said that President Grange was in his bedroom and had retired for the night.

Director Fredericks said, "Please call President Grange to the Oval Office and let your team know that we will be confronting the president and expecting him to resign, effective immediately. We will wait for him in the Oval Office."

Fredericks motioned for Adam and David to follow him. They accessed the Oval Office and Fredericks stood in front of the Resolute Desk. Vice President Powers, Speaker of the House Michaels, Senate Majority Leader Rossi, and Supreme Court Chief Justice Roderick were already there, seated on the two couches facing each other. Adam and David stood near the wall out of the way. A few moments later the president entered the office dressed in a robe, followed by two Secret Service agents. He closed the door, shuffled to his desk, and sat down. He rubbed his eyes and looked at the people assembled and said gruffly, "What is the problem and why couldn't it wait until morning?"

"I'm sorry for disturbing you this late, but this couldn't wait until morning. We have evidence of your involvement in treasonous activities that will be explained by those in the room. Adam, will you detail the evidence?" Fredericks said.

Adam, feeling the weight of the world on his shoulders in that unprecedented moment, took a couple of deep breaths. His heart was beating fast, but he stood straighter with his shoulders back and, in a strong voice, introduced himself. He carefully explained the evidence that has been collected against President Grange.

The Senate Majority Leader, Ginger Michaels, stood up and said, "We have reviewed the evidence and have sufficient reason to immediately begin impeachment proceedings. Mr. President, it is my recommendation is to resign—effective immediately—so that the presidency is transferred to Vice President Powers for the remainder of your term and for the good of our country."

"I agree with Ms. Michaels' suggestion, Mr. President. The House will also immediately launch impeachment proceedings in parallel with the Senate. Please take her suggestion and resign now," Speaker of The House Rossi said.

President Grange, still sitting at his desk, looked dumbfounded. His heart was racing, and his eyes were rapidly blinking. He looked around the room at the assembled leaders. His heartbeat was pounding in his ears, and he was having a hard time concentrating on what was being said. *"What!"* Grange yelled. *"I'm the President of the United States. You can't force me to resign."*

Chief Justice Roderick stood to his feet and approached the Resolute desk and stood before President Grange. He stared Grange in the eyes for a long moment, making him feel even more uneasy. He spoke in a quiet but firm voice saying, "Mr. President, I have reviewed all the evidence, and it is solid. We will prosecute you and you will be found guilty. You were elected to serve the people of the United States and agreed to follow the Constitution. This evidence suggests that you are not fit to be in this position. I firmly suggest that you resign immediately."

Vice President Powers joined Chief Justice Roderick in front of the Resolute desk facing President Grange. He had in his hand an envelope with the logo for the Office of The President on the front. He opened the flap of the envelope and slid a piece of paper from inside. He carefully placed the paper on the desk and turned it facing President Grange. He slowly slid the paper in front of the president.

"Mr. President, I am deeply ashamed of your behavior. If I had known that you would have engaged in corruption and put yourself and greed in front of the American people, I never would have joined you as your VP candidate. Your actions will always be attached to me in some way. I will have to work very hard to distance myself from you and may not politically survive. I trusted you and you betrayed me and the rest of the American people. I took the liberty of preparing a resignation letter for you to sign," Vice President Powers said.

He removed a pen from the inside pocket of his suit coat and placed it on the resignation letter in front of Grange. "Please sign the document as your last official duty as President of the United States."

Grange was trembling and sweating. His mind was trying to figure a way out of the situation; he always found a way out. It was quiet in the Oval Office and the only sound that was heard was the short, sharp breaths of President Grange. After several minutes, it was clear to him that he really had no choice. He figured he might survive the prosecution and be able to retire to his South African estate if he played his cards right. He decided that he could deceive the courts and get off with a minor conviction and disappear to South Africa.

He looked at the document and read through it slowly. It was only a short paragraph stating that he would resign effective immediately for private, personal reasons. His trembling right hand slowly picked up the pen and looked at it, then he quickly signed his name to the bottom of the page. Just like that, he was no longer the president.

"Mr. Grange, you have the right to remain silent. Anything you say can and will be used against you in a court of law. You have the right to an attorney. If you cannot afford an attorney, one will be appointed for you," Fredericks said and gestured to his agent-in-charge to put handcuffs on the former president and detain him.

Fredricks told his agents, "Please escort Grange to the White House Brig for temporary holding and process the arrest paperwork." He turned to Vice President Powers and said, "Mr. President, well done."

"Thank you, Fredericks," President Powers said.

Chief Justice Roderick stood and walked to the small

bookshelf in the Oval Office and picked up the Bible. He stepped over to President Powers and stood in front of him and administered the oath of office. He then handed a document for President Powers to sign officially transferring him to the office of the president.

"Thank you all for the work that you have put into this investigation." He gestured to the government leaders in the room and said, "We have a lot of work to do. Let's put together a plan. The rest of you can leave while we try to contain the fallout from this nightmare."

Fredericks sighed, turned to Adam and David, and gestured to the door. They walked out silently. Once outside of the Oval Office and the door was closed, he said, "What a night. Let's get you out of here before the media gets wind of this. It's going to be a zoo for a long time. I'm tired already."

"Thank you for your help. We need to get to Stevens' house for his arrest," Adam said.

They walked to the security station where they came in and Fredericks bid them goodbye. He turned to the security agents and put the White House in lockdown.

Adam and David drove fast, breaking speed limits from the White House to the assembly location near Stevens' house. Beck and Tuck were already there when Adam and David skidded to a stop near an assortment of FBI and private vehicles. The four men were directed to Ben Walters, acting agent-in-charge of this operation.

"Hi Ben, we made it. Grange resigned," Adam said.

"Hi Adam, we have Deputy Director Stevens' house under surveillance. He's there with some woman. The lights are all out. We are ready to go and have a SWAT team standing by. Are you ready? I thought you would like to make the arrest, since he betrayed you and tried to have you killed," Ben said.

"I'd like that very much," Adam said.

"Let's go then," Ben said as he led Adam and the team to Stevens' house. Ben and Adam walked to the front door. There were two FBI agents standing on either side of the door with their guns drawn.

Once everyone was in place, Ben knocked loudly on the door. The lights were off in the house, and Ben knocked again. A light finally turned on in the master bedroom.

"*Who is it?*" Stevens yelled from inside the house. He reached the front door and yelled again, "*Who is it?*"

"*FBI. Open up or we will break the door down,*" Ben said loudly.

The light behind the peephole darkened a moment, then the locks were released and the door opened. "What is the meaning of this?" Stevens said forcefully.

"Deputy Director Stevens?" Ben kindly asked with his hand on his weapon.

Adam was standing next to Ben. Stevens was looking back and forth between Ben and Adam. He was confused and a little disoriented. His hair was disheveled and his eyes were bloodshot. His robe was open at the top revealing a mess of stringy, gray chest hair. He looked at Adam and said, "Yes... Adam?"

"Deputy Director Stevens, you are under arrest for treason. Please put your hands on top of your head and lie down and spread your legs," Adam said.

Ben nodded to the agent next to him and said, "Place Deputy Director Stevens under arrest." As the agent was reading the Miranda rights and putting handcuffs on Stevens, the rest of the agents flooded inside to clear the rest of the house.

Stevens was dressed only in a robe and was told to sit on the couch. His hands were cuffed behind his back.

Adam stood in front of him and stared at him a moment then said, "Why? Why did you betray me? Why did you try to have us killed? We were expendable to you… Money. We were betrayed for money. We were nearly killed for money. Your self-serving corruption is despicable. I will make sure that you rot in prison for what you have done," Adam said as he shook his head and continued to stare down Stevens.

A moment later, an agent came down the stairs with a young woman in custody. She was wearing a thin robe and was told to sit across the room from Stevens while the rest of the agents finished clearing the house.

Ben sent one of the agents up to the master bedroom to get some clothes for Stevens. Stevens was hostile and yelling, *"I'm not a traitor! You don't have any evidence of that! You can't arrest me!"*

"Stevens! Please be quiet. You have been read your Miranda rights. We will question you in the office," Ben said as he nodded to another of his agents. "Please put him in the car and stay with him."

He turned to the woman, who didn't look over sixteen or seventeen years old. Her long, blonde hair was messy, and her makeup smeared. There were the beginnings of bruises on her arms and wrists. She was shaking and her blue eyes were full of fear. "Who are you and what is your relationship with Stevens?" Ben asked gently.

With a shaky voice she said, "I didn't know his name. He hired me to spend the night with him. He was disgusting, but the pay was good."

"How old are you?" Ben asked gently. "We are not here to get you into trouble, but we can help you."

She frantically looked around the room and said through tears, "I'm fifteen. This is my first job."

"You are too young to be in this business. We can help you. We will need you to make a statement and testify against Stevens. We can get you into a good home and help you start a better life," Ben offered as he gestured to one of the female agents to come over.

"What he did to me was awful. I don't want to do this, but I didn't have any choice. Will you help me? I will tell you everything," she said as she sobbed.

The female agent approached, and Ben quickly looked at her identification badge reading her name. "We will help you. Agent Sandy will take you upstairs to get dressed and she will escort you to our office to get an official statement. Is that okay with you?" Ben asked.

She nodded as tears were streaming down her face.

"Please take the handcuffs off her. She is in your custody Agent Sandy."

Beck, Tuck, and David were standing in the doorway watching the arrest. Adam walked over to his team and said, "We got him. It is in the hands of the FBI now."

Ben joined Adam and they all shook hands. "Thank you for your assistance," Ben said.

"Thank you—and the FBI—for your help. Grange and Stevens were apprehended. It was a successful night. Thank you again. We should get back to the airport," Adam said.

They all shook hands and walked back to their cars for the drive back to the airport. They were the last of the team to arrive at the airport. It was late, but they were all amped on adrenaline and knew they couldn't sleep, so they decided to fly back to the ranch.

Ian and David were in the cockpit and the rest of the team talked of their experiences with the arrests. A few hours later, they arrived at the ranch just as the sun was beginning to lighten the eastern horizon in a warm glow, promising a sunny day.

CHAPTER FORTY-TWO

NORTHERN MONTANA

The day was sunny and clear, and Montana was living up to its name as "Big Sky Country." Adam emerged from his room and looked around. It was afternoon. He yawned and stretched, enjoying the cool air scented with earthy pine. He gazed at the blue sky and thought, *It really does look bigger here.* He walked up the path to the main house hoping to find Ally.

The walk was brisk and felt good to his body. When he rounded a corner and could see the house, several of the team members were sitting on the deck enjoying the sun. Someone said something he couldn't make out, but he heard a squeal of delight.

Ally ran down the steps and flew into his arms. They hugged and shared a quick kiss with everyone watching and cheering. They both turned toward the onlookers and took a bow. Everyone laughed as they ascended the steps of the deck hand in hand.

Adam and Ally both kept looking at each other and Adam didn't notice that everyone had finished their lunch. Ally guided him to a chair at the outdoor table and had him sit. She kissed him on the cheek and said, "I'll be right back."

Adam turned and admired her as she walked away with a bounce in her step. A quick shake of her hips as she turned out of sight made warm color rise in Adam's cheeks.

Ally brought Adam a plate of lunch that the staff had prepared for him. She served him and sat down next to him and put her arm around him as he ate his lunch.

"I thought that you wouldn't ever wake up. I was starting to get worried," Ally said.

Adam grinned. "It must have been more stressful than I thought. I was surprised at the time when I awakened."

"Well, good things come to those who wait." She patted his knee and winked. "We have a meeting in the hangar at 3:00 p.m."

"Has there been anything on the news yet?" Adam asked.

"Yes. President Powers was on TV a couple of hours ago and spoke about what happened. He promised to hold a press conference tomorrow with more details. The media is blowing up and the markets have taken a tumble."

"That was to be expected," Adam said as he finished his lunch. "Let's walk to the hangar. I need a little exercise."

They walked to the hangar together holding hands and enjoying the peace of the ranch. Several ATVs passed them with hoots and hollers as they walked. Adam didn't care. The mission was successful, and he had the love of his life next to him.

Adam and Ally were the last to arrive to the meeting. They took their seats at the conference table. Ian started the meeting by saying, "Good job, everyone. That was a remarkable first mission. It turned out much bigger than anyone thought when it started out as a simple rescue mission."

Ian looked around the room and said, "We have some business items that we need to discuss. I had a meeting with our benefactor and discussed the mission. He has been able to secure more funding for our organization—enough to last for decades. We would like to offer permanent positions to each of you. Tuck,

Beck, and David have been on board for a while helping with the planning. Adam, Ally, and Emily, we would like you to stay on full time. We will provide cabins for you here on the ranch if you want to stay here full time."

They all agreed immediately.

"Great, Johnny and I have been talking about having multiple locations for our organization, but we still haven't decided on a name yet. We'll discuss your ideas on that later. Johnny and Emily were able to acquire a large estate in South Africa for a backup headquarters, thanks to Grange. He and Emily will also have a backup computer lab in Grand Cayman. Emily will work with Johnny in the computer lab and with handling the missions."

Ian looked at Adam and Ally and said, "Adam, you have proven yourself as a resourceful agent. Your knowledge and instincts have proven to be just what we need for a mission leader. Ally, you have also proven yourself as a valuable asset performing well in the field and in the computer lab. Your flexibility will be very useful in our future missions. As a wedding gift, we would like to provide you two with your own cabin on the property here and a home in the location of your choice. Ally, you and Emily expressed a desire to learn to fly. David and I will teach you and you will get your pilot's licenses. Any questions?"

"Thank you, Ian. There aren't words to express our thanks for the generous gifts," Adam said.

No other questions were asked.

"Does anyone have a suggestion for a name?" Ian asked.

It was quiet in the room as everyone thought. Ally spoke up and said, "I've been thinking about a name. We are in Montana, but don't want a name that might be associated with clandestine work. So how about 'The Beartooth Institute?'"

Everyone nodded and they thought about the name.

Ian said, "I like it. It doesn't sound like a clandestine organization but gives a nod to our area. Let's vote. Raise your hand if you like the name."

Everyone raised their hand. The Beartooth Institute was born.

"One more question. What about the Al-Mumeet and the Russians?" Adam asked.

"That is our next mission," Ian said as he ended the meeting.

EPILOGUE

WASHINGTON, DC

President Powers, sitting behind the Resolute desk in the Oval Office, was reading over his speech that he was about to give to the American people. The live broadcast was scheduled to begin at 9:00 p.m. The lights and cameras were in place and the heat was stifling. The videographers and lighting technicians were busy setting up their equipment getting all the lighting, microphones, and cameras in place. Occasionally they would ask for a sound check. *I will be glad when this is over,* Powers thought.

"Five minutes to live," the director said.

President Powers closed his eyes, took a deep breath, and slowed his breathing. It would be the most important speech of his career.

"One minute 'til we are live," the director said as he looked at his camera operators. They each gave him a thumbs up. The director held up one hand and counted down with his fingers from "three." When he reached "zero," he pointed to the president.

"Ladies and gentlemen of the United States. As you know, these last few weeks have been a tumultuous and sad time for our great country. The arrests and prosecutions of former President Grange and CIA Deputy Director Stevens have revealed that our country can still stand strong and united even though there was corruption in our midst. I would like to send a 'thank you' and 'well done' to the citizens of this great country that uncovered this corruption. Our country is truly grateful for your hard work. Rest assured, the country is still strong, and our founding documents have systems in place that allow the peaceful transfer of power. The presidency has been transferred to me and all branches of government have been involved in this transfer of the presidency." President Powers looked into the camera and took a breath before continuing.

"I have worked with my advisors and have appointed Megan Espinosa as vice president to complete my term. She will be a great asset to my team. Her credentials are impeccable, and she has served as governor of the State of Arizona. Her extensive experience governing the great State of Arizona, working with the Mexican government to increase the security of our shared border, and negotiating with both sides of the aisle will serve the United States well." The president paused as the camera angle showed Vice President Espinosa standing in the Oval Office.

"Thank you, Ms. Espinosa, for serving our great nation in the Office of the Vice President," the president said as the camera angle switched back to him.

"The Office of the President will support and assist the legal proceedings against former President Grange and CIA Deputy Director Stevens. As we move forward, our country will experience times of great sadness and anger at the actions of a few that tarnished our reputation in the world. Rest assured, your government is not defined by these actions, and I will work tirelessly rebuilding our worldwide reputation. It is with great pride that

I serve this great nation. Thank you for your time tonight. God bless each one of you and God bless America," the president said as the red light on the camera went out.

President Powers stood from behind his desk and walked to Vice President Espinosa, shaking her hand.

"Well done, Jack," Espinosa said.

"It's going to be a lot of work. Thank you for helping, Megan," Powers said as they both headed for the door, eager to get out from under the hot spotlights.

Adam and Ally were sitting on the couch in Adam's parents' home in Pennsylvania, watching the televised speech by the president. When it was over, Ken picked up the remote from the table next to his chair and turned off the television.

He turned to Adam and Ally and said, "Well done. The speech was short but full of confidence. I hope that the American public will see his dedication and devotion to this country. I think Vice President Espinosa was a good choice and will do a good job. We'll see how it works out. What is next for you two?"

"Well, we set a date," Adam said softly, and Ally smiled.

"When?" Susie asked with an excited voice.

Adam and Ally looked at each other and Ally said, "We would like to have the ceremony on New Year's Day in Hawaii!"

"We spoke with Ian, and he is going to fly us and the Beartooth team to Kauai. The benefactor of the Beartooth Institute has a large plantation and villa there that he has allowed us to use. He won't be able to attend, but we will have full use of the plantation," Adam said with a grin.

"I can't wait! Ally, will you take me shopping? I need to find a new dress," Susie said, beaming.

The ladies were talking about dresses and shoes, so Adam and Ken stood and headed for the kitchen. Adam said to Ken, "We will have a short honeymoon, but then we will be back to work tracking down the terrorist organization and the Russians behind them. I have a feeling that we will be busy soon."

"I'm sure that you will. Be sure to take time every day to show your love to Ally and build your relationship. I am proud of you, son," Ken said.

"Let's put those steaks on the grill. They may be talking for hours about the wedding!" Adam said as he opened the refrigerator.

ACKNOWLEDGEMENTS

I would like to take a moment to thank all those who helped me finish *Corruption in our Midst*.

Thank you, Jon L. for reading the rough manuscript and providing feedback.

Thank you, GeorgeAnn N. for providing feedback on the front and back matter.

Thank you, Rey L., Pam L., Mike C., Donna L., Alissa E., Emily P., Ben C., Michelle C., Debbie L., Sheryl P., and John P. for their feedback on the cover art.

Thank you to the rest of my family and friends who had to listen to me talk about the book.

Thank you, Erin Young for your expertise in copy editing. This book would not be what it is without your expert knowledge and valuable feedback.

Thank you, Ray Braun for your thorough and comprehensive proofread. You were able to catch many small typos and even some areas that needed a bit of help. I felt great going to publishing with the final draft.

Thank you, Christian Storm for your awesome cover art and typesetting. The professional look of the final book was beyond my expectations.

Most of all, I would like to thank my wife, Susan. She endured many hours of me typing away and her encouragement helped to make *Corruption in our Midst* the best that it could be.

ABOUT THE AUTHOR

Kendall Carlton is an electronics engineer. He retired in 2024 after a distinguished thirty-four-year career.

Growing up near the Navajo and Apache people of Arizona gave him a unique childhood. His unassuming character, spirit of adventure, and desire for learning have served his creative mind well.

He and his wife split their time between the mountains of Colorado and the deserts of Arizona. They have children and grandchildren across the country.

His debut novel, ***Corruption in our Midst***, is a fast-paced thriller that you will want to read non-stop. Check out him out on Facebook!

https://www.facebook.com/kendall.carlton.author/

www.ingramcontent.com/pod-product-compliance
Lightning Source LLC
Chambersburg PA
CBHW031118160726
47991CB00004B/1442